DOORWAY TO THE MOON

PARRIS AFTON BONDS

NEW YORK TIMES BESTSELLING AUTHOR

Blue Bayou	*Made for Each Other*
Blue Moon	*Midsummer Midnight*
The Calling of the Clan	*Mood Indigo*
The Captive	*No Telling*
Dancing with Crazy Woman	*Renegade Man*
Dancing with Wild Woman	*Run To Me*
Deep Purple	*Savage Enchantment*
Dream Keeper	*The Savage*
Dream Time	*Snow And Ice*
Dust Devil	*Spinster's Song*
The Flash Of The Firefly	*Stardust*
For All Time	*Sweet Enchantress*
Kingdom Come: Temptation	*Sweet Golden Sun*
Kingdom Come: Trespass	*The Wildest Heart*
Lavender Blue	*Wanted Woman*
Love Tide	*Widow Woman*
Wind Song	*When the Heart is Right*
The Barons	*The Brigands*
The Bravados	*Doorway To The Moon*

Doorway To the Moon

PARRIS AFTON BONDS

Published by Motina Books, LLC, Van Alstyne, Texas
www.MotinaBooks.com

Library of Congress Cataloguing-in-Publication Data

Names: Afton Bonds, Parris

Title: Doorway to the Moon/Parris Afton Bonds

Description: First Edition. | Van Alstyne: Motina Books, 2021

Identifiers: LCCN: 2021937218 | ISBN-13: 978-1-945060-30-4 (hardcover) | ISBN-13: 978-1-945060-29-8 (paperback)

Subjects: BISAC: ROMANCE/Historical | ROMANCE/General

Interior Design: Diane Windsor

FOR PHIL BISHOP

IN GRATITUDE
FOR THE FRIENDSHIP THAT GOES BACK TO OUR
YOUTH AND CONTINUES FORWARD INFINITELY

AUTHOR'S NOTE

In college, I opted to take a Southwestern Lit course, and one of the required readings was the soul stirring *Bless Me, Ultima* by Rudolfo Anaya. In its preface, he states, "The Golden Carp of the novel is my myth, for as a storyteller, I am, also, a mythmaker."

His myth of the Golden Carp inspired my *Doorway to the Moon*, but my Golden Carp is the myth of the mermaid of Puerto de Luna, New Mexico.

PREFACE

I am a verra auld mon now. Barely able to heft me hoary body from the slat-back rocker. It is positioned on the Luna House veranda to catch the golden, warming rays of New Mexico's famed sunlight.

Few visitors come around anymore. Sometimes the braver lads and lassies of Puerto de Luna, nigh a ghost town these days, venture to sit as close as the veranda's bottom steps and beseech the story from me yet again.

The story of the auld days. When a love so great could triumph over terror, betrayal, or even death. When one might sight, if lucky, the Golden Carp that turned into a mermaid. When one man actually did. Or, so me story goes.

Enjoy me spun story, the children might. But leave they do, with a roll of their eyes and a snicker shared among them, alas.

They scoff at the idea of holy wells, at the idea that it is human instinct to return again and again to that water, the source of our origins.

And as for meself, I know tis no myth, the Golden Carp. Aye, I change a name or place here and there with each recounting of me story.

Nonetheless, if a person believes in the healing power of the holy water of a well, does it not follow that any fish found in that well might be magical and, aye, miraculous? In the auld country, such a wonderful, mystical fish is thought to be, in reality, a naiad, a lovely maiden.

While nymphs be said to guard mountains and forests, naiads — they be said to watch over wells, rivers, and creeks. Naiads have powers to heal or inspire those who drink their waters.

Unlike nymphs, naiads are immortal, to be sure.

Like love. Aye, never underestimate, I tell those willing to listen to a batty ol' man, the power of love.

CHAPTER ONE

Puerto de Luna, Territory of New Mexico
April 1878

Miles Neville dismounted and planted dusty boots securely on the steep slope of El Rito Creek, where it united between low, fissured cliffs with the Pecos River. He flapped open his equally dusty denim pants to piss.

Arms akimbo and whistling, he scanned the opposite bank of cattails and rushes and cottonwoods. Their fluffs floated lazily on the morning breeze. Nearby, among the tall goldenrod, bees buzzed. The morning air was as dry as talcum powder. Glorious compared to the numbing gray drizzle that so often dampened the British Isles.

The enormous expanse of blinding blue horizon might overwhelm others, but, fettered by impossible expectations and torturous obligations most of his thirty years, his own spirit soared.

This was a land of limitless possibilities. Vast areas were still unsurveyed. Considering this was semi-arid high desert, a surprising lush land this territory was. Nursed by the Pecos, the land's grass grew exceptionally tall.

He ceased his whistling to tip back his beat-to-shit cap and grin. He had done well, buying out, just barely, the English syndicate of financiers in the cattle venture. He could almost smell the earthy, rich scent of gold, long buried.

He went to tuck himself in, when he heard the rustling. His right hand whipped to shuck his Smith & Wesson.

"Are ye an eejit?!" On the opposite bank, a young woman in a forlorn-looking, wide-brim straw hat sprang up from the rushes. Her sleeves were rolled to mid-arm, and one hand clutched a gunnysack, the other a hand trowel.

He blinked his astonishment. "What?" He holstered his practically useless revolver, with its mainspring badly in need of replacement.

"Ye're desecrating holy water, dinna ye know!"

He couldn't help but stare at the shabbily dressed creature. A wraith of Medusa hair meandered from beneath the droopy hat, bereft of either ribbons or flowers. "You'll excuse me, miss. I'm not from these parts."

"*Me vale verga.*" With the same Irish brogue, she tossed off the mild Spanish profanity, indicating that she didn't care. She nodded toward his denim's open fly. Surprising him, her glance skittered away, as if with a maiden shyness. "Speaking of parts, ye might want to cover that part of yuirself."

Fearing the sprite might disappear as easily as she had appeared, he quickly rearranged himself and rebuttoned his fly, all the while talking. "But animals can?" He glanced pointedly at his heavily saddle-packed sorrel, tail raised and now relieving itself. "Pray tell, wherein lie the difference?"

She rolled her eyes. "The birds and beasts on this side, they know nae better. Well then, the Golden Carp, she does. But she's of both sides."

"Uhhh, the Golden Carp?" Her brogue was familiar, reminiscent of County Cork inflected with the rich Spanish drawl of the American southwest. Red hair and cream-colored skin, rare in a countryside dominated by the dark features of its Moorish conquistadores and the even more ancient indios, snared the attention.

"And now that ye know better, ye would do well to beware of desecrating this part of the creek and the Pecos. Everyone – Mexican and Indian, Catholic and Pagan alike – aye, they know there is healing power in waters in these parts."

"As I said, I am not from these parts." He took reins of his blaze-faced sorrel and picked his way down the steep slope. In a seemingly leisured manner, he meandered across the rocks bridging that chunk of El Rito Creek to make his way toward her. "I only arrived today, by way of California, and I confess to being somewhat ignorant of your myths."

"Myths?" Her narrow shoulders pinched and her sharply

forged features challenged.

"Legends, history, whatever."

To her credit, she held her ground and watched his approach speculatively. "Then, if ye're planning on staying, ye need to know the other holy waters here, as well."

"Oh, I'm planning on staying." Appearing to dally, he hunkered to one knee on the shaley creek bed. He tugged off his neck's faded red bandana, dipped it into the pristine water, and swiped his sweat-dusted face. "Putting down roots, you might say."

He stood, a step closer now, to dwarf her. A closer inspection revealed little more than an unkempt and dirty peasant, much like those tenants on his family's holdings in County Cork. Actually, *his* holdings now.

Her sun-yellowed white cotton blouse was unbuttoned to below the bony juncture of her collarbones. Scuffed huaraches peeked from beneath her faded black skirt's dusty flounce. Staring at him rather oddly, she fingered her necklace, as if the leather cord's old, pitted gold cross with its tiny, tawdry bit of turquoise was a talisman. "*Pues*, the entire area is sitting on a huge underground lake."

"Then that would include a *huge* area of holiness," he countered drily, "that would by necessity exclude all human habitation here abouts. Including the pueblo of Puerto de Luna. So, how do you know about this underground lake?"

Exasperation huffed from her soft mouth. Still, there was a strange, inviting sweetness about its shape. "I hae swum between its underwater passages. At least, those shorter ones afore I lost me breath. Here, this exact place, is holy, like I told ye. The exact spot where Coronado is said to hae built a bridge. But other holy water places, there be, as well."

He tamped down his expression of excitement. What all might she know? "Aye," he prompted, "the legend goes the conquistador was seeking the Seven Cities of Gold."

All seriousness, she enumerated on her fingertips, blood-coated, no less. "There is the Blue Hole – bottomless, it is, and Hidden Lake and – "

"Hidden Lake?" He was most interested in what was hidden and what was underground. Like gold coins and ingots.

"Aye, where the mermaid lives. But she travels underground between all the holy waters as the Golden Carp. And, then there is the site of the giants who once stalked this land.”

She truly believed all this lunacy? Giants and mermaids and golden carps?

Coronado’s gold, of course, was another thing. The story went that the Spanish explorer had spotted the moon rising through a mountain gap to the east, Table Mountain. At certain times during the month the moon purportedly shone through, bathing the river valley in moonlight. “Puerto de luna!” Coronado had exclaimed. “Doorway to the moon.”

Miles found it curiously ironic that it was a couple of centuries later the Luna family, Spanish for moon, was awarded what was then a million-acre land grant. Some of its descendants were said to still scratch out a living here like chickens.

“And ye can find remains of the giants’ weapons at Blackwater Draw, although its creek is nearly dried up.”

He jerked alert. “Blackwater Draw?”

“Aye.” Her eyes narrowed to mere strips of dense, dark lashes. In that deceptive sunlight, those eyes, from what he could make of them, were either the rich shade of old gold or merely the common brown of dirt. “Why do ye start so?”

His callused fingers tipped the narrow brim of his sweat-and-soil stained cap. “Miles Neville, out of Blackwater, Ireland.” He refrained from adding the formal address of its 7th Earl of Blackwater. No grievance there that his old man, the 6th Earl, had, at last, met his maker, surely old Mephistopheles himself, three months prior.

“Ahhh, I see.” Her head tilted, and that altitude’s magical sunlight revealed the upsweep of her cheekbones above twin hollows and the freckles mottling the bridge of her strong nose. “But then nothing is ever by coincidence, is it?”

“What?”

“Ye hail from Blackwater, Ireland. Here we hae our Blackwater Creek. Me paternal ancestors hail from Eire’s Blackwater Valley. Ye ’appened here for a reason.”

“Most decidedly no coincidence. And you? You are . . . who?”

Her oval chin tilted imperiously. “Mhaire O’Moore.”

She slung the small sack over her shoulder, as if preparing to leave, and, both amused and bemused, he forestalled her. He nodded at her bloodied hands. “Mhaire O’Moore disguised as Lady Macbeth — or Pontius Pilate?”

A flicker of a smile tipped her lips. "Neither, I should hope."

Then she was well read. As for himself, he had been educated at Manor House school in Cheswick, followed by harrowing years at London's Harrow School and Christ Church, Oxford, where he gained first class honors in classics.

Absently, she glanced down at her short, slender fingers. "The blood is from one of me patients – a Regulator. Took a bullet in one of his limbs, he did."

It was all he could do to keep from rolling his eyes. Another frontier charlatan, no less. But a trace of the sweet fragrance of herbs drifted from either her or her gunnysack or both. "Regulator?"

"I forget ye're no' from these parts. The Regulators are deputized law enforcers. Ye may hail from Eire, but your accent . . . English born and bred, are ye?"

Her expression and tone placed his origin of birth slightly above that of a chimney sweep's. He nodded.

She went to turn away, and he detained her yet again. "Can you provide directions to a local house I am seeking?"

"Ye mean the Grzelachowski House in Puerto de Luna? Tis the only place in the area that serves as an inn."

"No. The Luna House. Do you know where it – " He broke off as her lithesome body stiffened like a six-hour-old corpse with rigor mortis.

"Why the Luna home?"

"I own it. And all its holdings – the Luna land grant. Or the 350,000 acres left to it, I believe."

"357,123 acres, to be exact – and ye're mistaking me fer a fool, sir. The Lloyd Group oot of London owns it."

"No longer. I bought out its partners."

He grinned. She did not. Her brows, dark as bat wings lowered. Her eyes turned the blistered black of coals. "Those scurvy pieces o' dung." She spun from him and scrambled like a goat up the bank's profuse vegetation, surmounted by a short but steep rocky cliff.

With something akin to dismay, he shook his head, then grinned. "Well . . . well . . . well." He was looking for gold in this isolated terrain and found right here the eighth wonder of the world.

CHAPTER TWO

How Mhaire loved the magic and mysticism of her sleepy little town of Puerto de Luna, with its 1500 souls, either saved or damned, depending on Father Ignacio's point of view. And that differed, depending upon his state of inebriation.

A transient, William Bonny was undoubtedly considered of the latter, damned. She empathized with the wild youth. Of about the same age – he, nearing twenty, and she twenty-one – they had both been orphaned at fourteen give or take a year. The Kid had lots of friends in Puerto de Luna, and he would come here, when things got too hot in Lincoln, to cool off.

She planted a smile in her tense jaws and closed behind her the door to the last of the ten rooms off the Grzelachowski House's hallway. Predominantly ranchers and traders stayed at the friendly stopping place that adjoined its mercantile operations. Its owner, Alexander Grzelachowski, also served as postmaster and town sheriff.

"Bonnie Billy Bonny, ye looked bored. I do believe ye missed me."

The wiry young man was stretched out on the bed, his injured right leg propped on a doubled pillow. He was pitching checkers into his floppy felt hat, turned upside down on the nearby pine dresser, the only piece of furniture in the small room, other than the iron-framed bed.

His grin showed his overlapping front two teeth. "Like a hole in my head."

"Or the one in yuir limb." His pants leg was ripped from hem to thigh. Earlier that morning she had pried out a bullet with a pair of sewing scissors.

Termed a curandera by the locals, she had learned curative skills from Elsa Anderson. Seven years before, the Danish woman had taken over mothering Mhaire. Periodically over the years, uneasy whispers would circulate that Elsa was a *bruja* – gossip abetted by the grisly view of the left side of her head, bald and crisscrossed by pink and puckered seams.

Witch or not, that did not stop the townspeople, when ill or injured, from traveling the four miles to Elsa's remote straw-and-mudbrick adobe. Dubbed the Turquoise Door, it was open seven days a week to the ailing seeking Mhaire's curative prowess.

They would risk Elsa's possible curses for Mhaire's cures, never guessing that it was the fifty-year-old woman who had taught her not only the rudimentary knowledge of healing but also healing remedies of the ancients – the Indios and those of the old, old country, the Moors.

Mhaire crossed to the dresser and dribbled water from the pitcher into the chipped porcelain wash basin. In the Navajo fashion, Elsa would have added a wad of spit. From the gunnysack, Mhaire fished out the tender shoots of yerba mansa she had collected that morning and set about pulverizing the plant with her pestle.

Her thoughts dwelled on the Englishman she had left there at the Pecos Pool, where the outpour of the Blue Hole, El Rito Creek, joined the Pecos. Miles Neville, of hair as black as his English soul. Miles Neville, of the timber-rich voice that resonated through her like a lightning rod. She could still feel the starburst of his vitality, a flame heating the morning air.

"Hey, Mhaire, how about getting gussied up and go to the fandango next week?"

The Kid was good looking with that head of longish butternut curls and a delightful presence of mind. "With that plug in yuir limb, ye won't be dancing soon. Besides, ye know I'm already betrothed."

He snorted. "Horse troughed more like it!"

"How came ye by the plug, Billy? Yuir luck run out?"

"Durn lucky I was, Mhaire, considering I shot the sheriff."

Her head whipped around. "Brady? Go on with yeself!"

One thin shoulder lifted in a slight shrug and a faint grin eased the pallor of his narrow face. "It was either Brady or meself that would cash in the chips yesterday, and I jist felt the corrupt old bastard should have that honor first."

Billy had been arrested at sixteen for stealing food. Next, he had been arrested for robbing a Chinese laundry. Recently the Kid had joined the Regulators. Even though the local justice of the peace had sworn them in, she had misgivings about their vigilante-like reprisals.

The fevered Regulators were composed of numerous small ranch owners and cowboys who had formed ostensibly to protect the area from livestock rustling – but in actuality who had united to oppose the corrupt territorial criminal justice system controlled by Emmet Sullivan. A mercantile store owner and banker out of Lincoln, Sullivan backed the rustling and opposed any resistance.

"'Sides, Mhaire, Brady had a hand in gunning down Tunstall, and the Englishman had always treated me squarely."

The sheriff of Lincoln County, Brady had been in Sullivan's pocket. Backed by the territorial capital's Santa Fe Ring, Sullivan ran the town of Lincoln and surrounding county of Lincoln as though the area were his fiefdom. Any business transaction of consequence in the county passed through the Irishman's bank.

She turned back to the bed with her medicinal compound. "By all the calendar saints, Billy, this is one fer which ye're sure to swing."

"What would you have us do, Mhaire? If we don't stop Sullivan's ruffians, who will?"

Five months before, the thirtyish Sullivan had stopped by Puerto del Luna. Before riding back to Lincoln, the burly Irishman rode out to Elsa's adobe, on the pretext of seeking Mhaire's care, after his thumb had been popped off by his lariat's hondo weeks earlier.

She did not like him, did not like his energy. She had not invited him in but stood in front of the turquoise door, barring his entrance. She merely gave the ruddy and rucked stub a once-over glance. "It's healing on its own fairly well, Mr. Sullivan."

He stuck his pinky finger in one of his big ears, cleaning it vigorously. "Heard you once healed John Tunstall of a bad bout of poison ivy."

She said nothing.

He wiped his waxy fingertip on his fawn colored sack coat. He always dressed spiffily. "For all the good it did. Tunstall died anyway."

"Not from poison ivy, Mr. Sullivan. From pistol shots. His body was riddled with bullets – and there was a major hole in the back of his head."

His expression was pure calculation. "Siding with the

Regulators, Miss Luna, can be dangerous for the health."

She had spit in the dirt after he had cantered away.

She dropped down next to Billy on the mattress ticking stuffed with straw and began applying the medicinal paste. "Ye'd been better off had ye paid Elsa to place a curse on Emmet Sullivan than openly opposing him."

Certainly, she had no intention of openly opposing Sullivan's all powerful mercantile and banking operations, connected as it was with the notorious Santa Fe Ring and known collectively as The House.

All she wanted was the Luna House back.

She wanted it and its immense land grant with soil that contained the blood and sweat, the laughter and tears, and the heartaches and joys of generations of Lunas – and that was now saturated with those memories and emotions of her own.

With roots going back more than three-hundred years, she was a Luna on her mother's side of a long line of distinguished Luna ancestors. They had followed the conquistadores' footsteps in 1541 and settled the vast emptiness.

She had held out hope that the English syndicate, which had bought out her over-extended father for far less than pennies on the dollar seven years before, would continue to administer affairs from afar.

This the syndicate had accomplished through Guido Jaramillo, whom her father had early on hired to manage his interests – his estate's irrigation projects, agriculture products, timber cutting, and rents . . . and, eventually, herself.

At least, that had been her father's fervent hope, a suitable marriage with the stalwart, older Guido to safeguard her, after her father took his life – but not before selling the land grant for piddling dimes on the dollar to the English consortium.

Her fervent hope had been stomped like a grape this morning by the arrival of the man who had bought out the syndicate. Last month's terse telegram from the group had informed only that a proprietor, not which one, should be expected, but no definite date. And not a *new* proprietor.

The proprietor was this Englishman, an earl no less? Mother of mercy. Her shoulders began to shake, and the shaking moved down her arms to wobble the pestle and wash basin she clenched.

"I'm thinking the old witch Elsa placed a love curse on me for 'ankering after you, Mhaire."

"Go on with yeself, Billy." Many a female fell for his boyish charm. She finished wrapping his thigh's wound with strips of bedsheets from the Luna House's once plentiful linen closet. "And I am serious this time. Go on with yeself – leave the Territory fer a while until the 'eat dies down."

She collected her gunnysack, but as she swept past, he leaned out to catch her wrist. The silky fuzz on his upper lip danced with his smile. "My heat for you will never die down, darlin'."

With a teasing one of her own, she shook loose his hand. "Cold cash fer me services would be more welcome than your free flirtations, William Bonney, to be sure.

"Aww, Mhaire, I left a chicken carcass fer payment on your doorstep last time."

"Aye – one stolen from our own henyard."

Another kind of heat – unlike Billy's immature one – licked through her as her buckboard traveled the green River Road to Elsa's adobe. A sizzling heat, much akin to a blacksmith's forge, it was generated by the despicable Englishman, who had bought her homeland. Worse, she did not know if this heat was due to her understandable animosity or inexplicable attraction. Or both.

And at the sight of tall, lean man, there, in the front yard of the Turquoise Door, she might as well have been instantly immolated. How else to describe the push-pull feeling that seized her legs and lungs and heart?

His sinewy weight braced on a back leg, he stood supremely confident beneath the desert willow shading the adobe, as if he owned that, too. Horse reins were draped from his fist on one hip and from his other hand his dingy round cap with its slight brim.

His stance was only slightly different from earlier that morning when he had stood astride the creekbank's slope, his heavy genitals displayed in a bold glory that rivaled that of mythical lustful Greek satyrs.

And like all tragic Greek myths, no good would come from her fanciful feelings about him. That fancifulness had made mundane demands of survival after her father's suicide something more than tolerable.

Halting the donkeys Bray and Neigh, she yanked up the

wagon's brake. Burlap bag in hand, she dropped down from the seat to warily cross the sandy yard dotted with buffalograss. She saw now that the Englishman was chatting with Elsa, hunched among the medicinal plants that banked that sunny side of the adobe's garden beds.

Certain ones of the thriving plants, including the highly prized manzanillo, unavailable in that area of the Territory, had been brought from the mountains to the west, in trade for Mhaire's curative services. Most people did not understand that the plants had spirits. Or revere the dew-kissed spider webs. Or divine the pulse of the earth beneath the bare feet.

The man seemed not at all put off by either Gruff the goat attempting to nibble at his cap, nor by Mhaire's pet pig, Pork, lounging in the garden dirt – nor by Elsa's marred visage, as many were at first sight.

Elsa appeared to be listening to the earl, but above stark cheekbones her intelligent hazel eyes, the left one's lid tugged slightly upward by a scar, were doubtlessly taking his measure.

Drawing closer, Mhaire noted he had his own scars. One neatly bisected his right brow. Another stitched just beneath his lower lip, nudging it into a tempting fullness. His overly long hair, an unruly burnt black, curled at the ends. The deep-set drowning-blue eyes kept secrets. The wide, magnetic smile was meant to charm. But it was nowhere nearly as harmless as the Kid's boyish one.

Pork scrambled its bulk to its cloven hooves and waddled eagerly toward Mhaire. Pushing up off her haunches, Elsa's knobby fingers briskly brushed the dirt and twigs clinging to her calico skirt. "Mr. Neville has come to collect your house keys."

Neville's square-set jaw, badly in need of a shave, swung toward her. "The Luna House belongs to *your* family?"

"It *did*." In her ears, her voice sounded as grating as her pestle against its mortar. "To me da, James O'Moore." She bent to pet Pork's dirty flank. "I'll get the keys." Chin high, she strode past him and Elsa to the adobe.

Inside, the ring of keys hung from one of the cup pegs beneath a window shelf supporting potted plants. More plants fought for room on the wrought-iron bakers rack. She turned her face to the deep-set window, its crazily tilted slatted shutters thrown wide open, fortunately. She needed the morning sunlight to warm the chill of despair running through her.

Piece by piece, letting go ties to mother, father, and brother. And now this, her last tie to her home, where once she had lived like a lady – as had her mother, a Spanish aristocrat who had married a common Irish buffalo hunter, Mhaire's father.

When she returned, Elsa paused in whatever she was telling Neville to note undoubtedly Mhaire's glistening eyes, then finished, " . . and she keeps the Luna House in order."

"Monthly cobweb cleaning," Mhaire added to the explanation. "Checking fer rodents. That sort of thing."

As if it were mundane work for her. No, she would lovingly rub the Luna House's balustrades with beeswax, polish the brass door fixtures so that they gleamed like sin, shine the multitude of windows until they sparkled with the sunlight of the high desert and radiated with its brilliant moonlight.

And several times, she had slept in her second-floor bedroom on the great feather mattress, but the ghostly whispers of memories were too painful, and she would invariably return by the dark of night to the Turquoise Door and her wool fleece mattress on the rope-slung bed next to Elsa's.

She proffered up the key ring. "And I helped our manager, Luna's caporal, Don Guido Jaramillo, with the quarterly reports made to the syndicate. Ye'll be wanting to review them."

After her father conveniently held his Remington's barrel beneath his double chin and taken his life, Guido had continued to oversee the many ranch operations as designated in her father's will.

Neville took the key ring, and though their fingers did not touch, surely an electrical current arced through the ring's metal. Odd that, when she wasn't sure if this stranger was worth tolerating. Usually, she read people easily at first sight.

His eyes, igniting to the blue that was the core of the candle flame, that hottest part, flashed his surprise, as well. But his tone was as mellow as the sunlight. "Where can I find this manager?"

Still startled by the tingling rushing through her, she cleared her throat. "Guido runs sheep on 750 acres of his own as well as the Luna cattle on the acreage belonging to the syndicate – to yeself now. I'll see word gets to him ye're here."

"Then, I would appreciate it if you could show me my new residence. I'm eager to get settled in. And, frankly, I'm bushed from a month of traveling.”

The morning that had begun so promising was evaporating more quickly than the dew. Repressing her irritation, Mhaire explained, “Me house – the Luna house – is another three miles north. Give me a few moments to wash up.”

Thumping the adobe’s dirt floor, hard packed with ox blood, Elsa’s huaraches trailed Mhaire to the bedroom they shared.

“Have nothing to do vith zis man, *havfrue*. He vill steal your power.”

She turned from the wash basin atop the row of stacked wooden apple crates, serving as a bureau, between the two beds. Her smile did not reach her eyes. “And I tell ye, Elsa, tis his power *I’ll* steal. And steal back me home here, as well.”

CHAPTER THREE

Alongside Miles, Mhaire climbed the steps of the Luna House's wrap-around veranda to the imposing front door. Its stained-glass panels reflected colored prisms like the wings of a dragonfly.

Her lips compressed, she watched the invader insert the key and throw wide the huge door to stride inside. "While ye take a look around, I'll open the blinds and curtains and remove the dust covers."

He paused midway in the entrance hall, his gaze raking over his acquisition. From the doorway behind them, sunlight slanted through, entangling their shadows on the sweep of the stairwell beyond. The high desert wind whisked in and swayed the round iron chandelier above them, its creak echoing eerily in the grand entry.

Her father had ordered the two-story, red-brick home built in the English Baroque style and had ruled from it like a feudal lord . . . until Emmet Sullivan, backed by his Santa Fe Ring cohorts, happened on the scene.

Completely out of keeping with Puerto de Luna's simple adobes and wood-frame shanties, the house was the only one in that part of the Territory of New Mexico containing indoor plumbing and was wonderfully combined with Italianate and French Empire details.

"The office is the first door to your right. Next to it is the library. Ye'll find tomes ranging from Plutarch to Des Carte to Nathanial Hawthorne."

The Englishman turned his head toward her and raked a brow at her erudite explanation.

Over the years, her father had ordered the volumes for her brother, Riley. Half the Territory of New Mexico's population was illiterate, and her father, who could barely read and write himself, was determined his offspring would not be. Even Mhaire's mother, though born an aristocrat, had little schooling, or need for it, in that far-flung outpost of Puerto de Luna.

This was going to be more difficult than Mhaire anticipated. A stranger. An Englishman. A Protestant. Living in her home.

He sent his cap sailing onto the hall tree and headed for the office, what she thought of as the Trophy Room.

She swerved left, into the parlor. Blinking back a surprising well of moisture, she crossed to open louvered blinds, framed by royal blue swags and floor-length chenille curtains. A quick swish of a dust cover unveiled the beige camelback sofa, bearing the scars of her brother's childhood spurs on the curve of one rosewood arm.

Another swish uncovered the card table and its boxed, handmade chess set. Riley might have excelled in sports, but she had beat him more often on the field of the chessboard.

"Zounds!" The exclamation was followed by a low appreciative whistle, which drew her footsteps back to her father's office where its mounted trophies of game and fish stared vacantly.

Fists on hips, Miles was surveying one wall, with its array of firearms – horse pistols, derringers, revolvers, rifles, and shotguns displayed in the wide cases. "When I read the house contents were included, I had no idea these were among its possessions."

She wanted to scream, *Dinna touch them!* Instead, her voice was calm. "They hae no' been fired in over a decade."

"No, I was talking about the fishing rods." He opened the wall's side case, containing a half dozen of them, and withdrew one of the rods from the rack. Experimentally, he snapped its length through a back-cast's arc. "Capital action!"

"Mind ye, if tis thinking about fishing ye are, all water is sacred within a league of the Blue Hole, as are the fish."

He half turned, an imperturbable smile showing teeth a startling white against his sun-browned skin. He flexed his wrist, and the tip of the fly rod flicked her hat's wide brim, flipping it back to dangle by its chin strap against her shoulder-blades. "And are you that Golden Carp, that mermaid you spoke of?"

Her resentment boiled to the top. "Careful fer yuir blatant disrespect. The Golden Carp may well cast an evil spell on yeself."

Put a scare in him, she would. Mhaire's mother, clutching her rosary's gold cross, had known something about the Blue Hole. Had tried to share the sacred secret in those precious moments before she uttered her last exhalation. That gold cross, now suspended from Mhaire's throat, was all she had left of her mother.

His head canted. Leisurely, his eyes perused her length. "I used to fly fish in Ireland's River Blackwater for the King of Fish, the salmon. I wonder which is the most revered, a mere carp or the salmon?"

She spun away. In the dining room, she snatched the dust covers from the lengthy trestle mahogany dining table and its dozen ornately scrolled chairs. Then, picking up her skirt, she shot up the runner rug of the expansive staircase with its gas light sconces to reach, first, the round music room with its windows' panoramic view of a limitless horizon.

She came to a breathless halt, the frayed hem of her skirt rustling around her ankles and her hat flopping to a standstill against her shoulder blades. She swallowed back a childish snivel and advanced to the Viennese fortepiano. Circumventing its stool, she rucked back the dustcover and lifted the keylid. Her fingers plinked a melody from her youth's woefully lackadaisical lessons. Mozart's sonata K. 448.

Behind her, Miles said, "You surprise me. Well read. Accomplished. What other talents do you hide behind this . . ." his palm swept to encompass the five feet of her height, " . . . this Arcadian beauty?"

Her hackles rose at the term, and her fingers paused on the keyboard. "I beg your pardon. Rustic? Simple?"

"No. Nature's splendor." He crossed to stand next to her. Bending near, he let his fingers idly and easily pick out the sonata's duet accompaniment on the keyboard. "I remember reading the Syndicate reports – of course, I didn't know they were yours. Your mindset is that of an analytical bookkeeper, yet your spirit would seem to be . . . uhh . . . otherworldly. Quite a contradiction."

She resumed trilling the notes, her small fingers edging nearer his much larger but also agile ones, then skittering away as the piece called for. "As are yeself. At the same time both a lord and a weasel."

He smirked. "Quite often, I have noted the two are found to be one and the same."

She slammed shut the keylid. His dexterous fingers danced out of harm's way, just barely.

She whirled and reflexively headed down the hallway's rooms for her bedroom. Here, the dustcover had long ago been discarded next to her dressing table. The luxurious marseilles counterpane and feather pillow held her body's indentation where it had last sunk with a sigh that still released the fragrance of lavender.

Realizing her error in selecting her bedroom as a place of refuge, she whirled and returned to the darkened hallway, only to collide with the Englishman. He caught her shoulders to keep her upright. Not that his supposed solicitousness staved off the arc of electricity sparking between them and tingling her most uncomfortably. In the corridor's dimness, she could barely distinguish the man's features but could distinctly feel the life force that bound his soul to his body.

"Whoa, there. Look, I just want to settle in. Can you help me here?"

She felt more than saw the avaricious heat of his stare.

"Uhmm, I could, also, use a housekeeper of sorts. You know." His upper lip came into focus, shadowed by stubble. His overconfident mouth tightened abruptly, as if, on its own accord, it had misgivings. "Well, every now and then."

Her very bones stiffened at the offensive suggestion. "The Second Coming will come first."

Continuing his hold, he studied her through puzzled eyes. "I have my doubts you are a Christian. More likely, a pagan masked as a practicing Catholic, what with your golden carp crap and all."

What was this . . . the feeling of the floor quaking beneath her? Eyes glistening, lips tighter than piano strings, she stared up at him. "Was not the fish the symbol of early Christianity? And does it matter? The answer be still the same."

"Now wait just a minute. You – "

Her hands shoved against his chest, and pivoting from his grasp, she flung over her shoulder, "The master bedroom is the next door down, to yuir left."

Downstairs, she yanked open the front door – only to crash headlong for the second time with yet another male. She looked up into Guido's resolute face, shadowed by his ornamented sombrero.

His hands steadied her shoulders. Above blunt cheekbones, his dark brown eyes scoured her expression with concern. "*Que pasa, mi querida?*"

She glanced over her shoulder at Miles, casually descending the staircase. At the sight of her in Guido's arms, he paused. His slash of black brows edged closer toward the high bridge of his nose. Then, his teeth flashed. "Well, what do we have here?"

She stepped away, and Guido followed her inside, shutting the door behind them. She nodded toward her lifelong friend. "This is Luna's manager, Don Guido Jaramillo."

Guido removed his hat. By habit, his hand drifted to relax on the pistol at his side. An outdated Colt Dragoon, it reassuringly represented the gentleman's saber of the Old World order. He glanced from her to Miles. "My presence was requested?"

The shorter of the two men, Guido carried his spare frame with the inflexible dignity of an aristocrat, while the stance of Miles's, the titled Englishman, appeared loose and rangy and with the implied threat of reckless adamancy.

The Englishman's male arrogance reminded her of her feckless, irresponsible father and brother Riley. Their libertine attitude had taken life and women far too lightly and thoughtlessly. Eight-years-older, Riley had been willed the paltry profits of the land grant sale, with the stipulation he was to care for her until she came of age at twenty-one – when she was to marry Guido.

That winter following their father's death, the profligate son had been seen gambling in Lincoln. That spring, when the snow had thawed, his remains had been found in a narrow mountain pass of the Sacramentos.

Gone, both Riley and the proceeds of their inheritance.

If it had not have been for Elsa's intervention, taking her in, Mhaire would have been homeless . . . or married at fourteen to Guido. Something to which she had not been able to bring herself to commit, although it was not unusual for girls that young to do so. Time had softened somewhat the idea of marriage to Guido.

As a choir boy, he had entertained ideas of becoming a priest. To this day, honor and righteousness stamped his Spaniard's hawk-like features. The pious expression in his stone-brown eyes and his firm mouth proclaimed he was a man who would not compromise his principles.

At that moment, she felt like a novice of a religious order. Now that at twenty-one she had come of age, there would soon come that day when she would have to commit either to being a wife to Guido or a curandera to her community. For Guido, it was either/or.

Following that first year that Elsa took her in, she, but fifteen, and Guido, an experienced twenty-four, had dallied along the banks of the tree-shaded acequia, an irrigation ditch that looped from the Pecos around the Turquoise Door and back. She connected the pleasant sound of the chuckling water with Guido's pleasant kisses. Those hesitant kisses had aroused more her curiosity than her ardor . . . or else, she suspected, she would have rendered up her maidenhead then and there.

But then the considerate and courtly man had abruptly ceased with his heated ardor, gently explaining it was his desire to keep her chaste for their wedding. And she had been young and understandably more curious at that age about the source of the firefly's glow than the lack of her own ardor.

She delivered an affectionate smile up at him now. "Guido, this is the new owner of the Luna land grant, Miles Neville." Her lips twisted up at the Englishman. "The Earl of Blackwater."

His expression remained amused. "Lord of Luna will do." His gaze, with the Devil's own deep blue eyes, shifted from her to Guido. "I assume I can count on your diligent services to continue under my ownership?"

The Englishman had not addressed Guido by either his formal title or given name, and she did not miss Guido's slight rigidity at this neglect, intentional or otherwise.

He inclined his head but barely. "*Claro, que si*. My services, *señor* – although not that of my fiancée's." He paused only fractionally for emphasis, then he allowed a brief but cordial smile. "You see, we are to be married later this summer, and I do hope you will honor us with your esteemed presence at our nuptials."

"Really?" Miles Neville arched a brow at her.

She sensed he was enjoying himself at their expense. She merely nodded.

As if he felt it necessary to explain, Guido said, "I have known her since she was a child."

"That long?" The Englishman strode to him and clapped him on the shoulder. There was no hint in his feigned bonhomie of Guido's candor, magnanimity, or dignity. "Come, come, what kind of wedding announcement is that? You Latins are famed for your passionate nature. A demonstration of your continued devotion is required. Like this."

Startling her, he turned, positioning himself between her and Guido, and took her hand, lifting it to his lips. From beneath his whiskbroom lashes, his taunting gaze peered up at her – even as his warm lips grazed overly long across her work-reddened knuckles. Was that his tongue she felt, tipping the indenture between each knuckle.?

She gasped and at the same time glanced anxiously at Guido. His expression indicated that he was taken aback at the Englishman's presumptiveness but not certain as to the best approach to this outlandishness.

When Miles released her hand and straightened, Guido's tone was cuttingly reproachful. "Even in affairs of the heart, propriety is a hallmark of a caballero, a gentleman, *señor*."

Miles grinned affably. "But, of course." He slapped the rigidly dignified Guido on the back this time, while throwing open the front door. "The world knows how cold natured we blokes are. No sense of propriety, right? I'll get back with you on the details of managing Luna's livestock soon." He propelled her fiancé through the door and closed it.

Then, he looked back at her with a semblance of what she would have surmised was compunction in anyone else. In him, it was smug satisfaction. "He's known you most of your life, and he lets propriety stand in his way?"

She was furious – mostly with herself, with the way her stomach had dropped at his salacious kiss on the back of her hand, when that very propriety would have demanded she react with an indignant slap on his impudent countenance.

With a violent movement, she swept back a loose swath of her hair. "Ye wouldn't recognize propriety if it slammed ye in yuir smirking face." She yanked open the front door – and *slammed* it behind her.

Guido, the braided leather bridle of his appaloosa in hand, was waiting for her. He grasped her elbow to boost her up into the buckboard. "What was that all about, Mhaire? His coming brings trouble, I fear."

Taking up the reins, she looked down at his disturbed gazed. Reassuringly, she placed her fingertips on his sunbaked hand. "He is a foreigner. He does not know our ways, Guido. He will soon leave the care of Luna back in our hands, and all will be the same again." Although something visceral in her screamed otherwise.

His dark brows knitted over his hooked nose. "There was John Tunstall, the wealthy Englishman, who came to ranch in Lincoln the year before last."

"Aye, and ye saw what happened to him, did ye no'? Murdered by The House. Nae, this Neville is but one hombre. We can handle one mere hombre."

CHAPTER FOUR

With O'Moore's fishing pole slung across Miles's shoulder and the deceased land baron's net swishing from his belt, he sauntered down the slope, slabbed with shale, then picked his steps more carefully where the scree made the slope more slippery.

Below it, El Rito Creek burbled into the Pecos Pool – the site where he had first met the water nymph or, more likely, the belle from Bedlam. Mhaire O'Moore was either certifiably crazy or brilliantly imaginative.

Wearing the old man's rubber Wellington's, Miles waded gently midway into the rocky shallows. Swarms of sunfish, perch, walleye, and catfish squiggled past. Whistling, he cast out, quartering upstream, then began mending the line so that it looked natural to the fish, and stripping fast enough before the slack could build up.

Fly fishing was second nature to him and had a special allure, representing unique challenges. He never grew bored. Even the ethereal scenery around him could not distract him. He had done enough fly fishing in Ireland's River Blackwater, with its broad valley, pastures, woodlands, and series of grand gorges.

The Blackwater was famed for its salmon and trout fishing, but angling for salmon and trout on the Pecos was not his purpose. Here, he was fishing for something greater.

Gold.

The great wealth the Spaniards took when they conquered the Inca of South America and Aztec of Central America had only fired beliefs that still more riches lay somewhere in the interior of what was now the Territory of New Mexico.

In 1530, the Viceroy of New Spain had in his possession in

Mexico City an Indian, native to the area of Jemez Canyon, near Santa Fe. The Indio, wearing a gold bracelet, claimed his father had often returned to the village with a large amount of turquoise and gold.

Next, in 1539, Friar Marcos had returned to Mexico City from near this very area of Puerto de Luna to proclaim he had seen the legendary Seven Cities of Cibola, first reported by Cabeza de Vaca in 1536. Friar Marcos confirmed that its walls glistened with gold and that its doors were studded with turquoise.

With that, the conquistador Francisco de Coronado had been commissioned in 1540 to find these Seven Cities of Gold. The caballero Pedro de Castaneda, who was a member of the expedition, later reported witnessing numerous clay jars of gold nuggets being buried somewhere along the Pecos.

Where *exactly* had Castaneda seen these jars being buried?

As an awkward, gangly youth, Miles had avidly consumed at Harrow a rare edition of a book chronicling Coronado's search for gold. From that time on, Coronado's thrill became his, a pulsing vision that made seasonal returns to the bleak Blackwater Castle bearable.

Using landmarks described – namely a bridge said to have been built by Coronado across the Pecos – Miles determined the conquistador's army of seventy-five mail-clad horsemen had marched southeast from Cibola and then down the Pecos – near to what was now Puerto de Luna. The area's history included the recounting of such a bridge.

By Miles's calculations, Coronado could well have buried his hoard of gold somewhere in the same area that the looney lass warned the Golden Carp ruled.

Nearly 350 years had elapsed since Coronado had passed through. The landscape would have changed. The river's banks could have been eroded. Its channel could have shifted numerous times.

Nevertheless, all the while casting and reeling in, Miles's gaze studied both shorelines for clues. He had prospected in both Canada and California and knew better than most tenderfeet signs of gold deposits. But he was looking for human tampering, not nature's.

In childhood, he had learned to interpret telltale signs with something that amounted to a preternatural sixth sense . . . the tone of his father's voice, the nuance of his every word, the subtle warnings in his body language, the pace of his footsteps, the threat of his very energy.

Miles was not only his father's heir, he was, also, quite possibly not his father's son. And for this his father, a British MP, had browbeat him with his words and judgments, followed often by his volatile violence. The reprehensible behavior of his father, a tyrant, betrayed his insecurities and suspicions.

Suspicions even of his wife's fidelity. She was the sole heir of her father, the Earl of Blackwater. A Peeress in her Own Right, Kathleen Neville Drummond had retained her title of countess after marriage. But, at the behest of her husband, she had conveyed the title of earl to him, via special decree of the Crown.

Miles's early family life was loveless, a circumstance common among the British upper class. He had seen little of his parents. When duty or necessity compelled them to take notice of him, they were formal and formidably frightening.

But, after the death of his mum when pitched from a horse, he had loss her protection, such that it was – her occasionally mild objections to Charles Drummond's overbearing conduct toward their son.

The suffering and shame Miles underwent were nothing compared to that feeling of waiting for the other shoe to drop, the sword of Damocles to fall. Waiting for his father's footsteps. Waiting inspection.

The constant anxiety took its toll. Every moment was laden with the possibility that in the blink of a lid his father's mood would shift from irrationality into an overbearing rage and ultimately a violence, which his mother gave a wide berth.

It was the eternally vigilant waiting that unraveled the boy Miles. And his father had known this and used it against him quite effectively. He never cried. Well, perhaps on the inside. Instead, when he came of age, he revolted and took his mother's family name of Neville.

It was the fly fishing that had taught him infinite patience. The Blackwater estates' head gamekeeper, the well-read Finian Selkirk, had taken the lonely boy under his wing and taught him fly fishing and much more. Resilience. Trust. Confidence. All this from a substitute father's loving care.

Mile's was expecting Finian's arrival any time now. On Miles's instructions, the Irish gamekeeper had traveled to France to meet with the inventor of a hand-held device that detected buried metal.

Just as Miles was reeling in a vigorously resisting fish, women and men, maybe a dozen or more, trooped single file toward the very spot he fished. Aghast, he watched from the opposite bank as, one by one, they waded into the pool created by the confluence of the Pecos and El Rito Creek and submersed themselves.

Mhaire O'Moore was the last of these interlopers. When she emerged, dripping wet, his wellies charged across the swirling pool to the shallows of the opposite bank. He got furious words past gnashing jaws. "I thought you said this spot was sacred?" Too late, he heard his father's scathing tone in his own voice.

Her fingers flung back from her face the mass of dripping ginger hair. Through water spiked lashes, she blinked her surprise up at him. "Tis our monthly Sunday sacrament."

He reined in his wrath. "What?"

Her expression took on that of a patient school marm with a slow child. "Ye see, since we hae nae parish priest, some of us cleanse ourselves of our sins by dipping our bodies into this sacred spot, afore lighting mass candles."

He snapped the rod and its catch, a miserable common carp, landed at her small, mud-splattered bare feet. The startled expressions of toothless toddlers and haggle-toothed ancients alike locked on him. "Well, this bloody sacred spot belongs to me now," he explained with his own forced smile of patience, "and your sinful souls are trespassing."

She gasped, her mouth forming an O of astonishment. "Ye canna be seriously thinking now to forbid us worship here?"

That patience he had summoned evaporated. The last thing he needed was a pilgrimage of petitioners spying on him. His hand flicked dismissively downriver. "Find a spot closer to Puerta de Luna and its church, for God's sake."

She raised a cool brow, "Oh, so ye believe in God, do ye now?"

"What I don't believe in is this Golden Carp of yours. A mermaid, you would have it! Can you get any crazier without being committed?"

"But this is the closest holy water to our town. We've been coming here for years."

"Well, all good things must come to an end. Now get these people out of here."

Her hands clenched into hammerheads. Her plump lips

thinned like barbed wire. He could almost hear her teeth grinding. "In that case, I place a curse on yuir miserably vile self. That ye be forever obsessed with the one thing ye cannae hae."

He smacked his forehead, as if struck with an epiphany. "But of course – that would undoubtedly be peace and privacy here at Puerto de Luna."

Her small chin shot up. She waved to her companions to come ashore and follow her. As he watched her flounce off with her motley group, a shiver slithered up his spine, and the fine hairs at his nape bristled. As if he bought into her supernatural rubbish.

Exasperated, he packed up his fishing gear for the day. Upon returning to the Luna House, his foul mood dissipated at once.

Finian Selkirk waited for him in O'Moore's office. The rawboned man ceased his restless prowling and, with a twinkle in his periwinkle blue eyes, glanced at Miles, then at the shaggy buffalo head mounted over the fireplace. "According to talk on the stagecoach, I expect to see yuir head mounted up there soon, if the Santa Fe Ring has anything to say about it."

Miles restored the fishing pole to its rack and wrapped the man in a bear-hug. "Or if the local mermaid has anything to say about it."

The grizzled droopy mustache waggled along with the dark brows. The thick head of hair, threaded with charcoal gray, had once been coal black. If the flirtatious gazes cast by both the comely and the homely was anything to go by, Finian must be considered a handsome roué still. "Mermaid?"

Hand still on Finian's shoulder, Miles ushered his old friend down the hallway toward the butler's pantry. Dusty boots clicked alongside worn-down brogans on the Saltillo tiles. "A most peculiar little thing, she is. But that's a cockeyed story to share over a tumbler of port in the smoke room, where you can, also, regale me with which of my dastardly deeds has aroused the interest of this Santa Fe Ring."

"Buying out the cattle syndicate aroused their interest. Taking occupation of the Luna House, perceived as a threatened takeover of the area itself, aroused their suspicions."

"Bah, humbug, and all that bloody rot. More importantly, were you able to secure the metal detector?"

The axel-rods that were shoulders sagged slightly beneath Miles's palm. "Och, well then, mon, ye know about the Moirae?"

He plucked a dust-filmed bottle of port from the pantry's wine racks. "To be sure. Irish goddesses who controlled everyone's fate." Was everyone around him caught up with nonsense like fables and myths and such hooey?

As if he were snoring, the ends of Finian's mustache fluttered. He tucked his thumbs beneath his canvass suspenders. "Well then, if the Moirae have anything to say about it, yuir fate as far as the metal detector is concerned is fooked."

§ § §

As Finian had put it, Miles knew his fate was fooked, or would be, if he did not repair his ill-considered interactions with the locals. Their good will might mean the difference between his achieving his goal or not there at Puerto de Luna. But, jeezus, if that bloody looney of a young woman did not set his teeth on edge.

Be that as it may, he readily accepted Finian's suggestion to attend the ice-cream sociable, the notice of which he had seen posted upon his arrival at the Grzelachowski Mercantile stage-stop. Apparently, the social was a project of the Nuestra Senora del Refugio church to raise funds for the construction of a cathedral.

"Think of it, mon, ice cream – here in the desert!"

He was thinking more along the lines of how he could turn the fiasco the week before into an advantage.

As if the dry and dusty desert were a delight, Finian extolled its beauty, as only an Irishman could do. The view from the O'Moore buckboard, traversing the continuing flat expanse, gave no hint of the abrupt landscape transformation to come.

Then, suddenly, cresting a slight rise, the winding gorge of Pecos canyon was exposed to the startled eye, and the spectacular view elicited a momentary, awe-inspiring silence.

"Will ye look at that, laddie! Paradise in the road rising up to meet us!"

Well, not quite Miles's idea of paradise, but the imposing panorama did offer a certain bizarre enchantment. Towering mesas of orange and red intermingled with green arroyos and contrasted with the morning's clear turquoise sky.

Here, where the road closely skirted a bluff of the river, its roaring volume was amplified. As the Luna backboard's white-oak wheels rolled alongside the river's rushes, a flock of geese beat a rapid retreat.

After passing an irrigated alfalfa field, where a mule deer grazed, and a field of tasseled corn, a cluster of squalid shacks came into view. Their rusted tin roofs were ornamented with drying green chiles weighted by rocks to hold them against the desert wind.

The shanties heralded the outskirts of Puerto de Luna. An oasis of humanity in that overwhelming vastness that could make one feel puny and insignificant, the pueblo was a riot of color.

Red geraniums spilled from a porch's terra cotta *maceta*. Last year's maroon ristras draped from a portico's whitewashed house. Outback, yellow hollyhocks climbed its animal pens. Neat adobe homes were clad with blue and purple flowering vines. Between the homes, their corrals were filled with fine prancing horses or bawling cattle.

Establishments with gaudy signs banked the plaza, and dozens of people milled in its center, where ruckus boys and mangy mutts darted in and out. The focus was the three wooden-staved tubs, around which the townspeople were congregated.

Women with parasols in hand and men with tankards watched the volunteers, perched on milking stools, turn the cranks of the three ice cream machines.

At Miles and Finian's approach, the crowd's joking and gossiping ebbed like the sea just before a storm surge. Finian fingered his mustache, concealing his mumble. "Och, laddie, looks like word of yuir fiasco last week has spread already."

"And readily repairable. The only thing worse than being talked about, Finian, is not being talked about."

Idly whistling, he strode over to the long, linen-covered table. At one end was an array of bowls and spoons, awaiting the creamed mixture to freeze. At the other end, backed by an arrangement of fresh flowers, reposed a large cut crystal bowl. It was filled with donations — an assortment of coins and a few tattered greenbacks and a wad of nearly worthless Mexican pesos.

He dropped in his own wad — four $5 bills, issued by the First National Gold Bank of San Francisco. He repressed a groan at this ostentation. He was all too aware of the desperate need to keep the Luna estate operating while he pursued his plan.

Behind him, he heard the all but smothered gasps at his lavishness. All at once, he and Finian were being clapped on their backs.

A robust and bearded older man grinned broadly. "Right generous of you, sir! Grzelachowski's my name. Alex Grzelachowski. Owner of the mercantile store across the way there."

An older, pigeon-chested woman, wearing an outrageously beribboned and plumed hat, beamed up at him. "God love ya."

There were others extending their hands in hearty welcoming shakes, but Miles only saw the woebegone straw hat shading a mouth that gave no quarter. The hat's lop-sided brim alleviated the severely strong molding of Mhaire O'Moore's features – all but her eyes. They flashed fire like a double-barreled shotgun aimed directly at him.

She flipped over her left shoulder one tatty end of a maroon shawl that had more holes than a sieve and sidled next to him. Tilting her chin up, she smiled, but her words, meant only for him, were a ferocious snarl. "A typical English chancer, ye are. Working all the angles."

His mutter was an equal growl. "Well, well, well . . . if it isn't one of the pesky ants that always manage to spoil an outing."

If possible, that smart-ass mouth widened its grin even farther – and then abruptly the lips twisted liked a corkscrew, and her hand went to the gaudy cross of her necklace. He followed the direction of her eyes, narrowed like snake slits.

Heads turned toward the man strolling indolently through the crowd. Of medium height and bullnecked, he wore a bowler and three-piece suit, its tan jacket flipping open with each stride to reveal alternately a scabbarded knife, then pistol. Following in his wake were three men who might have been taken for cowpokes but for the guns slung low on their hips.

The chap paused near the ice cream tubs. The trio of hand crankers, two older gents and a snaggle-toothed boy, halted their churning and stared up at him. He nodded. Hands on his lapels, he rotated back to the townspeople and singled out Grzelachowski. "Raising funds for a holy house, are you?"

Grzelachowski's beard parted in what could be taken for a friendly grin . . . or grimace. "Doing our best, Mr. Sullivan."

The man turned to Miles. That close, the chap had an oily face nicked and pitted by man or nature or both. "Emmet Sullivan." His granite gaze surveyed Miles's inordinate height. "And you are?"

The bloke didn't offer his hand. Neither did Miles. "Neville.

Miles Neville."

"Ahh, yes. I've heard about you." He sported a fancy bolo string tie, while Miles's bandana, knotted at the back of his neck, was looking rather ragged for the wear.

Dismissively, Sullivan turned to the clusters of townspeople, nervous smiles plastered to their faces. "For a reasonable down payment, my institution would be willing to finance the construction, and you'd get your church underway immediately." Disparagingly, he flicked beringed fingers at the three ice cream machines. "Rather than this penny-ante piddling."

Now Miles remembered the man's name from the Syndicate's report. He had thoroughly investigated both the Luna estate and its territorial governing affairs before risking the buyout of the venture. Emmet Sullivan was a gunman cum banker out of Lincoln, who made sure he had no competitors.

"Reasonable – or sizeable?"

Sullivan swung back to him, then glanced pointedly over his shoulder at the three gunmen accompanying him. His grin was fool's gold. "You willing to make a better offer?"

Miles easily identified the fissure in the man's façade – he did not like being challenged. For too much of Miles's life, he had backed off from such a countenance, reminiscent of his father's.

He chose a bland smile to meet Sullivan's threat. Why Miles even bothered was absurd, since in the long run these people served him no purpose. "I am *willing* to point out that a down payment is not a good investment. It benefits the bank, because the bank has a lower risk of losing money. If there is a default on a mortgage, the bank would foreclose, sell the building, and keep the equity."

Sullivan's responsive smile was as oily as his face. "You are failing to note that borrowers, as long as they don't default on the mortgage, are building up equity in the church building."

Miles shrugged, tucked his thumbs in the riveted pockets of his denims. "That buildup in equity occurs with a mortgage – or without one."

Sullivan blinked. Obviously, he had not anticipated analytical opposition. During this exchange, Miles could feel the weighted attention of everyone present in the plaza – including the young woman beside him and Finian, who had his back. Now, all breathing seemed suspended, waiting for Sullivan's reaction.

So was he.

Sullivan's furrowed features clearly said he was canvassing the situation. A showdown here in the people-filled plaza was not good for business. His smile smoothed out the furrows. "Too bad, then. Without my financial backing, it would seem hell will come to Puerto de Luna before heaven does."

Watching Sullivan and his three faithful followers ride south down the dusty, rutted road leading away from the plaza, Miles sensed Sullivan might be right, that hell was coming first – if for no other reason than the thin line of angry, rust-colored clouds roiling over the red mesas far off to the west.

CHAPTER FIVE

Disappointment eddied from Mhaire's sigh. The Englishman's manipulation of others was astounding. He outmatched P.T. Barnum in showmanship. At least Emmet Sullivan let his casualties know up front they would come up on the short end of the stick.

But Miles Neville defrauded through charm and deception. He cared naught for the townspeople and their strifes nor the church's construction nor the area's holy waters.

He wanted the fabled gold, it was that obvious.

She shouldered through the subdued attendees of the ice cream sociable to Ritter's Stables and her buckboard. Bray and Neigh lazily swished their tails at the flies, unaware of her agitation.

It only increased as she drove out of Puerto de Luna. Across the horizon, an ominous red curtain boiled taller and wider in scope even in the few seconds in which she took note of this ominous significance. A massive wall of sand.

The townspeople would make it back to their homes in time. They would know what to do. Primarily, stay indoors and lay wet rags across all windowsills and thresholds. Except, she was not at home. Home was still miles away. She popped the whip over the pair of furred rumps, urging the donkeys faster along the River Road. Toward shelter for them and herself.

Sand eddied in drifts across the rutted track, heralding the devastation to come. At last, the buckboard reached the path, bordered by sage and feathergrass, that departed the River Road for the Turquoise Door.

The sand was blighting her vision now and abrading her face.

She tilted it away from the direction of the stinging wind. It was growing, growling. A deafening sound. The wind tore back her hat, and its thin chin strap bit into her throat.

How far was she from home? Had the buckboard clattered across the acequia's wooden bridge yet? Minutes later, a horde of tumbleweed came roaring past, startling Bray and Neigh. They took off at a pounding clip-clop. Her arm muscles were strained, trying to control the reins. Now, the air was so dense with sand she could barely make out their pair of long ears, and the sand was blasting her skin.

Her sense of direction was lost. Worse, breathing grew difficult. Her teeth gritted with sand. Darkness swirled around her. Focus in that murk was impossible. But, surely, she was close to the adobe.

Within minutes, the wind was of gale force. It whipped the rein from her left hand. Mary, mother of mercy! Blindly, she groped for the rein. Neigh and Bray seemed to sense her panic. Their loping picked up to a frantic galloping gait. They plunged down in and up out of a dry gull wash.

Suddenly the bouncing buckboard was tipping. Her remaining grip hauled sharply on its remaining rein in a vain attempt to upright the wagon. Over onto its side it skidded, hauling the donkeys up short – and thumping her up and over.

She lay there, supine, her breath jarred from her lungs. Moments later, air crept back in, laden with sand that scoured her windpipe with each inhalation and exhalation. But feeling did not return. Stunned, she tried to find sensation of some kind, a tingling, something. How long had passed. Seconds? Minutes?

Meanwhile a blizzard of granules and dust whirled around her. No light penetrated this blackness. The roaring wind smothered all sound but for the occasional faint hee-haw bawling of the donkeys, who must have broken loose from the traces. Sandstorms could rage through for minutes or hours – or even days. How long before she would be found?

She thought she was afraid of nothing. The loss of her mother, father, brother, her home, financial resources . . . everything had been taken from her. What else did she stand to lose? But this . . . this incapacitation . . . it was terrifying. It stole her breath like the sand never could. Her heartbeat throttled to a painful pace.

Something – a snake? – slithered up her calf. She thrashed

wildly at her skirts and opened her mouth to scream, only to choke on a shovelful of fine sand.

"Good!" Satisfaction saturated the shouting male voice. "You're not seriously hurt."

"Ye – ye degenerate arsehat!"

He tsked loudly. "My, my – such language from a lady."

She went to swat away the man's hand, but both it and he himself had vanished into the blackness. She scrambled to sit upright. "Mr. Neville?" She hated the anxiousness in her voice.

Then, he was back, hunkering next to her. The air was so dense with the sand, she could barely make out his face. His bandana masked its lower half. Not that she could open her lids beyond the barest slit.

He leaned close into her and captured her chin firmly with one hand. She tried to twist away. A finger coated something acrid, lard-like, inside her nose, first one nostril, then the other. "Axel grease. From your wagon wheel."

She slapped at his wrist.

"It'll keep you from drying out." Then he ran his finger lightly over her cheekbone, down to find the indenture of her bottom lip, making her shiver. Slowly, with infinite care, he painted her mouth with the grease.

Her body was responding treacherously to the heat stirring between them. She pushed at his forearm. "Shelter! We need to get out of this!"

"We're in the safest place for now – on the leeward side of your upended wagon." He fumbled for her shawl, drawing it up across the bridge of her nose to cover her lower face. Shot through with holes as the shawl was, it offered little protection.

"My donkeys – "

"I've already set them loose. They'll find their way back to the your stable. Which means we're sharing the wagon's protection with my sorrel. Bronco won't mind, if you won't."

He didn't give her a chance for a rebuttal, but slouched next to her and, surprising her, turned to arch his upper torso over hers, so that his head was buried in her wind-whipping hair, his breadth of body shielding hers.

It was as if they were encased in a vacuum. The air scant. She felt dizzy. Could swear she could hear her heart drumming a rapid tattoo. Or was it his she heard?

"You ever been kissed?"

Mierda. Crikey. At a time like this . . . he would ask a question like that? What to say? "Have yeself?"

She sensed more than heard his low laughter. "Yes. Been kissed. And I have kissed. A pleasure I most enjoy bestowing. And you would enjoy experiencing."

What pomposity. Her teeth ground the sand wedged between them. Again, she perceived his intolerable amusement – and at her expense – rather than heard anything beyond the roaring in her ears.

Until he leaned his lips next to them. "And, bye the bye, you did not answer my question. Have you been kissed? Properly?"

A tremendous gust danced a whirlwind around them, saving her from responding. She clung to him – and then, suddenly, everything was still. Lemony sunlight, extravagantly beautiful, poured down upon them. The sandstorm had passed.

And so had the moment. They drew back . . . stared aghast at one another over the rims of their protective demi masks . . . then hastily got to their feet.

He brushed his palms together, shaking off the sand, and yanked his bandana down around the base of his muscular throat. "Best get the wagon upright. Take the far end, and when I say 'heave', give it all you got."

Something teased the back of her mind – beyond the need to grouse at his brusque high-handedness – but she followed his orders and braced her palms against the floorboard. With his order to heave, they righted the wagon fairly easy, though its springs groaned with the jouncing

Whistling cheerfully, he harnessed Bronco to the wagon. The sorrel shillyshallied, indignant at being subjected to a chore beneath its breeding.

After the wagon was back on the road, it took her a while to realize what was nettling her. "How did you know where to find me?"

He broke off whistling, snapped the reins, then glanced over at her briefly. "After you flounced away from the ice cream sociable, even a dunce would be aware you find my company . . . disturbing. I seek to make amends, Miss O'Moore. After all, we're neighbors . . . more or less."

"So, was that a neighborly kiss you were discussing back there – or a proposition you were importuning?"

His strong profile against the setting sun challenged nature and her. "Perhaps both, the kiss and the proposition."

"Like what kind of proposition? Because if tis that position of 'housekeeper' ye be thinking, then you can think again, Mr. Neville." Not for the world would she address him as 'your lordship.'

"My thoughts were more along the line of your helping keep the Luna estate books, as well. After all, you've been doing it for so long."

"And how do ye know I won't stiff ye?"

By this time, they had reached the wagon yard behind the Turquoise Door, and he braked the wagon. A smile softened the harsh countenance he turned on her. "I've learned there's a price for everything, Miss O'Moore, be it personal or business."

At that, he dropped down from the wagon seat to unharness his sorrel. His gaze between the sorrel's ears pinned her. "The question is – will the payoff be greater than the price? If so, then go for it with gusto."

Sourly, she noted he had not even bothered helping a lady descend the buckboard's cast-iron step. Which put her in her place. The smile she bequeathed was just as sour. "Keeping the books for yeself, would never be worth any price."

He sprang back aboard the wagon and winked. "Just so you understand your Sunday pilgrimages to the Pecos Pool are off limits."

"Trusting ye enjoy yuir afternoon ride back to the Luna House with equal gusto, Mr. Neville. Fare thee well, cheerio, adios, and all that blather."

Arsehole. *Pendejo. Cúl tóna.*

CHAPTER SIX

Poultices and potions were most effective if their medicinal herbs were gathered daily. When Mhaire returned home early that afternoon with her freshly filled gunnysack and hand trowel, five patients awaited her curative care – and one visitor her personal attention.

The most urgent of the patients was fusty Alberto Reyes, who had almost chopped off his left big toe with a hoe the Sunday before – the same afternoon of the sandstorm, when Miles Neville had forbidden her and the villagers access to the area's holy sites. She had tended to Alberto that evening, but now he was back.

As the four rickety chairs that crammed the *sala* were already taken, he hunched on the tall, staved butter churner. The little adobe's thrown open shutters cast merciless light on his gnarled foot.

Crouched before it, Elsa's knotty fingers were working to peel away the dirty bandage. With alarm, she and the four other patients eyed the puffed foot, red-streaked with heat. Returning that week with their ailing complaints unchanged, the patients were thinking the same as Mhaire.

Why had their maladies not healed? Her various ministrations lately were not efficacious. True, occasionally, in the past one of her prescribed therapies did not work. Naturally, that was to be anticipated.

But she strongly suspected that her many therapy failures lately were due to Miles Neville – to his desecration that day he relieved himself in the Pecos Pool and his supposed fishing expeditions since. She could only hope the spring rains would wash away the sins of his defilement and restore the water's full powers.

But not a drop of rain had splattered the thirsting land, so far.

Worse, with his arrival had come nameless, disturbing dreams to beleaguer her. Dreams that were more like vivid memories. Impossible, of course. Because these dreams vaguely seemed to take place in centuries past.

A male voice coming from the corner echoed her concern about Alberto's oozing toe. "Good God, even the docs at the Civil War's bloodiest battle had more to work with than you."

Gray bowler in hand, Emmet Sullivan stepped into the window's shaft of sunlight. Dust motes sluffed off the Irishman's compact body. He was a Union army veteran and capitalist – or swindler, depending on with which side one aligned. Her father had sided against him and lost almost everything.

His curly brown hair, receding at the temples, was pressed flat where his hat had set. He wore a starched wing collar with a four-in-hand tie, and his gray sack coat was carelessly buttoned only at the top, displaying his gold watch chain against his vest.

He nodded at the five villagers. "Do you have a moment – before you tend to them?"

She glanced questioningly at Elsa. The astute woman might as well have given Emmet Sullivan the evil eye. She shrugged shoulders of stout bone, then resumed unrolling the bandage from Alberto's ulcered foot.

Sullivan held the door open for Mhaire, and she stepped outside. Hands clasped before her, she turned to look up at him, though he was only of medium height. "Aye, Mr. Sullivan?"

Squared off hands, one minus its thumb, twirled his bowler in an obvious annoyed fashion. Nevertheless, he forced a curl of lips that revealed teeth yellowed by too much tobacco.

"Look, Miss O'Moore, what can you tell me about this English dude – Miles Neville – who bought your Luna land grant? What his plans are?"

She eyed him, his lips that rolled, his lids that pouched. The grooves running from nostrils to his mouth were seamed into hairlines of latent rage. Her gaze drifted lower, to his belt. She knew he packed on it both a revolver and a knife with which, if stories were true, he gutted men like field dressing a deer.

Her head canted. "Why do ye ask?"

"Word down from Santa Fe has it that this Englishman is an

earl. That he opened an account with a considerable deposit on its First National Bank.”

With no competition, Sullivan’s businesses in Lincoln charged high prices for their goods and high rates for loans, making him hated by farmers and ranchers alike throughout that part of the Territory. But the Englishman John Tunstall had taken on Sullivan – and lost. Did Sullivan see Miles as another competitor?

“Miles Neville, ye say?” Her mind’s eye recalled him standing on the Pecos shoreline, his male attribute boldly displayed. He reminded her of Pan, the god of the wilds and companion to the nymphs. She had to grin at the thought. “I’d say ye hae stiff competition, Mr. Sullivan.”

Those thick lips pursed, and his eyes skewered into slits of savagery. “I’ll see about that.”

“The Englishman’s not the kind to buckle under. Ye know, ‘The Charge of the Light Brigade’ – ‘ours is but to do or die’, stiff upper lip, and all that.”

He looked confounded by her quoting. He clapped on his bowler. “Sooner, rather than later, I know everything that goes on here in your backwater town. Everything that comes in, everything that goes out. You have a good day, Miss O’Moore – and I hope I shall be seeing you under more pleasant conditions, soon.”

“Ah, hope – tis a grand thing is it not? A guid day to ye, Mr. Sullivan, and haste ye back.” Ye rat’s ass. *Culo de rata. Fundillo.*

She may have dispatched Emmet Sullivan on his way but not so her worries about her continued failure to restore the health of her patients. As if word had passed around about Miles Neville’s profaning of the Pecos Pool, her patient visits dwindled.

The following Monday, only two patients showed up, a man who had crushed his hand in an inept attempt to dig an acequia and a boy whose sling shot had popped loose, swelling his eye socket.

Now, this sun-blasted morning, her sole patient was a mestizo mother with a wailing bairn tucked into the fringed *reboza* on her back.

When Elsa answered the next knock at the adobe’s door, Mhaire was expecting perhaps another patient and glanced up from the colicky bairn she had propped face down across her knees. She was surprised to behold the tall and lanky older man she had seen with Miles Neville the day of the ice cream sociable.

Seeming unfazed by Elsa’s ghastly features or the new

doorstop that was Pork the pig, he crunched his beret between his sunspotted hands. His eyebrows, the same shade as his hair and mustache – the fading black of a snuffed torch – pumped in agitation. "Miss O'Moore?"

"Aye?"

"Finian Selkirk. There's been an accident. Miles – Miles Neville – has taken a gunshot wound." The man's brogue was thick. So, Irish, this man was. He nodded behind him. "Me laddie's there in the wagon bed. Told me ye'd care for him."

Handing back the infant to its mother, Mhaire hurried to follow Selkirk outside to the back of the wagon. Among shovels and picks, buckets, and fishing poles, the barely conscious Englishman lay supine. A small, crimson circle splotched his denims near the groin area. Pain gritted words from between his clenched teeth. "Well, well, well . . . the Witch of the West."

She glanced back to the older man. "Help me get him inside."

When between them she and Finian hoisted Neville out of the wagon, he moaned, and she noted with real concern that the wound's perimeter was widening. His raspy breathing was labored.

"What happened?"

Wrinkles at the edges of Selkirk's blue eyes furrowed. His mustached twitched with lips that worked to hold back his worried tone. "We were, uhhh, fishing, when I heard gun shots. They were coming from somewhere along the opposite bank's marsh. Next, I saw me laddie buckle to the ground."

Her brow yanked up. "Fishing, ye say? More like digging, like all the other gold-dazed prospectors."

He fixed her with an implacable yet imploring gaze. "Know this, whatever gold be here, it means nothing to Miles, though he may swear differently. Tis the quest for it, the lure, the challenge, that fills his emptiness."

She sighed. "The result be the same – our soil plundered all for naught. The room to your right. And the plunderer still leaves, empty. Me bed – the closer one."

Making way for them, the mother, her bairn cradled in one arm, crossed herself and scurried away. Mhaire set to work, removing Miles belt and holster and unbuttoning his fly. To his friend, she said, "Take off his boots and socks."

At the doorway, Elsa said, "I vill heat the tea kettle and get the sheet strips for binding."

When Mhaire gently began to shimmy off Miles's denim pants, his eyes, the exact shade of the Blue Hole's fathomless water, shot open, and his white lips drew back in a snarl.

His underdrawers were blood-soaked, and she peeled back one flap to expose the wound, its pulsing spurts reeking with the blood's coppery tang.

Only then did she observe there were two wounds. The entry and exit wounds appeared high, just behind and in front, of the hipbone – meaning, hopefully, the bullet had plowed on through and, with luck, missed vital organs.

Of immediate concern was the urgency to stabilize the hip to staunch the blood loss. If she couldn't, he would die anyway. Even if she was able to stop the blood flow, he could still die of infection.

She glanced up over her shoulder at the older man, hovering at her side. He needed something to keep him occupied. "Get me something to secure his hip joint and thigh in place, something rigid, Mr. Selkirk."

"Finian, please."

"A ramrod, a branch, a branding iron, Finian – I dinna care."

She knew she sounded snippy, but, Holy Mary, Mother of God, if there was one person in whole of the New Mexico Territory she was reluctant to tend, other than Emmet Sullivan, it would be this man who was despicably English – and Protestant – and an occupant of the very home that had once been hers.

Gathering a length of the top sheet, she slid it beneath his hip and pressed the threadbare linen against the hip's front and back wounds. Too quickly, the clump of linen was soaked. Worse, his writhing torso was making it difficult. He was long-limbed and lean flanked. She pressed a becalming hand on his muscle-knotted stomach, and her fingers flicked back, as if singed by his flesh.

Aye, his skin was feverish. But something else had coursed between her and him. Once again. Exactly what she could not say. Yet, at her touch, he ceased his agitated stirring. She glanced at his ashen face. Lids closed, he was breathing shallowly. Perspiration beaded his temples and upper lip, faintly shadowed by stubble.

At that moment, Finian returned with what looked suspiciously like the yard-long hickory handle to her old axe. "Yanked the head from the axe, I did. Will it serve, lass?"

She contained a worried sigh. "'Ave to do, it will. Yuir friend should be immobilized fer a guidly while. He can remain here, abed." If he lives.

Elsa, sidestepping Finian, passed her the armload of sheet strips. "You can take my bed, *havfrue*. I vill make a pallet on the floor."

"No need fer that," Finian said. "The Luna House has bedrooms aplenty." He eyed Elsa thoughtfully, and Mhaire noted he flinched naught at that portion of the woman's ravaged head. "Can ye cook a mon a meal?"

Elsa turned her gimlet gaze on him. "And poison it, as vell."

A low moan returned Mhaire's diverted attention to Miles. "Will ye two fighting cocks back off one another? I could use some 'elp 'ere, ye know. Elsa, I'll need the willow bark paste – oh, and the dried white yarrow for the fever."

Elsa, with her own experience in the healing arts, was already headed for the kitchen. "And a sleeping potion."

Finian's large hands worried around the axe handle. "Ye'll take guid care of him, lass? A good egg, he is. Like me son."

"I'll do what I can." If he did not respond to her healing efforts, which were the complaints of her few remaining patients over the past days, that they were failing to get better . . . yet, she would swear the downturn had come with the Englishman's arrival. "Ready to help me restrain him?"

"I'll lift him – ye slide the axe handle under, lass."

The man bent over the bed and gently tilted him like a swaddled infant onto his good side. He half whimpered, half grumbled. His lids snapped open. "Bloody hell, Finian, an undertaker could better care for – "

With that, he mercifully passed out. Quickly, she and Finian bound the axe handle to his hip and thigh. By this time, Elsa returned with the unguents and helped her bandage the wound sites. His eyes opened to fasten on Mhaire, as if she was his saving grace. Then, she took advantage of his muttered groans to spoon a few quaffs of sedation between his parted lips.

At last, subsiding, he dozed off. She looked up at Finian. His lined face was nearly as pale as that of the Englishman. "I've done all that I can do for now. Why dinna ye get some rest? Ye can spell me tomorrow."

Reluctance to leave shadowed his eyes, a faded blue and

creased at the outer corners by time and weather, but he nodded. "Aye, lass."

Elsa's lips flattened to a determined line. "I'm staying, *havfrue*. You should not be alone with him."

Silently, Mhaire beseeched all the saints she could recall. "Elsa, he is too weak to harm me, and ye should know by now I dinna give a fig for what the townspeople might think. Now, go on with yeself."

From the turquoise door of the little adobe, she watched in the faltering light of day as Finian and a rigid-backed Elsa drove away in the wagon. Drove toward the Luna House. Mhaire's home.

Her former home.

She turned back toward the bedroom she shared with Elsa. Well, the bedroom she now shared with Miles Neville. The Earl of Blackwater. Lord of Luna.

Already, his restless sleep had reopened the wounds. Sighing, she leaned over him, her fingers gently prying loose the first layer of crimson-clotted, linen bandages.

His hand seized her wrist. Her breath caught. Her gaze swerved to his pain-wracked face. Even injured as badly as he was, his strength was superior. He fixed her with glazed, fever-bright eyes. "You are determined . . . to torment me."

"Tis trying to help ye, I am."

"Or kill me? Did you arrange for someone to ambush me?"

Ambush him? "Why, ye ungrateful slimebucket. No, but tis no' a bad idea." She focused on applying another coating of the willow bark paste, trusting it would soon serve as a sealant as well as calm his vile irritability. "Though, easier it would be to poison you here and now with one of Elsa's concoctions."

"That witch you live with? Was she scalped?"

"At eleven. And left for dead." She poked another spoonful of the sleeping draught into his mouth. "The Navajo, they found her."

"She calls you . . . what?" His tongue was stumbling with the medicinal concoction. "Half brew . . . something."

"*Havfrue.* Danish for Little Mermaid — after the story by her Danish kinsman, 'cause of me love for swimming."

"Is everyone in the entire county crazy?" Peevishly, he knocked away the spoon she proffered and tumped the lantern off the crate. "It must be something in the drinking water."

"And ye're no' crazy?" Summoning patience, she rescued the

upended lantern. "Ye and yuir friend digging fer the legendry gold on our holy land, were ye no'?"

No wonder her remedies were failing.

No response from him. She glanced over at him. He had drifted off again. Faint lines of fatigue bracketed his mouth and fanned the outer corners of his eyes. His profuse sweating had dampened his hair, making its ends curl. A curling swatch, as black as the Earl of Hell's waistcoat, slanted down across one eye. Even asleep, he did not have that boyish look, as men often did.

No, but he did look not quite so dangerous. After all, surely, he was like other men. Surely, he experienced instances of fear, of inadequacy, of need for something outside himself.

But she knew better. Knew that his greed, like that of all men sickened by gold fever, would destroy anyone and everything standing in their way to attain their goal.

And she knew it was going to be a long night, keeping vigil over him. Not that she would be missing any sleep. With his coming, her sound sleep had vanished along with her healing abilities.

And now came these disturbing dreams to plague her.

CHAPTER SEVEN

Agony and ecstasy alternated with darkness and light and fire and freezing.

In a blazing sweat, Miles thrashed against constraining hands and some kind constraining board that must have been used in the inquisition . . . and he thrashed against distressing images.

His father inspecting the way he combed – or did not comb – his hair. "Your cowlick is sticking up, boy." Or how he carried his school bag, the moves he chose in chess, the chores he mucked up. All for the opportunity for his father to vent his wrath with violence on the never-do-well who was his son. In and out of this delirious agony weaved a very real Finian, with his tender care and comforting brusque brogue.

Then there was the ecstasy. So different from anything he had known. A female's constraining hands, as well. Insistently inspecting and probing. Gently swishing the sweat from his naked body with a cool, damp cloth. And her soft, life-restoring lips, cajoling in her own lilting brogue.

Time's passage was distorted by what was surely delicious delirium. Oh, how he craved that comforting, reassuring touch. That craving was nigh a sensual need, a volatility that vibrated the air when he sensed that feminine presence.

Gradually, he became aware of tantalizing aromas. The air smelled of sweet corn and the richness of ripe green chiles, of the subtler scents of ripe apples and peaches, of pumpkins, and cinnamon. Or was all this merely hallucinations induced by his deliriums?

Gradually, he became aware, also, that he was naked, covered only by a thin muslin sheet redolent with breezy freshness and the outdoors.

Gradually, his crusty lids peeled open. He winced against the glare of daylight and the sudden awareness of the bitter taste of the sleeping draught . . . like the narcotic spell of the poppy flower he had once tasted in San Francisco's Chinatown.

His glazed gaze inched around his marginal parameters. On his left, another narrow bed, a meter away, was rope slung and unmade. In between was a stand of some sorts — double stacks of wooden crates. The stand danced closer and retreated, then edged close once more. A porcelain basin, lantern, and side-by-side books, looking like tin soldiers, topped it.

Then sounds penetrated his cottony hearing. Murmuring. Muttering. Mumbling. He peered toward the end of his bed. A leprechaun gamboled before him. After a moment, he realized the sprite was sprinkling the hard, dirt-packed floor with a copper watering can . . . and uttering what surely were imprecations in English, Spanish, and Gaelic.

"An awful eejit I am . . . a sure-fire sign I hae done something incredibly stupid."

Sunlight streaming through the small window glanced off the upward sweep of Mhaire O'Moore's glorious cheekbones to sheen her carelessly knotted hair. The sunlight outlined the long, graceful line of her neck and silhouetted the bud of one nipple, thrusting in dainty insolence beneath her threadbare muslin blouse.

At once, magnetic heat arced from his body and initiated a pernicious hunger in him. Although, there was no way under heaven that he could have gotten up his cock, fisting it or not. His blood loss had gotten the better of him, it would seem.

Like a doe sniffing danger, she paused. Her attention shifted toward the bed in which he lay. He watched through lowered lashes. Setting aside the watering can, she warily crossed to pause near him. Her expression eased somewhat.

Vigorously, she washed her hands in the nearby basin, and his nostrils picked up the scent of lye soap. She took his wrist, her fingertips pressing slightly on the inside of it for his pulse.

His body jolted, feeling the devastating power of a dust devil whirl around him.

At his pulse's rapidity, she frowned.

His mouth felt dry, but he managed to babble, "You kissed me."

Her gaze swiveled down to clash with his. "Nae. Ye're delirious with fever."

He ached all over, those aches drumming in every muscle and in his skull whenever he moved his eyes or even dared stir. "Those kisses . . . no figment of my imagination."

"Well then, I may hae kissed yuir forehead . . . ever so often. Tis a guid way to determine a body's temperature."

"Oh, to be sure." His voice sounded croaky. "You kissed that . . . and more." The hollow of his neck, for one. And the hollow of his palm. And where else?

A blush worthy of a Vermeer suffused her cheeks. "Now that ye're awake, I'll take a peek at yuir wounds."

He felt too weak to protest but gratefully realized he was no longer bound to the Inquisition's torture board or whatever it had been. "How long have I been . . . been here?"

"Nigh on three days. Yuir friend Finian has been to visit each of them. Angsting about yeself, he was." She shrugged, and a whimsical smile fleetingly curved her lips. "But then he could be merely eager to escape Elsa."

Elsa? His mind searched for recollection of the name. Then came the image of the older woman, strong as brandy but hideously disfigured.

The beauty beside him drew back the sheet. If she took note of his semi erection, a piss-hard it was, she said nothing but set about examining his groin wound. From that angle on the pillow, he could see the wound was rimed with dried blood and capped with some kind of thick poultice.

Her slender fingers with their short nails butterflied around the inflamed area. A sudden primal arousal, thumping his navel, responded to her flaming touch. She met his chagrinned gaze and lifted a brow. "A randy laird, ye be."

"So I have been told." After he discovered at twelve the pleasure his cock provided with but just a little manipulation and imagination, life took on a whole new aspect. But now was not the time to elaborate on this fine and valuable part of himself.

She continued her examination. "A wee bit better."

That potentially dire pronouncement saw his libido begin to subside, evidenced by his wilting cock. "A *wee* bit better?"

"Ye're no' oot of the woods yet. Now, let me hae a look at yuir back side."

Backside? Ah, the other sore that pestered him with pain. "Uhhh, I'm quite sure the wound there . . . is progressing at the same pace."

"Nonsense." Her hands went to shift him, ass exposed.

Seeking to divert her intention, he captured the small hands in his larger palm. They were not the smooth hands of a lady, untouched by work and hardships. "And your Golden Carp isn't? Isn't nonsense?"

"But yuir searching fer Coronado's legendary gold cache makes sense, does it?" Her tone was lightly derisive. "That Coronado buried his gold here is about as legendary nonsensical as the legend he buried his seed in a local Indian maiden."

She was quite annoying. "There's a difference . . ." he paused to catch a pained breath, " . . . between a myth and a legend. Legend is based on a fact . . . a logical explanation."

She looked down into his eyes, her expression momentarily serious. She possessed a bohemian beauty, totally unique. "If ye're among the more fortunate, ye will come to realize that not everything needs an explanation."

A sensible explanation for her insensible approach to life . . . and for his inexplicable fascination with her. Hells bells, she charmed logic right out of his mind.

She tugged her hands loose and went to turn his injured hip up. Abruptly, he bucked in resistance – a mortifying blunder on his part, because her hand slipped to steady him and inadvertently palmed his meaty privates.

Electricity charged the air. Blue sparks popped and snapped. A tingling shock surged through him. As it must have her, because her eyes flared and she inhaled sharply. Instantly, their aghast gazes darted – from her flesh conjoined intimately with his – to each other's startled faces.

It was too good to pass up. He couldn't help his smirk. "I don't suppose I could interest you in giving me a hand with my – "

"Nae!" Irritation matched with embarrassment sparked in her

eyes. She snatched back her hand. "Do no' test me. Sorely tempted still to let ye die, I am."

He eyed her curiously. "And yet you don't." If she would – let him die, she would once more have run of the Luna House until the next buyer took possession. Her heart and soul were invested in that house. Her curator's touch was evident in its every board and beam. He had felt her spirited force present in each room he entered.

Her shoulders, small for the responsibility they bore, shrugged. "Tis the ultimate sin, much worse than mere suicide, for a curandera to neglect any patient in her care. Her verra soul and those of her bairns are forever doomed."

"Ahhh," he murmured, feeling lassitude once more enveloping him, "then you are open to the prospect . . . to the, uhhh . . . act of procreation?"

From afar came her sharp inhalation. "Och, no – the prospect of – well, ye know – coupling with ye, a blighted, bloodsucking, greedy Englishman – well then, tis as likely to happen as the Golden Carp allowing herself to be seen!"

A man could only hope. But he found himself drifting, drifting, drifting.

§ § §

Elsa Anderson busied herself in the Luna kitchen. Its fire-dulled copper pans, cast iron skillets, fine bone china, and heavy hallmarked silver cutlery took up the entire wall of shelves built between the outside kitchen door and the one opening onto the hallway.

Ignoring needle-like pricking in her arthritic fingers, she turned out the ball of kneaded dough onto floured parchment paper and, taking the rolling pin, flattened the dough into a large, thin rectangle.

Next, she drizzled melted butter evenly over the dough and sprinkled it with currants, nutmeg, and sugar. Lastly, after opening the stove's iron door to lower the accumulated heat, she rolled the dough, pinching off its ends, and took up the knife for slicing the dough into a dozen cakes.

For a moment, she stared at the knife. Queer, how she could remember recipes from her childhood in Kansas – like Danish meatballs or rugbrød – or even the Navajo method of cooking fry bread and mutton stew. But she could not remember being scalped.

The breath-stealing terror before the Apache's knife thrust beneath her hairline, like a spatula scooping up a fried egg, aye. But not the pain of her scalp being hacked from her skull. Only the never-ending pain after all these years of people's horrified stares and dignity-robbing pity.

No surprise that a decade later, after she left the roaming band of Navajo sheepherders, she had sought shelter in the ramshackle adobe a goodly distance from Puerto de Luna.

Nor was it a surprise that seven years ago she took in the orphaned O'Moore girl. Elsa understood the fear quaking the heart at being alone, at the sudden loss of parents. Well, the loss of Mhaire' mother had not been sudden.

The Spanish beauty had faded and languished over years with consumption. In desperation, her husband had summoned Elsa. Over those last several months, she had used all the skills she had learned from the Navajo, with the young Mhaire anxiously watching, earnestly soaking in Elsa's treatments. But her efforts were to no avail. Magdalena O'Moore de Luna died a sweating, skeletal rendition of her former striking beauty.

A striking beauty, Elsa would never be. She kept no mirrors in the adobe. Did not need to be reminded of the horror presented by her left side, regardless that her remaining hair, draped in a healthy, thick braid over her right shoulder, was still a ripe wheat-field blonde with but a few, graying strands to attest her age.

From behind Elsa, a hand snaked past to snatch a roll. She whirled, the knife in her hand pointed at the thief's leather and fringe-vested midsection. Her hazel eyes glared into the Irishman's droll blue ones. Gaunt he was. Though only taller than she by a prayer candle, his shoulders were as broad as an ox's. "I did not give you zee leave to purloin my cakes."

Biting into the doughy glob, he grinned. "For all yer viper tongue and half-scalped head, ye're a right bonny woman, Elsa."

She gaped. No one, but no one, had the courage to address to her face the shuddering subject of her shriveled scars and whiskery-like yellow patches of hair that blighted the left side of her head. Only behind her back, the repulsed whisperings. Anger, the tightly closed lid to her tears, bubbled like an overflowing cauldron in her throat. "And you are a mush-mouthed man, Finian Selkirk."

He popped the rest of the doughy cake into his mouth and brushed the flour from his palms, the backs of their knuckles worn satiny as old bridle leather. "How did it happen?"

She turned to jab the knife tip into the cutting board, then whirled back to him, her hands on fleshed-out hips. "Uff da! Vat juicy bit of zee massacre do you vant to know? How my family and zee others in zee wagon train were hacked to pieces? Or how I crawled away from zee flames and days later avakened with maggots eating away at my butchered scalp?" Which, it turned out, was what had saved her from dying from infection.

"No, I'd rather know how ye hae braved oot yer life as ye hae. Quite admirable, lass."

Lass? He called her lass, at her age? She blinked. No, not after these years, no weeping and wailing now. Crying was not a luxury with which she could indulge herself.

She stiffened. Her jaw jutted. "By steering clear of busybodies. Now be gone vith yourself. And vile you're at it, you can brush zee flour from zhat mop of a mustache."

She turned back to the working table, only to feel a light sting on her bum. He had swatted her – there! Whipping the knife from the cutting board, she spun back to him. Anger boiled over. "Do that again, and you vill be missing some fingers."

"I was just brushing the flour dusting yuir . . . behind." His expression bland, he turned and headed toward the door to the hallway.

She hurled the knife, end over end, and it thudded in the doorframe, adjacent to his head.

He paused, his head turning slightly to take in the quivering haft. Then, chuckling and shaking his head, he strode on through into the hallway like a soldier of the Old Guard.

With a mighty clang, she shut the stove door, then swiped the flour smudges from her bum. Right bonny woman? The old fool. Both him and her.

§   §   §

Miles peeped through the tangle of ebony lashes at the titles of piled books to his left. *An Examination of phrenology.* Buchan's *Domestic Medicine. The Science and art of Surgery. The Germ Theory* by Louis Pasteur.

Next, his gaze strayed around the small room with its heavy beamed ceiling and flaking plastered walls to lock on the visage directly above.

"Welcome back to me world."

His eyes fought to focus and made out an impassioned oval face, radiant with energy . . . and both suffused with light and clouded with concern. "What happened?"

"Shot though yuir groin while ye *fished* for the gold." Scornful mockery pursed Mhaire's lips.

"Appears your local hunters are bad shots." Not that he believed it was a shot gone wild. He sighed. "My father always claimed my obsession with fishing would come to no good."

She sat beside him and smoothed a cloth damp with apple cider scent across his forehead. "Aye, but ye are a brawny lad who likes his fishing, do ye not – even if tis a holy place ye be violating?"

"Fishing is the one thing my father cannot do better than I." He had muttered his response without forethought and found himself puzzled by it.

"Mother of mercy, why could it not have been hunting or playing chess or lawn tennis instead of fishing?" Next, she was nudging a wooden spoon between his split, parched lips. "As ye plainly see, Miles Neville, ye are suffering these wounds fer yuir trespassing at a holy spot."

He swallowed the warmed, savory broth with a garbled grunt of irritation. "Miles will do. And, nonetheless, it would seem my black soul managed to survive the curse of my desecration."

"So far . . . Miles." Feeding him another spoonful of the broth, she raised a chaffing brow. "And no acknowledgement from ye t'was me ministrations to yuir black soul that kept it on this side of the cross-through? Or even mere gratitude from yeself?"

"Cross-through? What a little novelty you are. And as for gratitude, better late than never."

He captured her hand, holding the emptied wooden spoon, and drew the inside of her wrist to his lips, immediately picking up on her pounding pulse. Her lids flared. The spoon dropped, plinking on the dirt floor. The kiss had been meant more as a jest. One that backlashed on him. As puny as he felt, his body's immediate lusting response surprised him. He looked at her, as if to ask, *Did you feel that?*

But she was already stepping back, her expression reverting to neutral. She turned from him, knelt to retrieve the spoon, then stood and began to back away. "I hae an ailing bairn to attend in Puerto de Luna. Ye're on the mend but stay abed so ye don't bust loose the scabs a'forming. Yuir friend Finian should be coming around anon."

After she left, her fragrance lingered in the small bedroom, the fragrances of lavender and soap – clean and fresh.

And memories lingered, too. Of her haunting amber eyes straying to his exposed private parts. Her dexterous fingers unhurriedly tracing hits throat's thick cords, the bunched tendons in his forearm, the prominent line of his sternum. And exploring farther down to delineate his stomach muscles . . . and trailing the narrow path of crisp, black hair that shafted past his navel . . . alack, only to desert his heated flesh at that point.

She slept in the other bed, only a yard or so away, within his arm's range. He knew this because once or twice her distressed mutterings, from disturbed dreams he hazarded, reached through his own opiate-induced sleep.

Sometime later that morning, Finian appeared in the doorway. "Och, mon, ye're looking like ye might live to see yet another day."

"And I hear you've been seeing me *every* day." His voice, raspy though it was, did not hide his pleasure at the sight of the roué. When Miles was a lad, the thirtyish Finian had nigh every lass the length and breadth of Ireland pining over him.

"Aye, and helping Mhaire change your soiled sheets, I was."

He cringed at the thought of that significance. "Alas, yet another wound I suffer now, this one to my dignity."

Ignoring him, Finian grumbled, "'Tis the auld hen Elsa I would prefer no' to see every day." He crossed to ease his spare frame onto the bed opposite where Miles lay. "She fixes me with the stink eye and carps in spitfire Spanish spiked with what must be a mixture of Navajo and Danish when I light me corncob pipe, if I smack me lips at the supper table, and when I fail to wipe me brogans at the door."

He understood the thing about shoes. With a passion exceeded only by his lifelong vision, he loved his well-worn boots that fit his long, narrow feet like a glove. "You don't look any worse for the wear."

He rubbed his broom mop of a mustache. "Well then, her curses blare like a bagpipe, but she does cook like a French chef. And taken altogether she isn't bad on the eye."

For a moment, Miles had to wonder if they were speaking about the same woman, the maimed woman. "Were you able to scout the shore opposite where we were digging?"

"Aye, with nae luck. Nae spent cartridges anywhere to be seen. And, as for footprints, buffalo couldn't have trampled the area more that morning ye were ambushed than the Puerto de Luna parishioners."

He scrubbed his forehead. Mhaire and her followers were yet going to be the death of his venture, if not himself. His concern was not that they trampled the area – in fact, it might even help. Earth easier to prod through. But he did not want any bystanders when he found the jars containing their gold.

"Think tis the work of Santa Fe Ring," Finian ventured, "or Sullivan's goons?"

Or Mhaire? That singular young woman's' curse was tattooed on his brain. That he'd forever be obsessed with the one thing which he could not have. Gold or glory – or both – regardless, he *would* possess his obsession.

CHAPTER EIGHT

"W ith that bristly jaw and lip, ye're looking more like a wolf than a man."

On his elbows, Miles levered himself up from the bed and eyed Mhaire, standing in the bedroom doorway. For an apron, she wore what appeared to be a re-made flour sack. In one hand, she held a shaving mug with brush and razor. "A wolf can be a predator . . . or a protector."

Her head canted. "A threat . . . or an offer?"

"The offer still stands. As my housekeeper, you would naturally have my protection." He couldn't have been more appalled by his bald statement. The last thing he needed was a stranger watching his activities. Especially, her, a Luna.

She examined his features, one by one, as gravely as a doctor might a patient. "And who would protect me from yuirself?"

"I would never want to hurt you." And he meant it. The people he had hurt were legion, but, no, he would not let himself number her among them.

Her taut shoulders eased. "Not that the guid people of Puerto de Luna would let ye, so I need no protection." Her lips crimped in a half smile. "Besides, today ye're at me mercy." She brandished the straight razor.

Crossing the morning's sun-splashed dirt floor, she sat beside him on the bed. The mattress barely gave, so slight was her weight. Her hair was caught up in a crooked mass of damp curls atop her head. She smelled fresh, of soap and nature's wild herbs. Her face and throat were flushed, likely from the recent heat of bathwater.

As always, that close to one another, it was as if a magnetic field were activated. Her delicate fragrance, her fragile neck, her small, supple breasts . . . a desire as elementary as it was acutely irrational smote him.

He fixed her with a coolly amused gaze. "Planning on slitting my throat – so that the Luna House will be accessible to you once again?"

Shrugging, she set the mug next to the stand's water basin. "If no' you, someone else would eventually occupy it."

She leaned to wash her hands in the basin, then, taking up the boar's brush, she began to lather his lower face in circular motions. Her features were set in fixed lines of concentration – lids narrowed in focused attention, small nose wrinkling, lips pouty.

That close, with her eyes fixed on his jaw line, he studied her. Her sooty lashes were not necessarily long but were extraordinarily thick, as were her straight brows. Her lips were a perfect archer's bow. And her skin . . . what did her pearlized skin look like, unconfined by clothing? Would the thatch of curls nestled at her crotch be the same shade of honeyed red as the hair clustered at her crown? Would her nipples be as pink as her lips? And as puckered?

As if she felt the heat of his stare, her hand, feathering the leather over his flesh, faltered. She raised her dazed gaze to his and gulped in air to get out her tart response. "But I could threaten to slash yuir throat if ye do no' stop yuir digging fer gold on holy land."

Abandoning his childhood vision . . . that was a price he'd never pay to get in good with her. "Alas, that I cannot do. So best you take my life here and now."

"No need fer that. Because I shall simply suggest more frequent pilgrimages to yuir digging site at the Pecos Pool." She took up the sharply honed razor. "What with Sullivan's gang oppressing me people, we could use the water's miracles, to be sure."

"Miracles?" He tsked. "Childish superstition." But he could feel the ire rising in him like bad bile. "But I warn you, I want you and your blasted pilgrims off my land."

"Hold your mouth still." She squeezed his jaw tight and mimicked his tsking. "Dinna the Gospels mention the Pool of Bethesda as a healing well? And the Pool of Siloe, where Jesus told a blind man to wash his eyes – and when the man did this, his sight was restored to him? A curing of which I might say ye are in dire need! Ye are blind to everything but satisfying yuir own desires, Miles Neville."

He huffed, but she silenced his indignant rebuttal by leaning close to place her fingertips on the ridge of his cheekbone and gently stretch his skin for the downward path of her razor.

"And I tell ye now, we shall persist in our pilgrimages, beginning with St. Mary Magdalene's Feast Day, coming up soon. Besides," she continued, "if ye *persist* in yuir desecrations, only more evil will befall ye."

"Like what?" The question murmured out like a dying man's last breath, for one of her small breasts pressed lightly against his ribcage.

"Och, I dinna know. Mayhap, yuir wagon's axel will break or yuir barn will catch fire." She sat back and, head tilted for perspective, surveyed his face. "Aye, ye do look a tad more civilized now."

"For an animal?' He arched a scarred brow. "After all, we both know the English and Irish regard one another as such. As little more than animals."

She frowned and stood, taking a step backward, "Me young patient with the croup is nae better, and I need to check on him. But ye're better. Mayhap ye can leave on the morrow."

Like one of his feverish delusions, she vanished through the doorway, leaving him with an irrational craving. No, it was something other . . . most likely that perverse neediness that he had known even as a lad in leading strings.

§　§　§

Animal?

Did Miles Neville regard her as such?

Granted, since her brother Riley had absconded with her portion of the inheritance designated in their father's will, wee though the funds had been, Mhaire had been forced to scratch out a life little better than the chickens she now kept.

But animal? Nae, it was more like animal magnetism. At least, as far as she was concerned. A raw, starkly masculine quality that appealed to something disquieting in her. A primitive, dangerously burning need she had not known resided within. How else to explain this scorching yearning that left her warm and wet?

From both her observation of nature and her reading material, she knew enough about the reproduction process. How mere smell of the other could be arousing.

But this, this obsession . . . the very word she had used in jestingly cursing Miles for defiling the area's holy waters, obsessed with what could never be his. Now *her* obsession with *him* was playing havoc with her body. With her emotions. With her mind.

Even with her dreams lately. Farfetched but lucid dreams from another time that startled her awake, her body drenched in cold beads of sweat and . . . that constant wanting.

Wanting what?

Ridiculous this wanting. He was nothing but a splinter in her life.

A drumming headache accompanied her footsteps along the dusty River Road toward little Manny Aguirre's shanty. Inside, it was like a sauna. The child's mother sat on a hewn tree stump before the firepit and rocked the blanket-wrapped infant, cradled against her bony chest.

Hands behind his back, her husband paced a tight circle around the rickety table at the rear of the nearly bare room. The family was too poor to pay Mhaire even in eggs, a basket of which she instead intended to bring them later in the week.

She removed her shawl. "How is Manny?"

The sun-weathered young woman shook her head, and her long braids swished her prominent shoulder blades. "*Est peor.*"

Mhaire could hear the bairn's burdensome breathing in his windpipe and hacking coughs. "Ye hae been giving him the dandelion and yarrow mixture?"

"*Si.*" The expression on the poor mother's face was both pleading and frantic.

"Ay-ay-ay!" The husband closed in on Mhaire. "*Pobrecito mi hijo. Haz algo, por favor!*"

What else could she do? She had tried all the herbal remedies learned from Elsa and the advice gleaned from the few medical texts collected from the family library — texts ordered by mail after the consumption began frittering away her mother's health.

She took up the infant, letting the woolen blanket drop away. The wee body fairly sizzled the touch. She thrust her fingers into one of his armpits to determine the severity of his fever. Next, she rolled back his drooping eyelids and peered into his yellowed, fever-bright eyes. Then, with an ear pressed to his tiny chest, she tapped it with her forefinger.

Her shoulders rose and fell with her stifled sigh. The prognosis was grim. She knew many ascribed to the paradoxical theory that heat cured a fever, often tucking the ailing one into bed with several hated bricks. But not in this case, she thought. The laddie was far worse. And neither molasses and oil of turpentine for the coop or catarrh would serve this malady.

She reached for her shawl. "We're going down to the river."

Not a grand idea at that time, twilight – not that hour when all nature seemed to stand poised, when animal vitality was at its lowest ebb, when the healthy prepared to sleep; and when the sick often died.

Nevertheless, with infant Manny cradled to her bosom and his parents trailing, she marched to the sight of El Rito Creek's confluence with the Pecos. In the gathering dusk, she carefully threaded her way down the scrub-hedged path and the limestone slabs, past the cattails and bulrushes, to the edge of the Pecos Pool.

With its dark water lapping against her huaraches, she lowered the wheezing wee one into cooling ripples. It let out a startled yowl and thrashed wildly between her hands. After quickly submerging him, she raised his flailing little body high for the revitalizing breezes to restore life's vigor.

He seemed to freeze, then gasped sharply, and once again he was thrashing, but his flesh no longer felt quite so feverish.

Wearily, she handed the bairn over to his parents. "I hae done all that I can." She was trying to think clearly but her energy was ebbing. She had been doing double duty, caring for both her patient and her tormentor, Miles. "Keep Manny cool . . . and give 'im water. A lot." Water . . . water. . . .

Water was the answer to everything, was it not? It was the power with which St. Theresa de Avila believed strongly could repel evil and temptations. The saint had devoutly declared that nothing put the devils to flight like holy water.

Mhaire turned away, turned her footsteps in the now darkened evening back toward the little adobe she shared with Elsa. No, that she now shared with Miles. And someone else. An apparition? No, for this was . . . was what? His alter ego? But an alter ego not here and now.

She shook her head, trying to clear it. But the harsh, slashing features of another visage also haunted her footsteps.

Her head pounded with each dragging step. She laid the back of her wrist to her cheek. It felt hot but crackly dry. Her throat burned. Her breath rasped and rattled from deep in her chest. Had she caught the croup?

Her footsteps slowed, staggered, and eventually brought her within sight of the Turquoise Door. At her approach, the two donkeys brayed. Gruff, the nanny goat, bleated. And Cock the rooster crowed a welcome. Moo's bell tinkled impatiently, signaling the cow's need to be milked and turned loose.

Pork waddled toward her. She hadn't the strength even to pet the pig. A few steps farther and she felt herself pitching forward into the dangerous abyss of feverish hallucination.

CHAPTER NINE

Blackwater Vale, Eire
April 1691

Uneasily that afternoon Merrow O'Mordha hurried along the narrow path. It meandered through trees and shrubs that reached out to tear at her kirtle's brown woolen skirt, a sooty gray around its ragged hem from cleaning the hut's hearth that morning.

Ahead of her romped Rory, her red setter, tongue hanging to one side. By habit, he knew for where she was bound. Regularly, she made the trip to Tobar Na Croí Naofa, the Well of the Holy Heart, one of Ireland's many holy wells.

She felt unfriendly eyes watching from somewhere in that darkest and most overgrown part of the woods. Pausing again, she peered around, glancing back over one shoulder then off to either side. She had been careful to ensure she was not followed from the village.

Still, the last year or so, since 1689, with Williamites soldiers quartered in every house and hovel, she and her younger brother and other Jacobites from the village were constantly at threat.

At the well's pebbled bank, she toed off hobnail boots, too big for her and with holes in their soles. The boots, which had belonged to one of the Williamite's dead Dutch Blue Guards, rubbed blisters on her ankles, but they were better than nothing. She curled her toes into the damp dirt, delighting in the feel of the throbbing of the earth.

Next, she peeled off her coarse woolen hose, not the finely knit silk kind to which she had been accustomed. After that, she disrobed, beginning with her outer garments — the russet tunic, her kirtle, and, lastly, her chemise, discarding them at her bare feet.

Lastly, off came her tattered, red woolen scarf, binding from sight her hair. From its threadbare corner, she reluctantly tore away a patch. This she hung reverently from one of the limbs of the stately and scarred rowan tree, the Tree of Life, that shaded the well's spring.

Other clooties – rags, scarves, stockings, and such, most of them red in color – dangled from the tree forlornly. Once they rotted and fell into the pool, it was said they took with them whatever curse afflicted the owner.

She knelt beside the large, heart-shaped ballaun stone, as high as Rory's withers. Its hard surface was patinaed by thousands of supplicants' hands. Her care worn fingers lingeringly caressed the stone's hollow before scooping the rushing spring water to drink. The panting Rory was already lapping it noisily.

Like many other pilgrims, to assure beyond doubt her burning wish had a chance to be granted, she slid quickly, quietly, into the thigh-high holy water. Unlike other pilgrims, she bathed nude, loving the refreshing feel of the water flowing over her skin . . . cleansing all at one time her body and her spirit.

Would she ever be able to wash away the feeling of being dirty inside?

Even though it was April, the water was chilling. Rory was already romping in the spring. Hurriedly, she used the sandy grit at the water bottom to scrub clean every vestige of skin, including her scalp. "Ye could stand a guid bath, yuirself, Rory"

For a few moments, she reverted to her childhood and cavorted with the large dog, whooping and splashing and sloshing the water. It fed down into the River Blackwater, where it was said its sacred trout was worshipped as a goddess by her ancestors. Overlooking the river was the chief seat of the O'Mordhas, earls and marquesses and viscounts of Blackwater.

Well, goddess she was not. Nor, despite being the Earl of Blackwater's daughter, was she mistress any longer of the estates' majestic, crenelated castle.

No, at one-and-twenty, she and her younger brother Patrick, as of nine months before, now occupied a thatched-roof cottage – while her father reportedly rotted away in some prison, she knew not where, and her older brother, decapitated by a Williamite officer's sword, rotted on Drogheda's marshy, muddy battlefield at Oldbridge.

Her remaining kinsmen had long since been scattered, all but thirteen-year-old Patrick. She was still navigating through her grief, and she suspected so was he.

Finally, her ritual completed, she mimicked Rory, shaking water off his brilliant chestnut coat. She rose from the water and lashed her heavy, wet hair in an arc's spray around her hips.

Then, eyes closed, she lifted her too slender arms to the leafy cathedral and intoned solemnly, as invariably she did, "In the name of the Father, the Son, and the Holy Ghost, I plea for me heart's desire, the return of me family's O'Mordha estates."

At her side, Rory growled.

Alerted, she quickly swiped the water from her eyes and blinked. Blinked into vision a powerfully built man.

Arms akimbo, at fifteen paces distance, his leonine gaze was watching her every move. She froze, as still as a rabbit before the hound. That part of the woods was an isolated distance from the castle village. The rapier sheathed at the warrior's side gave him the advantage, if not his superior strength and height.

The supremely masculine features shapeshifted into a harlequin's mask of mockery. "It will take you a hundred trips to the well in a dozen lifetimes before the O'Mordha estates will ever be yours or your family's again,"

Her instinctive reaction to cover her nudity almost but not quite overrode the import of his words. "What?"

He wore the Williamite thigh-length, red jacket with its large upturned cuffs and officer's epaulettes. "I had wondered what had become of what was left of O'Mordha's family."

His eyes, the deep blue of the artisan spring, perused her insolently, and she flinched at their bonfire of lust. Her arms whipped in front of her, shielding as best she could her breasts and the curling red thatch at the apex of legs nearly as long as stilts. "Who are ye?"

"Fletcher Neville – a mere English commoner and baseborn." He swept off his plumed, wide-brimmed hat, revealing long, glossy black hair. Thrusting forward one shiny cavalry jackboot, he gave her a deep, exaggerated bow. "But now you see before your naked self no less than the lord of the drafty O'Mordha Castle and its Earl of Blackwater."

Fury overrode her humiliation. Her jaw was so rigidly locked mere speech was an effort. "So, it was ye – ye who had us turned oot of our ancestral home?"

Hard to conceive that now stood before her the legendary warrior upon whom England's King William had bestowed both the title of Lord Justice and her beloved estates in reward for the lieutenant's brutal bringing to heel the Irish Catholic rebels. His reprisals and severe governing of their countryside and its inhabitants far exceeded the Irish Catholic Jacobites' retaliatory scorched earth policies.

His smile bore the deadly curve of a saber. "My chamberlain reports you ran like rats only days before my arrival."

She bristled and all but snarled. "Muck like yeself is not even fit for me dog, much less me castle."

"Do tell?" He held out a gauntleted palm to Rory, who traitorously padded over to sniff it. "And you are – who?" He studied her with an unforgiving eye. "You, with the pink tips of your breasts peeking through your tresses would be . . . not Lady Godiva . . . but O'Mordha's daughter?"

His attentive and impertinent stare puckered her nipples. The chill goose bumping her flesh also chattered her chin. And indignant anger bit out each word from her tightened lips. "Merrow, Marchioness of Blackwater."

"*Former* marchioness, Merrow," he corrected with an implacable smile, so nearly a sneer. "'Mermaid – is that not the meaning of the name Merrow?"

She eyed him warily. "Aye."

Grinning, his fingers made a derisive gesture at her straggly russet hair lapping her bare breasts, their nipples puckered. "Merrow – replete even with your magical red cap. So that you can travel between deep water and land. Is not that how the myth goes?"

The despicable ass. He was amusing himself.

Suddenly, his head canted, as if his attention were elsewhere.

To her mortification, she saw in the distance beyond him half a dozen soldiers advancing through the verdant undergrowth. Long muskets were slung over their backs, and swords were anchored at their sides.

At once, he was shrugging off his red jacket and striding toward her to station himself between her and them. She retreated a step, but his long arm easily snared her and shimmied her arms into the sleeves of his heavy, red woolen jacket, so long its hem puddled at her wet, bare feet.

His arm encircled her shoulders possessively, and with a congenial smile he turned in time to face the arriving soldiers, all but one of them wearing black metal chest plates. "Apologies all around, men, but you are a wee bit late for the ravaging." He gave a lewd wink. "I lay claim to this particularly brutish female to mount and subjugate."

The purposeful look he turned on Merrow bore his intention to do just that, to mount her. To swive her. Fear weakened her knees. Fear . . . and something else as dangerously weakening. She twitched the jacket closed, as if that would protect her from him.

He addressed the soldier at the forefront, also clothed in the red of the King's colors. Substantial of build and older than the others, the man's flaxen hair jutted like straw from beneath his stockinged tuque. "Nielsen, bring my steed. Lady Godiva here needs a mount if she is to ride through the wretched hamlet arrayed as she – "

Taking advantage of his diverted attention, she whirled free of his confining arm. With Rory hightailing it on her heels, she struck out through the bramble. She stooped and scooted where the larger soldiers laden with their chest plates and weapons could not so easily charge. Twigs scratched at her cheeks, and stinging nettles pricked her soles.

A musket boomed, and she heard the soldier's commander, the Lord Justice, shout, "Hold your fire!"

She could hear pursuit close behind. She shoved aside the briars that clawed at her, as if to hold her hostage, despite every efforted step. Those frantic steps next plunged her into a bog. It sucked noisily at her feet. And next, weighted by the heavy military jacket, she sank more quickly, the bog rising to her knees.

Panic threatened to dominate rationality. The stinky, sulfurous fumes made clear thinking difficult. Every child was taught, if stumbling into a bog, to inch each footstep back, gradually, one leg at a time. And, if that did not work, to lay flat on one's back and worm the torso's way to solid ground, never stirring the extremities. But such tediously slow movements ate up precious time. The fecking soldiers might find her first.

Surely, this was but one of the nightmares she had been having since the Williamites conquered County Cork. Surely, she would awake and find herself back home, playing draughts with her mother in the castle's north solar or fishing in the River Blackwater with her brothers and father.

CHAPTER TEN

Puerto de Luna, Territory of New Mexico
April 1878

Knowing that it was imperative he return to his digging, Miles forced himself to get up, to stir his sluggish limbs. Though feeling marginally better, he had a filthy headache from being abed too long.

Gingerly, he swung his feet over Mhaire's low, narrow bed and sat up. Silent shrieks of pain emanated from his wounds. But, examining his nude, muscled haunches, he found the sores appeared to be a less angry red and scabbing over.

A paucity of clothing hung from pegs on one wall, but his wasn't among the feminine garbs. He found his neatly folded in the makeshift nightstand's bottom crate. Alongside it, in the next crate, he espied a pair of little worn high-button shoes – along with an irate-looking 8-inch centipede.

God's teeth! At once, he grabbed one of the boots and pounded the centipede to mush. Tarantulas, vinegaroons, Gila monsters . . . he suspected none of these inhabitants of the desert Southwest quite equaled the danger of Mhaire O'Moore.

Where was she? Hazily, he recalled her lilting voice more than the words themselves . . . something about leaving, checking . . . an ill child, was it? Or was she leaving him, ill as he was?

Clumsily dressing, he retreated to the narrow kitchen and found a battered tin coffee pot and a bag of Arbuckle's. He measured out the coffee and set it to brewing.

Then, gingerly, he began to move about, stretching the kinks from his muscles as he explored the mud-and-brick home with its chipped, white stuccoed walls and scant pieces of furniture – a small rustic dining table, a screen-door pie chest, a solid armoire, and a scattering of mismatched chairs.

In general, the place had a comfortable feel, despite it being as austere as a nun's cell. The castle back in Ireland, now solely his, had never felt comfortable, never felt like home. He had felt more at home in the woods or fishing on the River Blackwater with Finian.

He was searching the three-room adobe for small clues that would tell him more about this enigmatic young woman who cared for him with fierce determination.

Of course, her medical books confirmed her interest in the healing arts, as did the kitchen's arsenal of plants. Well, most likely, the plants were used for cooking, as well – or poisoning, if she so should choose.

He half smiled at what he hoped was an unlikely idea. He poured out a cup of the dark, aromatic coffee and continued his reconnaissance. A smoke-rimmed beehive fireplace with its pyramided wood, dominated the main room, the *sala*.

Aligned along either side of the fireplace, tin retablos painted with sundry religious images stared out vacantly. Nothing like the stuffy, ancient portraits that glared down from the corridors of his family's castle. His, now.

He peered more closely at the retablos. The Virgin of Guadalupe, naturally. Saint Joan of Arc. Mary Magdalene. And Airmed, whom he vaguely recognized as a Celtic goddess, of what, he couldn't recall.

Then there was the retablo of a golden fish, which could represent the Christian symbol, except for the retablo below it . . . that of a mermaid. But, of course. His amused smile went sour and with it the coffee's taste.

Just as he set aside the half empty cup, something drew his attention away from his perusal of her abode . . . toward its front door. A faint sound growing gradually louder. Curious, he crossed to open the door and beheld both an agitated, oinking Pork – and a gossamer-like Mhaire O'Moore, barely supporting herself against the doorframe.

"What the – " He caught her, lifting her frail, wraithlike body to cradle against his chest and headed for the bedroom. He lay her scant weight on the bed she had been using, next to where he had lain for nigh onto a week.

He felt her forehead, feverish and clammy. Her clothes were damp with sweat. A cold compress, that was what was needed. Linens would be where? The other room's armoire? He straightened to go in search, and she moaned.

"What?" He leaned over again, feeling the painful tug reopening his hips' scabs. Damn't. He lowered his ears to her lips. "What, Mhaire?"

"Water . . . water." Her jaws were clicking like castanets.

"Of course – I'll get you a drink now."

He went to rise, and her fingers latched feebly onto his cambric shirt's lacing. "No! The water . . . immersion . . . healing . . . " her voice trailed off to a faint sigh.

It took a moment for her request to register. Bloody hell! She wanted him to cart her to one of her fecking holy water sites and dunk her. But could he do any less for her than she had for him?

He paused, vacillating on the sites she had mentioned – and settled on what he reckoned as the nearest, the Blue Hole. As no chroniclers referenced it as possible location for Coronado's cache, he had yet to visit it. But from the age-old land grant plat he had studied, he knew it was, more or less, equidistant between the adobe and the Luna House.

He hoisted her lax body and felt the pull at his wounds again. If this did not set his recovery back, nothing would. He managed to get through the front door, with a determined Pork edging through, as well.

A three-quarters moon had already risen in the eastern sky, giving him a sufficient scrap of light to thread his way through the chaparral. Appearing to know a familiar route, Pork padded a few feet ahead like an advance guard.

Mhaire's small body was light enough that his lengthy strides covered the first mile rather easily and quickly. The second mile was a strain, with a nagging stitch in his side, and by the third mile, his arm muscles were burning and his legs felt weighted with lead. Sweat stung his eyes.

By now stars twinkled overhead like glowing embers. And moments later, the moon's silvery light lit the Blue Hole – a circle of rock-rimmed sapphire water, maybe sixty feet in diameter, there in the middle of the desert. A symphony of frogs ribbeted a nighttime welcome.

Huffing, he knelt to lay her supine on a limestone ledge, and, straightened. His recalcitrant muscles groaned after their lengthy inactivity of bedrest. His sleeves were damp with her body's perspiration, and his red flannel shirt was pasted to his chest and back, most likely from his own sweating. Next to them, Pork was snorting its consternation.

Hand scrubbing the back of his neck, he stared down at her, one arm flung over her head, her legs bent at the knees and doubled to one side. Her ruffled skirt was hiked to expose a tantalizing glimpse of one thigh.

Fecking hell, he wasn't sure which part of him ached more – his wounds, his muscles, or his bollocks. True, it had been rather long since last he knew the sweet taste of a woman, but this was something that was more than a connection of the flesh. No, it was more a faint, instinctive whispering around him, like moth wings beating around a lantern, insisting that something about him was imperiled.

Forcibly, he removed his glazed gaze from that length of pale flesh to scan the water's shoreline. His jaw dropped. There was no shoreline. Only a circular ledge of precipitous rock. From it, pristine water fell away, perceptibly mutating to darker blues the deeper it went until utter darkness pervaded far, far below. And there was something else. Something about the amazingly clear water that was overwhelming. A haunting, pulsating, inscrutable something.

His eyes shifted back to her. Her face was flushed, the tendrils of amber red hair framing it dripped with sweat, and her constricted breath wheezed in her throat along with her incoherent words. Nonsensical words. Gaelic?

No more delay. Insane, but this seemed to be what she wanted. Water . . . she fancied water as holy. A curative. A restorative. Yes, insanity.

Anchoring both her wrists in one hand, he rolled her onto her side and, clenching his jaw against the pain of his protesting wounds, nudged her over the rock's edge. He allowed her body to sink just below the surface. Her hair floated free of its loose knot and fanned about her – as did the leather cord from her blouse's décolletage. And, bloody hell, it was no pagan pendant suspended between her breasts but that shoddy Christian cross.

Tiny bubbles drifted up from her nostrils. Her lids flared open. Haunting muddy brown eyes stared up at him, importuning. Importuning what? Her wrist struggled in his grasp. Was she frantic to be pulled up – or to be released?

On one knee, he hauled her up and over the ledge. Ignoring the pain skewering his wounds, he released her wrists and grasped under her armpits to steady her – and she latched onto his forearms and tugged.

Off balance, in he tumbled. Shockingly cold, the water stole his breath. His weight – his boots rapidly filling with water – sank him like an anvil. He struggled to shed the boots. His precious boots.

Deeper he plummeted through the cylinder of stone walls. The gem-like crystalline water altered. To aquamarine. Darkening to lapis lazuli. Next the even darker navy blue of Davy Jones's locker. His lungs bellowed as if bursting. He fought the instinct to inhale. Starbursts of pain fired through him.

At last, he shucked free of his boots, and they plunged from sight. He shot upward, leaving behind the glistening magic of white limestone encircling him to ascend to algae crusted walls nearer the top. He surfaced, sucking air mightily, and clutched at the rocky rim.

Directly above him, Mhaire's face was luminous with the water's reflected light. She smiled softly.

Ribcage heaving, he rolled onto his back and propped up onto his forearms.

On both knees before him, she wrapped her arms around her shivering torso. "I feared ye'd fallen down the rabbit hole into the fantasy world."

Staring up at her, he watched her carefully through his water-laden lashes. "Did you now?"

Her spine stiffened and head jerked backed in indignation. "Ye doubt me?"

"I doubt that you are Alice." He raked a brow. "Perhaps the Queen of Hearts? You know, 'Off with his head.'"

"I might remind ye that I saved yuir soulless hide, plugged with bullets as it was."

"Saved my soulless hide? That's debatable." Would she dare

risk town whispers by letting yet another die in her care? When perhaps she had not counted on his surviving a gunshot? And now this . . . seeming to pull him down into the Blue Hole.

He felt a bewildering mix of anger, suspicion, and . . . crazily . . . an attraction. Mild attraction, he mentally amended, while grudgingly granting she exuded some kind of primeval feminine power. The kind that could peel the pretentious wallpaper off the Luna House parlor.

He pushed himself erect. Beneath his cold, soggy wet clothes, his flesh was goose-bumped. He was exhausted. He thought about the wounds he had ripped open, lifting and carrying her. "I'll see you home, then I am headed to mine."

"Well then, actually, tis *me* home ye're headed to."

His teeth ground. "It *was* your home."

In the near darkness, with Pork leading the way, they started out through the bristly brush. After a few minutes of blessed silence, she broke his brooding ponderings. She peered up at him. "Ye're home in Blackwater, what was it like?"

He shot her an annoyed look. He couldn't let her know how she affected him. The way her wet clothing clung to the pleasant roundness of her breasts, the firm curvature of her hips, and the inordinate length of coltish legs . . . hell, lust was incinerating him. "Why do you want to know?"

"In yuir fever, ye raved about it – that and yuir da."

"I don't discuss my father. And as for my home – it's a castle, more or less."

If a dangerously ruined, gothic castle could be called a home. The main tower was rubble, but a range dating from the sixteenth century was still livable. That substantial portion rose three stories above the River Blackwater's cliffs. Skinny dips in the river had taught him well about swimming . . . and the female anatomy.

He glanced down at her to see how she took the pronouncement that his home was a castle. Her disturbingly beautiful features were wistful. "Me da hailed from Blackwater environs. But from what little I glean, his home there was no' a castle but a hovel. Came to Philadelphia at fourteen as an apprentice to a watchmaker, he did, and took up fur trapping instead. Followed the buffalo herds all the way here to the New Mexico Territory."

He couldn't keep the derision from his voice. "Fur trapping earnings bought an empire like this?"

"Nae. T'was marriage to me mother. She was the Luna Land Grant heiress, Magdalena Luna." Her pace slowed and she turned her face up to his, watching his carefully. "While ye were down there . . . did you see . . . see the Golden Carp?"

"The Golden Carp? Hell, no, I was too busy worrying about my lungs to watch for gills." He was reminded of something else. Something he may have glimpsed beneath the water. A petroglyph of some sort or perhaps it was simply inscribed carving in limestone. Nevertheless, how was that possible – underwater carving at that depth?

He put the niggly thought aside for the moment. "Those tin retablos on your wall – "

"Aye, Joan of Arc, Airmed – "

"Airmed?"

"The Celtic goddess of healing and magic."

"Yes, yes – but the retablo of the painted gold fish." Could that have been an allusion to Coronado's gold? "What more can you tell me about the Golden Carp?"

"I already told ye. It can shift to a mermaid and back. And even then ye can only see her around midnight – and only if she wishes it."

"Yes, but how old is the myth? I mean, does it go back before the arrival of the Spanish? Or did they bring it with them to the New Wor – "

"Tis nae myth, I keep telling ye." Her full lower lip, the color of a peach, was thrust out petulantly, and he wondered if her mouth tasted as sweet as a ripe peach. As chilled as he was, he nevertheless felt the heat of arousal.

He ducked a bat swooping low. "Have you ever actually seen either – the Golden Carp or the mermaid?"

She huffed, blowing a damp curl that had fallen atop her nose. "I don't need to. Because ye can't see something, disna mean it disna exist. Can ye see the air? Or yuir mind? Yuir belief in yuir infallibility is appalling. As is yuir fixation with Coronado's gold."

"Well, the gold has been rumored to be stashed in dozens of places across the southwest. Hell, it could be even right here, in the Blue Hole. Ouch!"

A goat head sticker nailed the heel of one bare foot. How he had loved his dearly departed boots. Following years of adventuring, they had had come to mold his long feet in such perfect and comfortable support.

On one wobbly foot, he paused to extract the anchored sticker – and realized her arm around his waist helped support him. Her fresh scent mingled with the night's blossoms. Prickly blossoms, he reminded himself.

"'Tis sorry I am about your boots."

If he did not know better, the glance she spared him might be misinterpreted as enchanting. Hell, the night was enchanting. The whole damned area with its red canyons and blue waters and lush green grasses was enchanting. Maybe it was that, maybe he was bloody enchanted, damn't.

Better he set her straight now. He set off walking again, his strides lengthening, and she quickened her graceful pace to stay abreast of him. "Just so you understand, while I am grateful for your taking care of me, that doesn't mean I am going to tolerate trespassers on my land."

She made no reply, which he knew meant nothing. Especially not her assent. Her nimble, imaginative mind was likely spinning yet other means by which to thwart his purpose. As attractive as he found her, he would break her open like a shotgun if she continued to oppose him. But he did not want to hurt her, if he did not have to.

He did not want to be like his father, a raging browbeater. And yet, growing up in such a morose, violent environment, was it not conducive to assimilating such traits? Would he ever get this monkey off his back? The waiting for someone to come and inspect him. The dread of coming up, yet again, lacking in whatever fashion.

They walked beneath the night, and it was as if they were the only two humans on earth. Only the occasional hoot of an owl, the yip-yip of a coyote, or Pork's grunting broke the companionable silence. Yucca and mesquite and juniper, pungent with blueberries, stood sentinel in dark silhouettes.

With the sterling silver moon lighting their way Miles felt strangely content, moving in rhythm with Mhaire over the fecund earth. Noticeably absent at the moment was the tension, that constant anxiety, that knotted beneath his skull and rigidified his shoulders.

Thumbs tucked in his jeans pockets, he began to whistle softly, a tune he had picked up while in San Francisco, "I'll twine Mid the Ringlets."

"Me da said in the old country tis believed that whistling at night attracts bad luck. But I like your whistling." She paused, stooping to examine an odd-looking plant.

Somewhat surprised by this kind admission he stared down at her. "Do you now?"

Her curiosity regarding the plant apparently satisfied, she straightened and tossed an arch smile up at him. "Aye. Tis hoping I am that your whistling will attract bad luck for yuirself."

His shoulders rose and fell in a theatrical groaning jest. But his whistling was no jest. The whistling went far back with him. It offset the silence of his childhood.

As if conspiring with her prophecy of bad luck, the prodding Pork sideswiped him. Flailing his arms, he landed in a prickly patch. At once, Pork was slurping over him.

Smothering giggles with the knuckles of one hand, Mhaire offered her other to help him up.

Abashed, he accepted it and scrambled to his feet. Still holding her small hand, he found himself biting the inside of his cheek against the laughter threatening to escape him. He couldn't explain his good humor. Maybe it was the magic of the moon that burnished her beauty . . . or the Blue Hole's sparkling water he had inhaled that brightened his spirits.

Alarmed at his susceptibility to her odd charm, to the magic of the night, he released her hand like it was a scorpion. "I am thinking I should take up wearing garlic around my neck – to ward off evil spirts and such." He occupied himself brushing sand and barbed spines from the seat of his denims.

This time, she let her smile surface. "I did warn ye no' to traffic with the water naidids, though I grant tis a fine ass ye hae."

"Fine ass? Ass, you said? Fine ass?" Of course, when he was down and out with the plugged wounds, she would have seen his naked ass.

She affected shock. Her eyes narrowed a honeyed brown beam on him. "Nae, you misheard me. Whatever could ye be thinking? I said, ye hae a fine cast. Ye know, with yuir fishing rod."

Once again, he had underappreciated her intelligence and humor. "Yes," he parried with a sly smile, "I am often told I have a fine rod."

She dimpled. Then, they both broke out with laughter.

When their mirth ebbed, he caught her staring at him, as she would at finding another fascinating herb or fungus or whatever plant to investigate.

In mindful silence, he resumed walking, and she fell into step with him. Wind sang around edges of the cliffs, calling to him like a mermaid's song. Overhead, the stars were diamonds and the moon a rare conch pearl.

Reaching the ramshackle adobe, her hand on the turquoise door latch, she looked up at him. "'Tis too far to the Luna House fer you to walk at night barefoot. Stay the night with me. When Finian visits tomorrow, he can take ye back."

He hitched a brow. Was this a seductive ploy to defeat him without inflicting so much as a bruise?

The moonlight magnified her becoming blush. "In separate beds, of course."

He repressed a lust-soaked groan and followed her inside. She lit a beeswax candle and led him back into the bedroom. Arriving at the foot of the beds, he braced his hands on his hips. "Uhhh, I sleep in the nude."

Her smile held soft mockery. "Remember, I've seen yuir nude self, Miles."

The warm inflection she gave his name jerked at him, all the way down. He pulled his shirt up over his hand. Then, watching her expression, he loosened the flap button of his denims, now dry.

In that classic cameo-like face, her eyes widened, and her cheeks blanched. "I'll change into me nighty in the other room." She snatched the nightdress from its wall peg and, taking the candle stub with her, deserted the tiny bedroom.

Grinning, he shed his clothes and, peeling back the wash worn sheet, slipped his long frame into bed at an angle, so his feet would not hang over.

From the other room came the soft sound of her rustling clothing. Then the yellow light seeping across the bedroom's dirt floor was extinguished, and he heard her padding into the bedroom, drawing near him, pausing, as she sought out the other bed, then the swish of sheets. So near, he could fling out an arm and touch them. Touch her.

Hands clasped behind his head, he lay awake. Listening to her light even breathing. Was she already asleep? Sleep, he knew wouldn't come for him. He felt too invigorated after the dunking.

He wondered what it would be like to sleep with her. Just sleep with her, tugging her curving backside against his torso. He felt the unflagging desire knotting in him and knew tomorrow he would have to take himself in hand.

And then he did the last thing he would have expected, fell asleep . . . but with the disturbing and vague recollection that when he had undressed he had noticed no stitch of pain in his groin and, impossibly, only the faintest trace indicating there had once been a festering, fevered sore.

CHAPTER ELEVEN

Blackwater Vale, Eire
April 1691

For nearly three years, Eire's countrymen had battled England's Protestant King William for the right both to their land and to worship however their souls were called, and, thus, Irish farmers had eventually melted down all their scythes to create pikes.

But, at least, now the Protestant victors were allowing Irish blacksmiths' restoration of pikes back into scythes. Scythes to mow and reap Irish fields, pitted with mortar and now owned by the Williamites.

Catholic Jacobites' estates had been carved up to pay for arrears to King William's armies. Which meant that times were desperate. Astronomical prices were being paid in nearby Cork for bread. A single rat meant another day of life.

With long, rhythmic strokes, Merrow swung the heavy scythe so that the grass fell into neat windrows. She loved the pungent, tangy smell of the newly moan hay. Lizards, butterflies, moths, and bees, hearing the approach of her scythe's sharp blade, escaped in time.

Once the grass dried and was gathered, its seeds left in the meadow for next year could feed a pony through the winter. Not that she any longer had her beloved Pegasus. The Williamites had confiscated the Connemara pony for artillery transportation.

Her shoulders, lower back, and upper arms ached unbearably. New blisters oozed atop old calluses. Sweat coated her ribs and waist. And her bare feet were bruised and scratched. No wonder the scythe carried with it the connotations of death, the Grim Reaper.

And then, she glanced up to see just that, the Grim Reaper in the form of the new Lord Justice, Fletcher Neville, now Earl of Blackwater.

"I believe you stole my jacket."

Straightening, she swiped the perspiration from her brow with the back of her hand and stared at his scarred, sunbrowned hand, resting menacingly on the chased gold hilt of his sheathed rapier. Behind him, waited the massive older man in the stocking tuque.

From the edge of the field, Rory rose from where he was bedded down and padded over to lick the Lord Justice's bare hand. Swallowing her unease, she stared down both the defector Rory and the victor Neville. "Ye believe wrongly."

A black brow, sickled through by a scar, arched. His eyes narrowed, as if reappraising her. "I distinctly recall seeing you wearing my jacket as you scurried like a rabbit through the brush last week. And it is as 'my lord' that you may address me."

Gripping before her the hoe's upright handle for support, as the prisoner Samson must have the Philistine's pillar, she tried a shrug of insouciance. "Search me hut, if ye will."

She had rid herself of the enemy's offensive red jacket, giving it to a pig farmer's wife to cut into scraps of clothing. With all their pigs confiscated by the Williamite soldiers, the Flahertys and their five children were going both hungry and in rags. Not that her own shabby raiment was that much better.

Easily the man's long legs bridged the wide windrow, bringing him close enough that her nostrils quivered with his fresh, sunny scent. Whereas her sunny scent was sweat. Of course, he had the resources that provided regular baths and lavender soap. Her soap was the stringent lye and ashes, when she could scrounge up a small block, and her baths often less frequent, working as she did from six days a week, sunup to sundown.

His smile was both disarming and dangerous. "The red kirtle worn by the Flahertys' four-year-old daughter is quite becoming."

Surprise flared her eyes. Her heart teetered-tottered.

He inclined his head even closer, so that his hat's wide brim shut out the sunlight. "I know everything that goes on in this miserable hamlet. Everything."

She summoned the courage to risk begging her case. "If ye know everything . . . my lord . . . do ye know where me da is imprisoned?"

Ignoring her, he turned back to his aide. "Nielsen?" The man passed Neville something, what she could not see, until he turned back. "Your hobnail boots." Dropping them before her, he doffed his hat and, once more, swept her an exaggerated bow.

Hands palsied, she watched him rejoin the man called Nielsen, the two striding toward the edge of the meadow and their mounts.

She spun on Rory. "Traitor." His floppy ears and hairy tail drooped.

She finished out the day's last two hours of scything. She tried to reassure herself that Fletcher Neville could take no more from her than he and his Williamites already had . . . well, discounting her life, her younger brother Patrick's, and that of her imprisoned father's, wherever that might be.

Her maidenhead had already been ripped from her three years before, by one of the same nameless soldiers who had also raped the young peasant woman, whose parents' hut she and Patrick now shared.

With flagging footsteps, she returned to that thatch-roofed, wattle-and-dub cottage, nigh gutted by the Williamite raids. She set about kindling last night's ashes on the hearth.

From outside came the muted conversation of Betha and Patrick, most likely returning from harvesting honey. Betha's parents had been beekeepers, scythed down like wheat stalks during the Williamites' pillaging and plundering.

Merrow rose to await them at the open door. Both her brother and Betha reeked of cow-dung smoke and the male mallow mucousy juice smeared on their bodies to ward off bee stings.

"Ye must make sure ye mix thyme or pounded raisins with mulled wine," Betha was explaining to Patrick. "'Tis the best food for young bees – and makes for sweeter honey."

Patrick's mouth turned sour. His grubby hand shoved from his eyes the shock of raggedly chopped hair, orange as an autumn leaf. "And where would we be getting wine, pray tell."

"Begorrah, Master Patrick, yuir faith is faulty. So far, yuir sister has managed quite well to – " she broke off at the sight of Merrow, listening from the hut doorway. "And speaking of wine and honey –

och, ye dinna look so guid, yuir ladyship."

No matter how many times Merrow had remonstrated with the twenty-six-year-old woman that she and Patrick had been stripped of their titles, Betha blithely ignored her. "I had a run-in with the Lord Justice Neville."

"The devil ye say?" Her tiny rosebud mouth puckered like she might puke.

Discounting a front tooth she had lost in her struggle with the Williamite soldier, Betha was comely. Her hair, its braid an ombré shade varying from its roots of brown to its tips of gold, was uncommon. As was her snippety spark.

Alas, she seemed fated to remain a spinster. Injured when she fell from a tree as a youth, her left hand and arm were stunted. With her smaller arm permanently angled at the elbow, most domestic chores were difficult. And in these difficult days, a wife sturdy of body was highly valued.

"I *do* say." Carefully, Merrow opened wider the slatted door, hinged by only a single leather strap near the top. "And I doubt it's the last we'll see of that devil's hairy hide."

The hut, with but one small window, contained a single, nigh airless room and loft. Here chickens now roosted, and the place smelled of habitation at its worse. Betha filled a lamp with a lump of lard and struck flint to the wick. "Oh, so ye know what his arse looks like, do ye now, yuir ladyship?"

She nodded surreptitiously at Patrick, who was already plucking a seared barley cake from the pastry board. "Little pitchers hae big ears." As if he had not heard her being violated in the Minstrels' Gallery three years before.

"Bugger me blind, yuir ladyship, but yuir brother has seen farm animals mounting one another." Her wide grin amplified her missing tooth. "And, as for yuir Lord Justice – well then, we all know what happens to the king bee, after mating with the queen in flight. He loses his bollocks and falls to the earth, dead on the spot."

CHAPTER TWELVE

Puerto de Luna, Territory of New Mexico
May 1869

Guido Jaramillo prided himself on doing his duty. A man without honor and dignity was a man without self-worth. For that reason, he had continued management of the Luna Estates after Don James O'Moore's death. Pues, that and his devotion to Mhaire.

Since Father Ignacio only managed to make his rounds to Puerto de Luna once every other month, and that was if he was sober enough to remain astride his donkey, Guido had taken it on himself to assist in an additional mass, a vigil mass each Saturday night in the makeshift church, an abandoned adobe off the plaza.

From his days as an altar boy, Guido knew when to ring the bell, and he made sure candles were lit, copal incense burning in the chain censor, and the brass bowl on the rustic credence table filled with water.

He assumed these duties, because the townspeople were getting lackadaisical in their faith, evidenced, for one, by the boisterous fandangos at Tenorio's Bar. Saturday night revelry often meant Sunday no-shows at the improvised church. So, better to celebrate mass Saturday night before everyone adjourned to Tenorio's.

And everyone meant *every* one from far and wide – from infants openly nursing to senoritas with the artillery of the eyes, from half-breeds in leather moccasins to the common ranchero in long, dirty woolen stockings. Upon arriving for the fandango, the adults, one and all, gave the abrazo.

Tenorio's tables had been cleared, leaving sufficient space through the center for couples to waltz through. Already, a fiddler and guitarist were warming their instruments.

At these fandangos, it was not unusual to see an elaborately dressed matron in silks and high combs dancing with a barefoot peon or an eighty-year-old man dancing with an eight-year-old child or even men dancing with men.

He took one of the little sponge cakes from the end of the bar. His sense of decorum was disturbed that the crockery was not all the same set and the spoons were not all the same size. His free hand resting on his outdated Colt Dragoon, his gaze scanned the room. Its walls, whitewashed with gypsum, were covered with cloth to protect the many people, standing.

The one his eyes sought, Mhaire O'Moore, never attended the flamboyant dance. Etiquette required an eagle-eyed duenna accompany a young maiden, and, understandably, the ghoulish Elsa Anderson never ventured in polite society.

Not that Mhaire conformed to conventionality. For her, there was no black or white but everything in between. Chaotic color. Disorder that scraped his nerve endings. And, yet, when in her presence, light, be it sunlight or candlelight, seemed to shimmer with a luster, an incandescence, to be found only in worship.

His glance chanced to alight on Emmet Sullivan at the far end of the ring-stained bar. With him were three of his personal body guards, in dust-begrimed clothing and encumbered with holstered revolvers. All four appeared to have been drinking heavily.

One of the three hired guns, a swarthy man sporting a gold tooth, aimed a wad of tobacco juice at a spittoon. The *pistolero* missed, hitting instead one of the heavy, horseman boots of his compadres.

The man, his long and lank yellow hair stringing from his sugarloaf sombrero, jumped back. "Diego, you steaming pile of cow shit! I oughtta punch out that gold tooth of yers, for that."

The third henchman, wearing an eyepatch, laughed mirthlessly. "Hell, Cloyd, you couldn't box your way out of a flour sack."

Emmet Sullivan took the corn shuck with its rolled tobacco from the corner of his mouth. "Shut up, Eugene."

Guido had to give the nattily dressed entrepreneur due credit. A gold watch chain hung from his floral waistcoat pocket. Sullivan understood the importance of impression. Dignity conveyed authority.

Guido prided himself on commanding the loyalty of his vaqueros. The embroidered, cream-colored bolero jacket and tight pants he wore tonight were impeccable, despite the heat of the wrought iron candelabrum overhead and the press of people.

Abruptly, Sullivan rotated to face the clusters of gathered partiers. He flipped his *cigaretto* into the spittoon and pushed back his bowler hat. Bracing his forearms on the bar behind him, he crossed his highly polished spat boots at the ankles and glanced from surprised face to surprised face. "I'm looking for the Kid. William Bonney."

The tentative strokes of guitar and fiddle slowly screeched to a sawing halt. Shocked glances passed surreptitiously from one person to another. Sweat broke a sheen on many of the faces.

People liked Billy. He was convivial. Old Grzelachowski said the Kid often left money on the store counter for food or supplies he helped himself to during a night on the run. His easy charm won the hearts of the area's senoritas.

The potent aguardiente glazed Sullivan's eyes a cracked red. But his smile was deceptively benevolent. "Come, come, someone must know something. He's a wanted man. Killed one of my men over at Blazer's Mill. Any of you here harboring the outlaw?"

Still, the palpitating silence.

Sullivan's hand nudged his sack coat's flap back and tucked it behind his holstered pistol. Another holster sheathed a knife, its heft a deadly spike of silver amidst the golden light of the multitude of candles.

Breaths gasped.

But he only took out his pocket watch.

An immediate relieved sighing . . . hacked off by his next words. "All right, then. For every minute that passes without a response, a soul in this room will pass into eternity." He nodded at the greasy, yellow-haired gunman to his right. "That Mexican kid in the knickers, Cloyd. He goes first."

Guido knew the boy. Miguel, the son of his housekeeper, Sofia.

"Madre de Dios!" Sofia, cold terror on her brown face, plowed forward from the crowd to fall at Miguel's feet and wrap her arms around the child's thin body. He looked startled, confused. He glanced from his mother to Cloyd, standing with legs splayed and his revolver pointing dead center at Miguel's head of spiky black hair.

Guido broke from the refuge of his haughty silence. He stepped forward. His glance swept the mass of thunderstruck people to settle on the mother. "Do not give in. There is such a thing as principle. Today, your son, Sofa. Tomorrow any one of the rest of you." His hand swept the herd of dancers. "Appease this man now in the name of peace and none of us will ever know peace."

He turned to face Sullivan. "Murder one of us, you have to murder all of us."

Sullivan grew purple in the face.

Guido maintained his haughty stance. He was more than willing to sacrifice himself and the lives of the thirty-odd people in the room. Did they not see that to bow before a bully once meant bowing forever? He felt honor-bound to this land of his ancestors.

Tempers frayed. The four – Sullivan and his three gunmen – could easily mow down the lot of them. Diego jerked his pistol to eye level. "Let me plug him."

Shaking his head at Diego, a slightly weaving Sullivan shucked his .45 piece from his holster. "He's mine."

Sullenly, Diego held his fire.

Despite the mutters Guido heard among those behind him of "Dios, ayudanos" and the sweat blossoming beneath his armpits, he stayed his ground. Duty was everything, was it not, though Mhaire often chided his principles cloaked pigheadedness?

The dapper Sullivan shrugged and raised his revolver at chest-high level of the others. "Have it your way then."

Suddenly, the bearded Alex Grzelachowski lumbered hurriedly through the cantina's bat-wing doors. "Wait a minute, Sullivan!"

His expression one of disbelief, Sullivan's head jerked toward Grzelachowski.

Diego's pistol swerved toward the hefty man. Instantly, Grzelachowski shot up his hands. "Listen, listen. Don't you think anyone here, on the point of death, would tell you if they knew the Kid's whereabouts?"

Guido rebuked Grzelachowski with a frown, but the man's precipitous action seemed to make Sullivan think twice. He lowered his revolver, but only slightly, and stared at Grzelachowski as if he were a madman, when clearly Sullivan was *el loco*.

The ponderous Grzelachowski stuttered on with his violent outburst. "For God's sake, think, think, Sullivan — kill everyone here and you lose not only much of your capital investments but also draw down the U.S. Marshall on you."

Thoroughly agitated, Grzelachowski rotated his girth to Guido. "You're a deluded man, Don Jaramillo, to believe dignity is more important than life."

Disgust roiled in Guido's throat, but he refused to lose his temper. "That will do, Grzelachowski. I am fully aware of what I am about. Don't you see — *todos somos calaveras*. We are all skeletons. We are all the same."

Grzelachowski glanced askance at Sullivan. "No, God help us, Don Jaramillo, we aren't."

Sullivan shucked his silver Colt, a single-action army revolver strung low on his thigh. Termed the Peacemaker, it was hardly that in his hands. "You are an arrogant fool, Jaramillo — sacrificing the lives of others out of sheer stubbornness."

He signaled to his gunmen to back off, and the press of terrified people parted for the four as they made their way toward the batwing doors.

For Guido, it was hardly a decisive victory, because he felt uneasily in his bones he had merely staved off a showdown for some greater reason yet to reveal itself. Instinctively, his hand made the cross.

§ § §

With the month's blue moon to help light the way, Emmet Sullivan turned his roan in the direction of Lincoln. Behind him, the three hired gunmen were exchanging annoying quips.

"Didya see that *mamacita*, Cloyd?" Diego's chortle competed with the yip-yip of a coyote in the distance. "When you pointed your six-shooter at her kid, I thought she'd pee in her pants right there on the fandango dance floor."

Cloyd hee-hawed. Cloyd the clod, Emmet deemed him. The man was good for nothing but target practice. "Wheee, I'd sure enough like to cram my cock in her pants."

Eugene, the deadliest shot of the three, merely grunted. "Your cock could be crammed into a cigar band with room left over."

Emmet ignored them. The night air cooled the frustration simmering beneath his skin. He was not all that disappointed that his schemes hatched with the Santa Fe Ring were straggling.

The English interloper, Tunstall, had tried to break Emmet's monopoly in the county's banking operations. His gunmen had taken care of Tunstall. Just as, sooner or later, they'd take care of the kid, Billy Bonney.

No, it was another English interloper who worried him more these days. Miles Neville. The Earl of Blackwater presented a more formidable challenge.

How Emmet hated the English, with an iron grudge that knew no forgiveness.

His country's legendary forty shades of green had stained the lips of his starving family, who futilely fed on tufts of grass for survival, while their English overlords feasted. During the great potato famine, he and his family, their eyes as empty as their stomachs, had scrabbled Ireland's blighted fields with bleeding hands, searching for one, just one, healthy potato.

But, god almighty, the worse was the fat priest in his flat black hat and white collar. For precious pounds – when Emmet's family rarely had two sixpenny to rub together – would sprinkle the crops with holy water. Goddamned holy water!

And Emmet would be goddamned if he would let Neville have his way with the Pecos River valley and its goddamned inhabitants and its goddamned holy water with all its accompanying goddamned superstitions that hurt rather than helped.

And if this English earl wanted to play with dynamite, well, so then, could this Irish clover.

§   §   §

Watching Maria Jesus Lopez collapse over her husband's

lifeless body, stretched out on the couple's matrimonial bed, Mhaire's heart fell to pieces. The young woman's husband, a stocky man with sloping shoulders, had pulled a tormenting tooth on his own – neglecting her often admonishments about the need for hygiene. Days later, after Luis had turned feverish and his neck had swollen under his jaw, Maria Jesus had prodded him to see Mhaire.

She had done all that she could for the suppurating sore. Nae, she had done more.

When all her scientific knowledge, gained from her medical books and her poultices and potions and folklore traditions had failed, she had crept under the stealth of dawn down to the Pecos Pool – Mother of God, a trespasser on what had been her own property – to collect a canteen of the holy water. And this, despite Miles's stern warning against that very trespassing.

Later that morning she had gone to the Lopez home and dosed the now unresponsive young husband. It was all for naught. His fever and his pain had raged two more days until death relieved his body's agony. But not that of his young widow, Maria Jesus.

For the second time that month, Mhaire attended the funeral services at San Jose Cemetery, near Hidden Lake. The first time, she had wept for little Manny, whom she had been unable to save. This time, she was dry eyed with desperation.

The tragic deaths of both were heartbreaking for her at the soul level. With a sickening certainty, she felt that her healing powers were being syphoned. Syphoned by none other than Miles Neville.

Or it could be the distressing dreams that were giving her no rest?

Either way, his arrival at Puerto de Luna had without a doubt marked the downturn of her skills.

Not only that, but when he had removed his shirt the night after his immersing in the Blue Hole, her jaw had dropped. First, at the sight of his stomach's corrugated muscles. Next, slightly below them, she had gawked at where once had been his groin's appalling wound . . . yet nothing but a faint, healing scar had she detected.

Worse, now, it appeared he possessed the therapeutic power – he had made certain she survived that fateful night – and she no longer possessed that therapeutic power.

But she vowed she would regain it. How, she was uncertain.

Not when she was so susceptible to his blatant masculine appeal.

When Guido called upon her later that afternoon in their adobe's small space allotted for a *sala*-cum-clinic, his ascetic features indicated his visit was of a serious sort. Was this of a health nature or personal?

As there were no waiting patients that day, she settled on a rickety chair across from him, tucked her huaraches on its bottom rung, and, arranging her flounced skirt, listened to his quiet but determined voice. So different from that direct, deep, and mellifluous one of her ruthless enchanter, Miles.

Guido was truly a good man. While Miles clearly preferred recklessness over caution, the conscientious Guido, instead of rushing blindly, as he often condemned others' actions, preferred to review the situation, hold discussions, and draw up a plan of action.

Concho-banded sombrero balanced on his lap, he spoke with the ponderous dignity that politely veiled his belief in Old World superiority. Another suitor might have come straight to the point, but Guido was observant of ritual, so imperative was it to a caballero's comportment.

"Patiently I have waited all these years, *mi querida*. Since even before the day your father promised you to me. I waited, even after he took his life, even after your brother gambled with your dowry in Lincoln and was found murdered. Because I wanted you to come to me of your own accord."

He shifted his stiff weight to rest his palm on his Colt Dragoon, and the thatched chair protested. "Like Jacob did for Rachel in our Bible's story, I have waited seven years. Seven long years. Either you want me or you do not."

She rubbed her palms together with the same chaffing that plagued her mind and heart. "Aye, Guido, I want ye."

"But as your friend – or your beloved?

She bit her lip. "I confess, I still dinna know."

"It is this Englishman, this crumpet-sucker, he has come between us, *sí*?"

Guido's snobbery should not have startled her as it did. Despite his sterling qualities, he was an obsessive, deluded man. She reached out a hand to touch his work-hardened, brown knuckles. "Nae. Tis what I hae felt all along. God love ye, how can I no' be grateful fer all ye hae done fer me. And I do care about ye. Tis only . . . ."

His Adam's apple worked. "Only what?"

Only that with Guido never had she felt that dropping of her stomach . . . the flush of heat tingling throughout her, to her very fingertips and toes . . . that she felt at the mere sight of Miles Neville. And when he drew near, her heart would set to pounding so loud in her ears, she feared even he could hear. "Only give me more time."

He fumbled with his hat and came to his feet. His face might have been a tombstone. "No, *lo siento*, Mhaire, but my pride as a man will not permit that. I shall no longer look upon you as my intended." He put on his sombrero, drawing its strings' knot beneath his jutting chin. "My allegiance, my devotion, have reached their end."

She sat listening to the finality of the clink of his spurs exiting the *sala*. She knew all about pride. The O'Moore name itself derived from the ancient clan of the O'Mordhas, Gaelic for proud chieftains.

Her shoulders slumped. As the spring sunlight receded across the hard-packed dirt, she pondered her heart's heaviness. The loss of her patient Luis Lopez today. The loss of other patients in the last few weeks. The loss of the unfaltering Guido Jaramillo. They were all a thud in her gut.

But the loss of her faith in her healing gifts . . . that perhaps most of all. Or else, for what was her purpose in life? She had been so arrogantly certain it was to heal.

A shadow slanted across the floor in front of her huaraches, and she looked up to see Elsa entering, her arms loaded with a wicker basket of wet clothes that smelled faintly of lye and vinegar. "My bones are too old to be toting vash so far."

Mhaire shot to her feet. "And ye shouldn't hae to. No' with the river practically at our door." Well, Miles's portion of the river, that was. True, the acequia looped the Turquoise Door's plot of land, but the steeped-bank, dirt canal was conducive for irrigating, unlike the Pecos's shallow, stony banks, better for washing laundry – and sins.

She had to find a way to defeat Miles. The river's mythical gold was his heart's desire, but what was his Achilles' Heel?

"Next time, if I'm not here, wait for me. Let me carry the wash." She took the basket from Elsa. "I'll help ye hang the clothes."

It wasn't like the sitting room was overflowing with patients these days. And, then, too, Elsa's rheumatic fingers were not as nimble as her own with the clothes pins.

Out back, a breeze wafted the air with flowering sage, and Gruff was browsing bramble and random tufts of weeds. Mhaire secured a linen bandage strip to the wire stretched between the house and the animal shed. Another clothes pin between her lips, she retrieved a pair of knickers, faintly stained still with her monthly blood flow, and mumbled, "Those days ye spent at me home with the Irishman – Finian – did ye learn anything?"

Elsa snorted. "Ya. Finian likes his snuff and his ale. Once, he got tipsy and pinched my backside. I threatened to flay his old hide if it happened again."

She looked askance at Elsa, whose blush could be slightly detected just below her fair but weathered skin. Interesting. "But did he share anything with ye about the man himself?"

Lips pinched, Elsa hung a wrung-out dish towel. "Vell, it seems zee younger man did get his own hide flayed with horsewhip and belt and such. More often than zee Irishman liked."

"Who whipped Miles?"

"His papa. Bared a rib to the bone once. Zhat's ven he left home and school, at sixteen. Zee Irishman Finian, he vent vith him."

She thought of what Miles had said about his father, that fishing was something his father could not do better than he. So, the river was as important to him for more than just the fabled gold linked to it. As important to him as it was to her. "I am going to church tomorrow."

From the other end of the clothes lines, Elsa glanced over at her. "But it's not zee Sunday for zee Padre's visitation."

"Even if Father Ignacio does show up, he'd most likely be inebriated." Sooner or later though, he would make good his visitation, if for no other reason than to collect the tithes from his parishioners.

"Vell, since you all are now forbidden zee holy water sites, vhat vuld be zee point of going to zee church?"

"There will still be the candle lighting – and I aim to light a fire beneath our townspeople."

CHAPTER THIRTEEN

Blackwater Vale, Eire
May 1691

Momentarily, Merrow and Betha paused amidst the merrymakers to watch Patrick and the dozen other rowdy May boys haul bags of turf into the village's milking yard.

That evening, the turf would be used to build the two bonfires required for Beltane festivities. All about fire and fertility, Beltane had spread throughout the British Isles. It derived from the Druid equivalent, Samradh, and had been assimilated by the English in the form of the Mayday festival.

And, of course, the drunken English soldiers had already erected in the milking yard their version of Beltane – a maypole. Part of the spring rites to ensure fertility, the maypole was striped in spirals of reds and blues and festooned with ribbons entwined with flowers. Wildly fired carbine shots and smoky grenades flung like apples attested to the English idea of celebrating.

Though dusk was quickly crowding in, villagers were still participating in the day's games – archery contests, wrestling, running in sacks, and other foot races. Patrick, losing interest in building the twin bonfires, joined the Flaherty boys and other children in the game of chasing a skinny pig with a shaved and well-soaped tail.

Gaudily dressed merrymakers were already imbibing from kegs of whisky the Lord Justice Fletcher Neville had distributed. Not so much, she conjectured, out of formality or his good will but as an appeasement. Each family was expected to present to his lordship a sack of flour – and the chieftains, a hog, if one was to be had, or a barrel of brandy – before escaping to celebrate Beltane.

The remnants of dutiful peasants were lined up just inside the castle's heavy doors, ruggedly studded with wrought iron. They opened and closed as tightly as a safe. Betha and Merrow fell in line with others in the Grand Hall. There, Nielsen sat at a table, his wrinkly boots stretched out beneath it. Flanked by two attendant soldiers, he marked in a ledger the receipt of each family's payment.

When she and Betha came to stand before him and hefted over their sack of flour to one of the soldiers, Nielsen's quill paused in its scratching marks. He glanced from her upward to the area of the Minstrels' Gallery. No one was there, of course. But she knew, even as a child, of the small peepholes from which a lord could observe what was happening in the hall.

"Your homage is duly noted." He appeared to return his attention to the ledger, but then he added, "Come Candlemas, his lordship will expect your homage again . . . if not before."

Betha glanced at her with raised brows. She shrugged, then responded. "But, naturally."

Giggling like girls, she and Betha escaped the stronghold and hurried down the spiraling cobbled street leading to the hamlet at the castle's base. It was a crowded warren of narrow alleys, rickety tenements, an almshouse, and a tavern, stinking of piss and ale and the sickly perfume of filth.

If only the constant patter of rain could be heard on the high and narrow rooftops' leaky slates. But rain had been a reluctant visitor to the County Cork that year.

Discounting the Williamite soldiers patrolling with muskets, pistols, swords, and bayonets, a traveler would never suspect that the area was gripped by famine and war with not even oats or straw for the horses and with the common man sometimes eating rats and dogs and horse blood mixed with weeds for soup.

No, vendors gaily hawked shriveled fruits and brain-spinning beverages from their stalls. Floral decorations could be picked out amidst the area's rim of towering trees. Laughter and music, much needed, seized the occasion to ring the air.

Twilight had ceded to the night, and torches were being lit around the perimeters of the festivities. Merrow and Betha dodged an empty cart to enter the field of festivities and the communal area.

Like other village maidens that evening, they both wore their hair unbound, with garlands of marsh marigold around their heads. A light mist gossamered their hair. Merrow had donned her one spare garment, a nut-brown skirt and a white leather-laced bodice.

Fifers and fiddlers has struck up lively tunes for the revels. Through the mist, she saw Hugh Harrington approaching. He drew up before them and doffed his cap. "Lady Rh – Mistress Betha."

His empty linsey-woolsey tunic sleeve was doubled back and pinned to the shoulder. The former gatekeeper at O'Mordha Castle, of medium height and scarecrow thin, had lost an arm in the war with the Williamites the year before and was gradually learning to accomplish tasks 'singlehandedly', as he liked to joke.

Betha bobbed a curtsy, but Merrow merely inclined her head, out of habit rather than any show of superiority. She truly like the young man with the cropped light brown hair. After the Williamites had ransacked the area of its famed wool, cattle, and butter, Hugh began to drop by the hut with a hare or rook he'd snared for the three, and in exchange Betha would gift him with jars of honey.

He scratched behind his head, cleared his throat, tugged his cap back on. He gestured at the hornpiper, warming up to play a reel. "Thought ye might like to take turn around the maypole afore the evening gets really crowded, Mistress O'Mordha."

Merrow did not miss the flicker of disappointment in Betha's fair face. "I – I dinna know the steps. But Betha here, she – "

Betha's tight-lipped smile, concealing her missing tooth, was a thin disguise for her heartache. "Go on with ye, Lady Merrow. Tis simple enough. A step-hop and step hop around the pole till yuir ribbon is used up and then reverse."

Reluctantly, Merrow accompanied Hugh across the milking yard, where he collected two strands of ribbon, one purple, the other green. His smile rueful, he proffered them. "Forgive me for rising above me station, me lady, but tis plain desperate, I am."

"What in Hades do ye think ye're about, Hugh?" Without glancing at the strands' colors, she took one. "Did ye not see the hurt ye caused, overlooking Betha as ye did?"

He ducked his chin, then peered at her with appealing gray eyes. "Since little more than a laddie, I have been a'soldiering. Having neither wife nor sister, I know naught about the ways of the female,

Mistress O'Mordha."

"Clearly, not."

The hornpiper had launched into a reel, and with ribbons in hand the participants swung forward around the pole, forcing she and Hugh to fall into step. His mouth curled downward at its ends. "Mistress, pray pay me no heed. Maimed as I am . . . och, I only thought to make her jealous."

Amazing, he did not notice Betha, too, was maimed. But did not war maim everyone – victim and victor – in one way or another?

A little short of breath, she waited until they moved through the next round of step-hops. "Now, heed me closely, Hugh. We shall forego the expected kiss at the end of the dance. But, next, ye ask Betha to dance, and when it is finished, ye grab her around her waist and kiss her heartily. Make her feel special. Not jealous, ye eejit."

He slipped her a sheepish grin.

When the dance ended, she immediately sauntered away, back toward the communal area, where lit candles blazed brightly among the May Bough's thorny branches with its dark buds, an emblem to vernal light.

Further back, torches were being dipped in an old tar barrel and then put to the two stacks of turf collected by the May boys. The fires that leaped into life drew her toward them. With great incantations, farmers began driving their cattle and sheep between the stacks of growing flames in hopes to prevent diseases in the coming year.

After the bleatings and bawlings faded, hundreds of rollicking villagers, old and young alike, took their turn in leaping backwards and forwards three times over the flames. The light mist mingled with the smoke and exaggerated the leapers' contortions into macabre apparitions.

Maidens leapt to purify themselves for marriage. Males might leap to safeguard themselves on a hazardous journey. Later, when the fires burnt low, women heavy with child would leap for safe delivery. When those fires dwindled to ashes, parents would tote their infants across in desire for a long and goodly life for their bairns.

Her back to an oak, Merrow stood beyond the magical ring cast by the bonfires and wistfully watched the pleasant foolery. A gusty west wind licked the flames higher, whisking away the wreathing mist, and tousled her unbound hair. At that moment, the finer filaments of hair on her neck tingled. She had the uneasy sensation of being watched.

Then, across the flickering flames – above and beyond the heads of the revelers on the far side – she glimpsed the shadow of a mounted warrior. Gradually, his great steed moved out of the shadows. As it pranced between the gray plumes of the twin bonfires, the villagers at once made way for it. Dancing yellow-orange light played across the slash of high cheekbones of the rider and set eerily afire the deep blue of his eyes.

The Lord Justice trotted his warhorse up alongside her. For too long, he stared down at her, as if measuring her worth. Or was he waiting for her to curtsy and give the customary greeting for Beltane, "You're as welcome as the flowers of May"?

She couldn't bring herself to do it. Instead, chin tilted upward, she stared tight-lipped back at him.

"You do not take a turn at leaping. Mayhap to procure a husband?"

"I am betrothed." But his intelligent, watchful eyes told her he somehow already knew this.

"My Lord Justice. And I am quite certain, mistress, you will address me as such with as much joy as an heir to an estate her title deeds."

"*Imeacht gan teacht ort.*"

His snarl of a smile reflected his grim temperament. "Now what makes me doubt that is the Gaelic greeting for the Beltane?"

She forced a smile. "Ye would be right, sire. Tis Gaelic for the Beltane fare-thee-well." Wisely, she did not render him the exact wording.

"'That you may leave without returning,' is not that the literal translation?"

The Brit knew Gaelic! She swallowed thickly. Dipped a curtsey. "But not the customary."

His charger sidestepped closer to her, and she clutched at its braided bridle to keep from being nudged off balance. He leaned over her, and his gauntleted hand overlapped hers. Even through the gauntlet's leather, she experienced the triumph of his virility.

"Do not underestimate me, or you will rue the day." He

hesitated, then added. "Your father languishes at the stone-solid Kilmainham Gaol in Dublin."

With a mixture of perturbed gratefulness and growing alarm, she watched her persecutor trot away on his warhorse, disappearing into the enveloping fog. What perverse ploy prompted this seeming act of kindness?

CHAPTER FOURTEEN

Puerto de Luna, Territory of New Mexico
May 1878

Mhaire was armored in her shabby straw hat and equally shabby brown walking skirt and shirtwaist. Her only suitable dress, its puffed sleeves woefully were outdated. A large, frayed and drooping maroon ribbon flourished it at the throat.

As usual on Sunday mornings, Mhaire set forth alone. Understandably Elsa refused to take part in any community affairs. "I prefer Pork and Gruff and Cock to zee pious citizens of Puerto de Luna."

Well, Mhaire could argue if pious was wholly descriptive, not when a man slight of build staggered from Tenorio's Bar onto the sandy street and collided with Mhaire. Barely supporting his weight, she winced at his blast of whiskey breath.

"If it isn't Mhaire, heart of my hearts!"

"Billy Bonney, the devil take ye!"

Bleary eyed, he grinned, his protruding two front teeth somehow charming. 'I'd rather *you* did, darlin'. Take me to your bed, that is."

Mhaire sighed. "Take ye to church with me, I shall." Not much shorter than he, she easily latched onto the kid's ear and tugged the gunfighter along like a schoolboy, with a mongrel yapping at their heels.

"Aww, Mhaire."

"Hush."

A small adobe, fronted with a veranda's two square wooden

columns, served as a make-do church with all but the dimmest hopes of one day a grand cathedral to replace it. The house had been abandoned by its owner, a cooper, who left town for lack of work.

Inside, some parishioners were lighting votives on a sideboard where a hand painted wooden statue of the Virgin Mary presided amidst a profusion of wildflower bouquets. Along with the incense, the candle and floral scent cloyed the air.

The Rocky Mountains to the west and the Llano Estacado caprock to the east isolated Puerto del Luna from law and order, so the townspeople did not bother to check their firearms at the door, and neither did Billy his six-shooter.

Worshippers, heads bowed, were seated on the backless, wooden benches. In hopes of escaping the eternal torments of the afterlife, some were praying the rosary. A few others knelt in prayer on the wide plank pine boards and beseeched pardons for their burdensome sins.

At the sight of the churchgoers, Billy's sloped shoulders stiffened. "Aww, have a heart, Mhaire."

She shot him a blistering look and ushered him onto the nearest bench aisle at the rear of the room. "If ye move a hair, I'll have Elsa place a curse on ye."

From there, she advanced up front to stand before the hand-hewn pine box that served as a pulpit. She cleared her throat.

On the first row, the oddly-paired married couple raised their heads – the young Mexican woman Secundina, barely in her mid-twenties, and her decades-older husband, the Pole, Alexander Grzelachowski. Their six children sat docilely between them, doing their best to stifle giggles.

Behind them sat the soft-speaking farrier Benicio Moreno, his wife and their precocious daughter, Alma. From beneath her black mantilla, head turned toward the back of the church, she was casting coquettish eyes at Billy.

On the pew across from the Morenos perched the big bosomed milliner, Widow Singletary. Affecting a starchy, proper manner and nearing fifty, Gladys Singletary was known for her generosity of favors in her boudoir. Some townspeople condemned her for a hypocrite, but Mhaire certainly couldn't cast a stone, burning for Miles Neville, as she was.

As if prompted by the Holy Ghost, one head after another raised to give Mhaire attention. From the far side of the room, Guido's dark brown head swiveled toward her.

"As ye know," she began, somewhat uncomfortable with his earnest but unhappy attention and the others' quizzical ones', "coming up is our ritual torchlight procession held during the feast day of Saint Mary Magdalene de' Pazzi."

Grzelachowski hefted his bulk to stand, swishing his long, grizzled beard against his paunch. "Ya, but the new owner of the Luna land grant has posted 'Keep Out' signs up and down the banks at the Pecos Pool."

Crikey, the English scoundrel did not waste time. "Pfft! Meaningless."

"Heavens alive," gasped Gladys, a white gloved hand between her hefty breasts, "the new owner could gun us down for trespassing."

"Not on my watch." All heads swiveled toward the rear of the room. A swaggering Billy shot to his feet. Hat in one hand, he grinned and patted the pistol on hip with the other.

Mhaire clapped her cheek in exasperation, then glared at the kid. "Thank ye, Billy. However, that won't be necessary."

He smirked but eased his gangly frame back down onto the wooden bench.

Sighing, she closed her eyes momentarily. Oh, saints above help her.

Or in this case, Saint Mary Magdalene de' Pazzi. She was known as the patron saint of mystical ecstasy, despite having taken a vow of virginity at the early age of ten. Given Miles Neville's powerful virility, Mhaire doubted her own virginity would make it to the ripe old age of twenty-two – if she did not do something drastic to alter that course of collision.

England, Ireland, Canada, California . . . and now here, the Territory of New Mexico . . . he clearly was not a man to put down roots. Here today, gone tomorrow. She would be a fool to trust her heart to the adventurer.

"I urge all of ye – dinna forsake this holy ritual because of a few trivial posted signs. We can still make the pilgrimage to the Pecos Pool and purify ourselves there."

Hat in hand, Guido stood. His liquid brown eyes scanned the

room. He appeared to be speaking to the group at large, but she knew he was addressing her specifically. "I have met with this Englishman several times, and I feel he stands fiercely by his intentions."

And what were Guido's intentions toward her these days? Friend or foe? She suspected he still loved her, but on which side would he ultimately align, hers or Miles's?

"Under English common law," she parried, although she knew little about the subject, "the Luna grant's new titleholder does not own water rights – only the land's access to the water."

Old bespectacled Burt Lowry, the saddler, waved a hand, and she nodded at him "That's all well and good, Miss O'Moore, but we're not in England. We're in a free-for-all Territory."

Tom Broadbent, the young wheelwright, shot to his feet. "Begging your pardon, Miss Luna, but those two words – land's access – puts a dire damper on your suggestion." His lantern jaw worked like a cow chewing its cud, before he got out his concern. "We still gotta get down to the water, right?"

"No' at all a damper, Tom. We merely enter the Pecos 'ere at Puerto de Luna, free and clear of the land grant purchase, and wade along the shallow edges of the riverbank to the Pecos Pool. We ne'er touch dry soil."

Questioning gazes crisscrossed across the room. Some brows raised. Other heads nodded. She spread wide her palms in persuasive supplication. "I hae no fear of making the pilgrimage. Tis easy enough, I would imagine. Who's with me?"

§　§　§

After sundown of Mary Magdalene de Pazzi's Saint Day, the party of nearly thirty, give or take, set forth in a more or less devotional spirit to make the holy trek.

While Billy did not show up, Guido did. He walked off to one side and farther back of Mhaire, as if to demonstrate he was not fully in support of her reckless idea, but there, nonetheless, for her. A man of duty, as always. How admirable. Why could she not love him the way he wanted?

Unfortunately, the pitch torches that breezy but moonless night failed to light the hidden beaver dams and snags and stones beneath the shallow, gurgling water. People stumbled and floundered.

Urgently, she reminded them to refrain from sloshing ashore. Not that she feared being shot for trespassing at that time of night, but no point in giving Miles justification for more drastic measures later.

"Damn't to hell!" the barber sputtered, after tripping face first.

"Mr. Rawlings!" Ms. Singletary reproved. As if she did not nightly violate the Scriptures against fornication. The wind whipped her hat's festoon of flowers, and her torch's cinders whirled like fireflies.

"I've fallen so many times," Burt Lowry complained, "my rheumatism has got me bent crookeder than a knotty stick."

Over the next hour, one after another of the townspeople stumbled and was soaked in the water. This was not going at all as Mhaire had planned. Arising, muddy and wet and chilled by the night wind, many of the waders were even more frustrated to find their torches doused.

Apparently, though, not all the torches were extinguished, because just before the Catholic community reached the sacred Pecos Pool, drier brush just beyond the river's edge somehow caught fire with sparks dancing among the bushy clusters like Mayday candle lights.

Aghast, the parishioners watched as the flames quickly crackled past the bulrushes and cedar clumps. Then, the fire streaked like a lightning bolt across the winter's leftover dead sagebrush and chaparral and headed directly toward the Luna barn . . . just as Mhaire had taunted Miles could happen if he thwarted the Golden Carp.

"By all the saints!" she mouthed. "*Madre de Dios!* God Almighty! *Léan Dé*"

§　§　§

Even with the second floor's window sash hiked for the relief of the night wind, the billiard room sweltered. Perspiration tickled Miles's temples and trickled down his neck into the hair matting his chest. Naked to his denim's waist band, he bent over the four-pocket table, aimed his leather-tipped cue, and caromed the two red balls.

Finian blew on his chalk-dusted fingertips, gathered in the Gallic gesture he had acquired when in France. "By Jove, now there's a shot fer the records!"

Miles stood upright. His triumphant grin, directed at Finian, evaporated at the sight beyond his old friend's shoulder. Framed in the window's dark-of-night, a red-orange blaze sizzled directly toward the barn.

"Bloody hell!" Miles threw aside his cue and charged down the staircase and out the door. Barefoot, he raced to the barn. He yelled to Finian, close on his heels, "Save the horses!" and, without pausing, snatched a horse blanket from the stack near the tack room.

He sprinted around to the barn's backside. Already the brush there glowed with cinders, heralding the rapid advance of the inferno. He began beating at the advancing flame with the woolen blanket. Gradually, the flame engulfed his perimeters. He retreated. Goddammit! What he needed was a miracle. He needed Mhaire's blasted holy water.

And, as if his thought had summoned her, at some point soon thereafter she was at his side, along with the Luna foreman Guido and others. Some were flapping blankets at the raging fire. Others had created a bucket brigade linking down to the river.

He spared her a glance. "You?!"

She seemed to shrink as much from him as she did from the licking flames.

He returned his attention to the firefight. But it was of no use. Battle though they did, the conflagration consumed the barn. They all watched, as toward dawn, the flames flickered out, leaving a large rectangle of smoldering, red ashes.

Slumping to his haunches, he heaved an exhausted breath and turned a furious stare towards her and her cohorts who had gathered around, charred horse blankets and galvanized feed buckets in hand. He didn't need a soothsayer to tell him the cause of this conflagration. "Your pagan rites have brought about this."

Hurriedly, she crossed to kneel in front of him, and he could smell the stench of her scorched clothing and singed hair. "No, no. We meant no harm." She took up one of his blistered hands. "Oh, Mother Mary, let me tend to ye."

He shuddered at her mere touch. What power did she possess over him? He would not allow it. Scowling, he withdrew his hand. "You contrived this!"

"Nae, t'was an accident, I swear."

The backs of his hands and fingertips and soles of his feet were burning but no more so than his temper. His nostrils and throat were congested with smoke and ash, but his seared vocal cords managed to grit out words. "I distinctly recalled your curse about my barn catching fire."

Hands fisted, she shot to her feet. "If ye had possessed the sense God gave a goose, ye would hae kept the buffer path around the barn cleared of clumping tumbleweed and dead brush."

His gaze swerved from her, scanned the exhausted group, and found Guido. Sweat streamed paths down the soot coating the hidalgo's oblong face.

Addressing him specifically, Miles raised his file-rasped voice so all would hear. "I want you to run our cattle, horse, and sheep herds through the Pecos Pool every day from here on, until it is dry as dust, even if it takes to eternity."

CHAPTER FIFTEEN

Blackwater Vale, Eire
June 1691

The war between the Irish Jacobites and the English Williamites had created such a shortage of workers – craftsmen, servants, field hands, and other laborers – that often soldiers and clergymen and even an occasional nobleman were forced to thresh wheat and plough the land if they hoped for bread.

So, Merrow, standing at the rear of the threshing floor to catch a breeze, was not surprised to see a rider trotting toward the barn. Only a nobleman could afford to own a horse with such a superb conformation. Not a plow horse but a war horse.

At her side, Rory, his floppy ears perked and tail tucked with guarded tension, watched the rider pull up by the broken plow. He loosening a boot from the stirrup and dropped from the saddle to tether his steed.

As the rider strode toward the barn, she recognized that dangerous grace of the animal kingdom's predator. And as he drew nearer, she noted the determination chiseled in his jaw, the adamant set of his shoulders, the iron will in the muscles that roped his neck.

At once, she let fall at her feet the burlap bag of grain and tugged up around the lower half of her face the ragged linen scarf that protected her from the threshing's flurrying husks and straw.

Rory followed her as she stepped over the threshold, the doorway's board that held back the threshed grain from spilling, to face off with the Englishman.

He held forth a gloved hand to knead the scruff of Rory's neck, and she clamped back an exasperated huff as her dog, tail wagging, submitted with obvious delight. Her mouth twisted. A fine protector Rory was.

All the while, the man's magnificent indigo eyes were regarding her with what she could only interpret as baser instinct.

She noted he had not doffed his hat, as he would have had he considered her of the nobility. Rage as red as blood gushed from her like a slit throat. Her dragon's breath of irritation fluttered the scarf covering her nose and mouth.

He nodded toward the summit of the rocky promontory opposite the river. From their vantage point, irregular battlements and fanciful castellations and round towers rose heavenward to create a magical setting, for her, at least. His silken voice was amiable enough. "My castle is in need of a maidservant, primarily for the scullery."

You mean *my* castle.

She spared a glance over her shoulder for the half dozen peasants toiling, then turned a flinty expression on the unnerving man before her. "You will find no idle hands here in need of employment."

That near to him, the very air was afire. It seared her lungs. Even her speech was parched, as was the earth. The year before had been known as the hot Terrible Summer of 1690. In better years, the vale's marshy fringes turned to soup with the drenching rain.

He arched a brow. "My lord."

She inclined her head in the merest of assents. Behind her, she heard the scuffling of the straw and glanced to see Hugh and Alroy approaching with their winnowing forks.

The thickly muscled Alroy dragged one foot – not from any war wound but from an ankle injury when his cottage's burning roof timber fell on it. The ironmonger had been trying to save his wife and two-year-old daughter, trapped inside. These days, most villagers avoided working with the bitter man.

Idly, Fletcher Neville's gloved hand rested on his rapier's hilt. Overhead barn swallows squawked their warnings. "I want not your employment. I want a token of your fealty. Present yourself, maiden, to my steward and first in command on the morrow."

"Ahh, Nielsen, is it not?"

Hugh, the sleeve of his tatty jacket pinned to its shoulder, circled to stand beside her. "My lord, several years ago my sister served as a scullery maid in the castle, and I am sure she would be – ”

Neville never took his eyes off her. “Your brother Patrick O'Mordha – ten-and-three, I believe – is eligible to be conscripted in His Majesty's service. “I was that age when I went to war.”

And look at the hardened man ye are. Pure fury blazed in the back of her brain. But she couldn't afford to lose another family member to the Williamites. Patrick would surely be killed – or sodomized – within weeks if not months. A plague on Neville! She risked the dark promise in his eyes, and the words spit out of her like phlegm. “I shall present myself on the morrow.”

“My Lady Merrow,” Hugh protested, “this is asking too – ” He broke off at Neville's scorching glare, burning, it seemed, even her eyelashes.

However, the ironmonger hobbled forward. “Ye feckin' gobshite! Yuir godless soldiers stole the lives of me family and lay waste to me home!”

Before she could comprehend his actions, Alroy lunged with his winnowing fork to strike at the Lord Justice.

In what was a smear of motion, the Englishman parried the thrust, sweeping off his broadbrimmed hat between them, momentarily blinding Alroy and deflecting his jab. Next, with a lightning flash, the Englishman whipped his rapier from its scabbard and drove it up under Alroy's ribs, burying it deep enough that the blade's tip protruded from the other side, next to the backbone.

The winnowing fork dropped. Alroy doubled over, clutched at the rapier's bloody hilt. Baying frenziedly, an alarmed Rory bolted to corner him.

Neville placed his jackboot on the man's midriff and, shoving him over into a spasmodic heap, yanked out the bloodied blade. Neatly, he swiped the blade clean against one flap of his long, red jacket and sheathed the rapier.

Twined with her scream was Hugh's shout. “For God's sake!” Stunned, both their stares shifted from the still-twitching body back up to the Englishman.

He grimaced, then looked at her. “Yet another jacket ruined.” Once again, he scoured Rory's neck, its furred hackles falling back into place with his stroking, then he strode away.

Stricken, she watched him canter his mount back over the

nakedness of the scorched land. Her heart felt as dark as the land's furrows.

CHAPTER SIXTEEN

Puerto de Luna, Territory of New Mexico
June 1878

Mhaire hauled up on the wagon reins and stared dully at the gunky riverbed. Only a month before, the Pecos Pool was a vibrant, rushing water, swimming with myriad aquatic life . . . fish, crawdads, tadpoles, beaver, and dragonfly nymphs.

Now, the Pecos sludged in a diverted direction around rocks mottled with brown, dry moss. The banks of her beloved Pecos Pool, once thriving with lushly green vegetation, were trampled flat by hooves of Luna's livestock. And sandbars hung from what little water there was like tongues parching in the scorching sun.

Stories handed down from the hoary past said if a spring dried up, the naiad within it died. Mhaire might not be dying, at least, she did not think so, but she did feel as if inside her female parts were shriveling like sun-dried tomatoes.

Sitting beside Mhaire on the wagon bench, Elsa eyed her quizzically. "You are sure zis is vise?"

"Nae, I be sure of nothing these days." Especially not as muddled as her nights were, with dreams of a time long past but teaming with people as vivid as and real as her own skin.

Her healing services were little sought anymore. Feeling useless and foolish, she wandered around the Turquoise Door, piddling her time with hoeing the garden or feeding the chickens and shewing off a roadrunner hopeful to indulge its appetite in a raw egg.

Her gift for healing seemed to have dwindled with Miles's

arrival. He had dazzled her. Had she heedlessly let the steel of her shovel touch the tender roots of the plants? Had that brought down the curses?

The debacle of Saint Mary Magdalene Feast Day had left a bitter taste in everyone's mouth, most of all – and most obviously – that of Miles's. He had made good his threat.

Oh, she knew she could not blame him for her lackluster efforts at healing. She, with her bitterness toward him from the beginning, was solely responsible. How could she help heal anyone if she could not heal her own distressed spirit?

Then, too, she was even responsible for goading on the traditional torchlight procession. Something had to change, and, grudgingly, she conceded that change had to begin with herself. She cast a forlorn glance at Elsa's hatchet profile. "In fact, I hae me doubts talking to Miles Neville will make a difference, but I must make the effort."

Elsa appeared absorbed in paring a callus from her palm with her knife. For someone who had been scalped with a knife, the woman seemed to hold no horror of the blade. "Talking to you, it is not vat he has on his mind, *havfrue*."

"Well then, sleeping with him tis no' what I hae on *me* mind." Then grudgingly, "And even if it were, what guid could come of it?"

"Plenty. Zee Earl of Blackwater, he fuels your flame. And he vants you like a fire vants wood. Given zee good looks of you two, I have never seen a pair better matched. 'Sides, what have you to lose – other zan your maidenhead?"

The stirring of hope within her to end this foolish feud dueled with the cutting-edge of the heart's pain. She swallowed, then flicked the reins, and Bray and Neigh, ears perked, clip-clopped along the familiar route to Luna House . . . and her adversary.

§　§　§

Finian appeared at the study's doorway. "Uhh, you have visitors."

Miles glanced up from the latest dispatch from the Territory's Office of Comptroller in Santa Fe. It had declined his application to open a bank in Puerto de Luna, despite the obvious fact it was sorely needed, as there was only one other bank within a hundred-mile radius – and that one was owned by Emmet Sullivan, in Lincoln.

Clearly, Miles possessed the capital, meager though it was, to get his bank up and going. So, something stood in the way, and that something was Sullivan and his Santa Fe Ring, a shadowy cabal. And if Miles did not find a way to obtain return on his capital, then the funds would fritter away.

He was a man who always had a standby plan. The bank was just that, while he pursued his life's dream. If neither came to fruition, then he was the failure his old man had so often predicted he would be.

"Who is it, Finian?" His mild tone nevertheless shrieked of impatience. He needed to get back to fly fishing-cum-gold digging instead of this pestilence of paperwork.

"'Tis the lady Mhaire O'Moore and the Mistress Elsa Anderson."

He snapped to attention. "Show them to the library." Hurriedly, he finished fashioning what would be a telegram to the territorial governor himself, Lew Wallace. No use pussyfooting around with the bank deal. Because he sure as hell hadn't with Mhaire O'Moore.

With his herds befouling the Pecos Pool, he had been coolly anticipating what form her response would take. He had to admire her spunk. Enraged, she would most certainly be. But would she strike back or negotiate?

His terms? No more processions in the vicinity of his digging. No more collecting the damned curandera weeds, or whatever they were, in that particular area, either. His intestinal fortitude would not bend to less than what was his way.

At least, he thought so. Then, seeing her fingertips running across her beloved book spines, he had second thoughts. His impulsive, reckless temperament, not to mention his soul's discontent, was becalmed . . . and conversely his libido excited. Hell, he was besotted with her.

The afternoon sunlight shimmering through the window's gauze curtains cast her in an iridescent glow. Beneath her old, shingled straw hat, the mass of red hair clustered at her nape gleamed with gold. The sunlight shafted through her worn, sun-bleached cotton blouse and faded muslin skirt to reveal the delicate shoulders, a ballerina-straight back, and her slight curvature of her hips.

And he knew then and there, in the midst of his manipulations, he was somehow losing sight of his goal. His fierce need to succeed on his own was still strong, but he was wavering. Perhaps his methods in regard to her were a little extreme.

She turned to him with a nervous smile and held up her fingertips for his perusal. "Dusty. You need a housekeeper."

He grinned back. He knew now he had her at his mercy. "And a cook." Finian's cuisine suffered egregiously. "You are offering your services." It was a statement, not a question.

She sashayed closer, to the leather sofa between them. "Elsa can do that, too."

"Cook – and clean," muttered a voice beneath him.

Only then did he notice the dauntingly scarred woman, seated on the sofa below. She shot a scathing look up at him from over her shoulder. No sunbonnet or scarf for Miss Anderson. Scare the piss out of people, she would if she could. But not himself. Determined to string out Mhaire's surrender, he maintained his coolly amused smile. "And her wages?"

Mhaire's returning smile was just as cool. "You cease running livestock at Pecos Pool."

Leaning over, he braced his hands on the sofa's overstuffed back and stared her down. "And you and the townspeople will halt their trespassing?"

Only the small tick at the base of her throat revealed her tension. "After what happened that night, they hae no desire to . . . to make any further pilgrimages."

He had to concede they had joined in to help fight the fire. But he was not about to let her off the hook. Her pointing out in front of the onlookers that night that his burnt barn was his fault – a result of his carelessness in clearing away the accumulated brush – had made him feel foolish. He sighed, rightly so. "And yourself?"

She rubbed her palms together, her agitation visible. "I, uhh, I still require access to Pecos Pool fer me curandera work. And all the other sacred water sites on me . . . on the Luna land grant."

No way she was going to acknowledge verbally his ownership of the land grant, eh? "I can handle that. With the provision, *you* do the cooking and cleaning. You know, as a domestic live-in. Of course, with Sundays off."

She blinked. "Meself? But . . . but me skills are not in homemaking. They are in healing and easing the – "

"For God's sake, hop off that merry-go-round, Mhaire. We've been round and round this. You, not Elsa here, incited the pilgrimage. Pay up or forfeit."

All color drained from her oval face. Only her brows and lashes created dark arcs of despair. He knew he had her between the proverbial Devil and the Dead Sea. Return to her beloved childhood home while knowing the Pecos Pool was again fresh and sparkling – in exchange for abandoning her curandera calling.

She licked her parched lips. Glanced at Elsa.

After a long moment, the woman nodded her gristled head. "I can mind our place and zee animals."

Mhaire was yet to yield. With renewed grit, her chin shot up. "If ye not only agree to cease running cattle around the Pecos Pool area but also cease yer digging, too."

A fortnight ago, he would have told her there was not a chance on God's green earth he'd abandon his digging. His burning desire depended on retrieving the gold he believed Coronado buried there. But after his inadvertent baptism in the Blue Hole, his master plan now appeared to be taking a different direction. Hell, yes. "Granted."

Surprise that he should so easily capitulate widened her eyes. Then her head hung. "I'll send fer me trunks."

His moral recklessness had won out. Why did he feel such little pleasure?

§ § §

With viscous chops of the kitchen knife, Mhaire diced the potatoes, the mainstay of any Irish household. Except this particular household was no longer hers.

She would have thought living here at the Luna House again, even if only during the week, would be her fantasy realized. But it was the opposite. A nightmare. The longing for what was in plain sight but forever denied. The desert sojourner dying of thirst while the mirage of an oasis shimmered continually just out of reach.

But her nightmares featured more than the Luna House. The Lord of Luna dominated them. He . . . and another man, much similar, so that it was difficult to distinguish between the two . . . often plagued her unsettling dreams. Sometimes, she would awake, sweating and expecting to find Miles in her bedroom, only a door down from his own.

Was that what a repressed part of herself desired? A part that was even showing up in her dreams?

And was she the female ousted from the castle on the River Blackwater centuries before?

Both the press iron, heating on the kitchen stove, and its kettle's boiling water steamed her hair to an unmanageable frizz. A straggling lock flopped across her eyes. With the back of her hand, she went to swipe at it – when a glistening mass also flopped before her, this on the knife-scarred worktable.

Her glance swerved up from the dead eyes of the freshly caught string of trout at the same time her knife skittered around to encounter Miles's gut.

Fly rod slung across his shoulder, he hitched a cocky, daring grin. "Fillet them for the nooning." The backs of his fingers nudged away her knife point.

This wasn't going to work. She was used to being in charge of her life, not surrendering the order of her days to the whimsy of someone else. Much less surrender her nights . . . although, he had yet to take charge of those, unless it was through her dreams and his body double.

"Aye, aye, captain."

His glance ran over her appraisingly. "You're much too good for Jaramillo."

Her lips made a moue. "We are no longer affianced."

"Ahh, then you are fair game for the local bachelors."

Her knife pointed swiveled back to his fishing vest. "Nae, fair game I am no'."

Once again, he flicked aside the blade. "I won't deny I wanted you like I've wanted no other woman, from the first time I saw you, rising from the river rushes."

Despite his dispassionate delivery, she felt a rewarding prickle of harsh triumph.

He strolled toward the hallway door, then looked over his shoulder. "But don't fret over any amorous pursuit from me. Way before I turned fifteen, I learned that when the desire was mutual it was more pleasurable."

She yanked the press iron from the stove top but immediately reconsidered as ill-conceived the idea of hurling the iron at him. She hammered out a silky smile. "But then, ye know what they say, 'One man's pleasure is another's pain.'"

"Obviously, you have yet to experience the former." He winked and, whistling, left her there fuming.

After he left, she set about fileting, flouring, and frying the trout. She tried to sort out why she was perturbed. Because he had – gallantly, or rather, ungallantly – left the option to her? As if she would ever come around.

But that was her pride rebelling. That was the former Mhaire who had never known deprivation, who had no familiarity with death, who had never been shaken by doubt. Who had yet to lose her parents and her brother so early on.

Another part of herself appealed to her in soundless whispers to acknowledge her deception. That she was drawn to Miles Neville and had no defense against this irrational weakness.

Granted this Earl of Blackwater was handsome. Granted she was attracted to him, drawn by some magnetic force. But on which side of the earth's ley lines did that magnetic force reside?

§　§　§

Amidst the unfurling of fine linen napkins and the clinking of silver, crystal, and porcelain, Finian helped himself from the platter of steaming, butter-dolloped biscuits that Mhaire positioned close to his plate, then dipped a spoon into the peach preserves.

The long table could seat a dozen or more, but with a smile as sweet and chilled as ice wine, the cheeky lass had refused Miles's offer to take meals with them. "Hired help dinna dine with their betters."

And his laddie had responded as coolly with an indifferent shrug. "As you wish."

The table's center was taken up with fried trout, creamy mashed *potatoes,* and sautéed green beans, their savory flavors enough to make a man's mouth water. During Finian's quest in France for the metal detector, he had chanced across no chef who could have created tastier cuisine, despite Mhaire's decry that cooking was not her calling.

"Ye going to the town hall meeting tomorrow evening, lass?"

Turning away from the table, she paused, looked over her shoulders. Her brows knit with puzzlement. "I dinna know there was one."

He nodded at Miles, his loose-limbed body seemingly at ease in the heavily scrolled chair across from him.

Fork in hand, Miles paused, as if only vaguely aware of the lass serving them. Finian knew better. The laddie's attentive focus was surpassed only by his headstrong will. "I have called a meeting of Puerto de Luna's good townspeople tomorrow after church to discuss interest in my proposed bank."

Her inhalation was audible. "Ye cannae seriously be thinking of going up against Sullivan and the Santa Fe Ring?"

"That's my intention at this time. A biscuit, please."

Had he purposefully withheld the use of her given name as a reminder she was a mere servant? Finian doubted it. His laddie was keeping himself on a tight leash. The unseen but intense and edgy force pulsing between him and the lass indicated their towering yearning was going unslaked. He had the distinct feeling that yearning was burning on a short fuse.

She returned her attention to him. "Aye, Finian, tis Sunday – and me day off. I believe I shall be going, after all."

So was her companion, the formidable but estimable Elsa Anderson. That Sunday afternoon the pair rode with Finian in the Luna carriage. As he took Elsa's horny hand to help her alight in Puerto de Luna, she directed at him that basilisk stare that could shrivel a man's soul.

As if she were Queen Victoria, head held high beneath her lopsided crown of ruby-red scars and a braid the shade of moonlight, she descended without benefitting him with another withering glance.

Incredibly, people spilled out the doorway at Grzelachowski's Mercantile onto the boardwalk and into the dusty street. They had come from far and wide to listen to Miles's proposition. Beneath the intense sunlight, parasols bobbed, and sombreros and Stetsons shifted, straining to draw closer.

However, the crowd parted at once for Elsa Anderson, as if she were a leper. Finian ushered the two women inside. The rows of shelving in front of the counter had been cleared of merchandise – work gloves, harnesses, washboards, sacks of flour and sugar and other basic staples necessary to frontier life – and crammed around the stuffy room's perimeters.

The Danish woman sailed through the hordes inside to a far corner of the room to take up her vulture's roost near the Franklin fireplace stove and apart from the humanity that scorned her.

Her charge Mhaire, instead, edged closer to the front – as did the farrier's daughter, Alma Moreno. The ebony haired lass's reported adoration for Billy unrequited, Alma was now casting calf-eyes at Miles, standing behind the cleared front counter.

One hand was tucked loosely into the roomy pocket of his Norfolk hunting jacket, well-worn at its elbows. He was in the midst of a terse presentation.

"Governor Wallace turned down my application for a bank here in Puerto de Luna." He paused, looked pointedly around the room. "So, I am proposing a savings and loan association, owned by you, as depositors and borrowers. To start it up, I shall front the capital. I sincerely believe I can offer you and your families better terms than Sullivan's bank does."

"Eet's not about terms," Benicio Moreno called out. Thumbs jammed under his suspenders, the brown-skinned little man rose amidst the wary yet curious spectators.

A dry smile twitched Miles's lips. "Then what *is* it about?"

"It's about Emmet Sullivan et al," bearded Grzelachowski said, standing at the front of the gathered townspeople. As this was his building and given that he was well respected, his Puerto de Luna compadres gave him their ears. He locked beefy palms over his barrel stomach. "It's about survival. Sullivan holds our notes and can call them in at a moment's notice."

Miles's gaze scanned the room's intent faces. He nodded. "Fair enough. I'm willing to cover that. If you move your accounts to my bank, I pledge to cover those notes."

Brows peaked and people glanced askance from one to another. Slowly, some nodded. But then Tom Broadbent stood. The wheelwright rubbed his lantern jaw pensively. "Yeah, but can you cover us against retaliation from the Santa Fe Ring?"

Finian thought the bobbing heads and concurring mutters worthy of an Irish funeral dirge. A gloom descended on the room. Miles's offer was ready for a dismal burial.

A deriding voice from the back of the room sent all heads swiveling like owls in the direction of the buzzard. "You lily-livered men!" It was the harridan Elsa's voice, melodious yet biting. "You up and move your family to zis piss-pot on the edge of the vorld and zen don't have the bollocks to poke your head above your gopher holes!"

If cringing could make a sound it was the uneasy shuffling of the shame-faced men in the room. Throats cleared. Chins ducked. After a deafening silence, Grzelachowski begrudged, "Well, ja, I suppose I'm inclined to take a chance. We're so far from Santa Fe, I doubt the Ring will be bothering with us."

Of course, the White Elephant in the room was the Ring's accomplice, Emmet Sullivan. He and his gang were a much closer proximity. In the tense silence that followed, Finian noted that one by one raised hands indicated willingness to go along with Miles's banking proposition . . . at least, for the moment.

Afterward, Finian stopped by the counter to lean in close to Miles, conferring with an old coot about financing a vineyard. "Take Mhaire and Elsa home for me, will ye, me laddie?"

Miles's dark head swung around to shoot him a quizzical look but, apparently noting his determined expression, nodded.

With that, Finian shouldered his way through the press of people. His course was set directly toward the towering plumed hat, with its artificial flowers and even a bird nested among them. He swept its owner, the delightfully buxomed milliner, a flourishing bow. "Ms. Gladys Singletary, yuir smashing hat has laid claim to me heart."

The widow's excessively pleased expression was worth his sally. Her white gloved hand nestled suggestively in the valley between her ample breasts. "Why, sir, I have many more chapeaus in my shop, if you'd like to view them."

Her tiny millinery store was cramped with shelves of hats, bust forms, a sewing machine and other trappings, with which neither of them bothered. That evening in Glady's bedroom at the rear of the store was well spent, to which, undoubtedly, many of her male customers could also heartily attest.

He could only hope he provided the lively widow with as much pleasure as he intended to provide the next female in his sights.

§   §   §

The ride back early that evening from the meeting in Puerto de Luna was uneventful, if Mhaire could discount the Luna carriage's cowhide seats split by age, with wool tufts poking through.

And if she could discount the guilty and terrible pleasure roaring through her as she sat next to Miles. That debilitating pleasure was an emotional betrayal of everything she was about – her familial, political, religious, and national makeup.

Her gaze repeatedly strayed to his suntanned hands, strong and well-shaped with neatly paired nails. He handled the reins with sensitive finesse. What would it be like to feel that same touch on her love-starved flesh? Her sudden wanton weakness was fearsome, and she could only be grateful for Elsa's formidable presence on her other side.

The Danish woman's seamed mouth worked liked she wanted to spit out something unpleasant. When Miles halted before her adobe, she forthwith sprang down and muttered only a curt and distracted farewell in her guttural Danish. *"G'natt."* Surprisingly, she even swished by Pork, padding across the yard to greet her, and slammed shut the turquoise front door.

At once, Mhaire edged to the carriage seat's far side. She should have stayed the night at the Turquoise Door. But the carriage ride would save her the walk to work early tomorrow morning. And, if she were honest with herself, to leave Miles's side was like leaving a furnace's heat on a winter night. "Now, what has Elsa wired to the moon?"

He snapped the reins, and the carriage jerked forward. "I suspect her disgruntled mood is more likely attributed to Cupid than *la luna*. His arrow must have found its target."

Her head whipped toward him. His strong profile was etched against the golden haze of the gloaming. "Ye're talking about Finian? Tis no' possible. Elsa finds him . . . ." She hesitated, realizing she did not really know how Elsa felt about Finian. "Irritating," she finished lamely. "Elsa merely finds him irritating."

Miles emitted a dry chuckle. "I can empathize with her."

"What? Ye find yuir friend irritating, as well?"

"No. You."

She switched her gaze back to the faint white of caliche road bending out of sight beneath the river's trees ahead. "That can be solved easily. Dismiss me services at Luna House."

"You're free to go at any time, although I don't think Elsa will be delighted about taking your place. Not with *irritating* Finian there to plague her. Nor would you be delighted with Luna's *irritating* cattle running amok around the Pecos Pool."

Her mouth pressed as thin as a grass blade. "Ye've made yuir point."

Once back at the Luna House, before he could come around to assist her, she alighted from the carriage and hurried inside and up the spiraling staircase to her bedchambers. She sought the comfort that sleep offered the depressed, the lonely, the guilty. But for the longest time, she lay awake, staring up at the darkened ceiling.

At one point, she thought she heard Miles's lengthy tread coming down the hallway's runner. Thought she heard his footfall pause before resuming. But was not certain. She did not know whether to be relieved or not that she had locked the door. She feared . . . nae, she knew . . . she was weak in resolve whenever he entered a room.

At last, in her sleep, the iridescent blue-green of fish scales morphed to those of eyes watching her, wicked blue-green eyes of an entity that would sweetly torture and torment to gain its end. Even in her sleep a frisson of desire prickled through her lower regions. She moaned, spasming in the sheets that bound her . . . .

CHAPTER SEVENTEEN

Blackwater Vale, Eire
June 1691

Merrow descended the narrow, stone steps. The strong smell of mold, dust, and dampness drifted up from the buttery. Its cool cellar space stored barrels, bottles, and butts of spirits. Hurriedly, she searched among the rows of racks. She was seeking bottles of claret wine.

After nearly a month in service to the autocratic Lord Justice, she was learning servant rudiments that obliged she seek out cramped, dark, and forbidding places of which she had been but vaguely aware prior to the Williamite War. Rooms such as her present sleeping quarters or the dungeon, currently imprisoning several Jacobite rebels. But the dungeon was a far sight better than Kilmainham, where her father was imprisoned.

Fletcher had provided her with the whereabouts of her father. Why? And would he provide her with provisional papers to travel to see him? Or was all this an elaborate trap, set for both her and her father? By birthright, she imperiled the Englishman's claim to her county. Readily, he could dispose of her, arrange for her to fall to her death on these bloody slippery stairs, if he so elected.

A complex character, he was. Haughty, clever, savage, cold . . . but hotblooded with a vaulted prowess, if the kitchen gossip of the mistresses who warmed his bed were true. And, most likely, the wench with whom Merrow shared the sty that was their sleeping quarters, was doing just that. Phebe had not returned to her pallet until the light of dawn this morning – and her small teeth had gleamed with a sly, satisfied smile.

Finding the store of claret wine, Merrow selected the nearest and removed its cork stopper. She dipped her nose near the rim and inhaled the aroma of wild violets. A mere whiff transported her back to childhood, to her mother, to her mother's favorite fragrance.

Daily, her mother would place a vase of violets on the altar of the private chapel that adjoined the north solar. While on her knees before that altar and rosary in hand, she had been brutally pummeled by a Williamite soldier, wielding a club with nails stuck in it.

Briefly Merrow entertained the idea of adding a slow poison to the claret wine, but what would be the point? Only another tyrant would rise to take the place of his most honorable Lord Justice Fletcher Neville.

Aye, hated him and his kind, she did. But if she had to endure his heavy hand, better he than King William's Dutch general, the fat Godard van Reede who at the head of his soldiers had initially seized the castle.

With not a wee bit of acrimony, she had to confess Fletcher Neville was enormously more attractive than Reede. Alas.

She sighed and headed back up the moldy steps to the banquet hall and audience chamber. The Great Hall was so crowded a piece of vellum would be difficult to slip inside. The chamber's high walls were hung with French, Belgian, and Flemish tapestries. Above the oak dower-cupboard, the standard displayed the coat of arms of the ruling family.

After centuries, the coat of arms was no longer that of her family, the trout and the mermaid flanking a gold escutcheon. No, now Neville's coat of arms ruled – a black heart entwined by a red rose and flanked by red dragons.

Here, her father had dispensed judgements while sitting on the dais in his Chair of the Estate. Now, Neville sprawled there, seemingly bored. But she knew better. He was acutely aware of every person, every movement, every expression.

From the screen passage, she studied her adversary. Through the large mullioned window, late afternoon light played across his unforgiving features. Arrogant, strong-willed, and cold hearted. He wore the look of a gambler with no nerves.

With shock, her gaze next alit on the man seated next to him, in conversation. None other than her intended, Lord Alfred Dunhill.

At seventeen she had been betrothed to the twenty-eight-year-old widower, a Catholic of English stock. Throughout Alfred's courtship, she found him to be considerate and well read, an excellent horseman and a fine dancer – and so certain he knew what was right.

Though still betrothed to Dunhill, she had last seen him the day he went off to war with her father and brothers and other Jacobites. It appeared Alfred, periwigged in the latest fashion, now wore one shoe Irish and the other English.

She approached the dais. The Great Hall's raucous conversations and laughter drowned out the seemingly pleasant but idle conversation being exchanged between Neville and Dunhill. She set the three wine bottles on the linen-draped table.

He spared her not a glance. His entire attention was centered on Dunhill. But Neville's next words proved he was keenly aware of her. "You jump, Dunhill, as if in recognition." Then in a scathing undertone, "Are you *familiar* with the maid serving us?"

She tensed, waiting for Alfred's response. Was he overjoyed or would he repudiate her?

He shoved away from the board and stood. "Lady Merrow."

She dipped a low, graceful curtsey worthy of any high court. "My lord." She rose to face him. His naturally bulging eyes betrayed nothing, but did she detect a twinge of disquiet?

The abhorrent English commoner, now Lord Fletcher Neville, Earl of Blackwater, glanced up over his shoulder at her. "Ahhh, then you *are* familiar with one another." A statement not a question. She suspected he had known this all along.

Alfred sketched a swift bow. He was only slightly shorter than Fletcher Neville but substantially thicker through the shoulders and chest. Those lips that had urgently pressed that single kiss on hers before leaving for the battle front smiled blandly. "The lady is my betrothed."

"Now this is quite a novelty." Fletcher leaned forward to uncork one of the wine bottles. "You are betrothed to one aligned with the enemy you have come this day to profess?"

Her eyes widened. Then Alfred had, indeed, turned traitor.

He reached inside his waistcoat for his ornamental snuff box.

She knew Alfred well, knew this practice signaled his tension. "My regard for the Lady Merrow has naught to do with politics."

At that, she snapped. "Do ye two mind ceasing discussing me, as though I were no' here?"

His expression amused, Fletcher held up the bottle. "Pour Lord Dunhill and myself a glass."

She snatched the bottle from his large, battle-scarred hand and sloshed the claret into the two brass goblets. She was not fooled. Fletcher Neville was in some way engineering things to his own advantage.

He held aloft his goblet in a coldly silent toast. Then, quaffing the claret slowly, he eyed Alfred over its rim. "King William could find consorting with his enemy treasonous."

Less harshly sculpted than Neville's face, Dunhill's blanched. He glanced up at her, then nudged aside his goblet. Leaning forward, hands the size of Clydesdale hooves clasped between his knees, his lowered tone would seem conspiratorial. "Lord Neville, I assure you that this is not a politically arranged marriage but one purely of financial convenience."

One of financial convenience? For three years straight, he had sought her father's permission for her hand in marriage, appearing often at O'Mordha Castle, when weather permitted travel from Kinsale. What about the longing looks he had cast her way, the opportunities to touch her fingers, the back of her waist, her shoulder?

His courting approach she had found both interesting and amusing. He was not that bad looking, and she had been amenable to making a life with him.

The snake. The serpent in her Garden of Eden.

"Convenience?" Only now did Fletcher allow his gaze to dwell on her. It was a slow perusal, unknotting her scarf, loosening her blouse's laces, baring her small breasts. He dragged his gaze from her and broke off a hunk of warm, perfectly round brown bread. "Then you will have no objection should I enact my privilege, that of the *droit du seigneur* the night of your wedding and bed her first?"

She gaped at him, struggled for words at such effrontery. "Ne'er has that primitive privilege been enforced here in Éire!"

Her eyes arrowed next to Alfred. His pale hazel ones were staring at her with abject futility. He licked his lips, then attempted a weak smile. He turned to take up his goblet, downed its contents, then shrugged. "Tis of no consequence to me, Lord Neville. As I said, it is merely a marriage of convenience."

"Good then." Fletcher was watching her, even though he addressed Alfred. "When is the wedding set, Dunghill?"

Alfred's chest puffed like a pouter pigeon's. "Dunhill."

Both amused by Fletcher's turn of wording and distraught by this calamitous turn of events, she eked out a stringent smile. "There is no date. No wedding. And, thus, no rights of the manor lord."

Fletcher returned her smile, his superior. "Then, as Lord Justice, I shall set a date. Say the full moon following Lughnasa, the beginning of the harvest season? Will this arrangement work for you, Dunghill?"

Alfred let this second mispronunciation of his name pass by. He shrugged heavy shoulders and nodded. "As you wish, my lord."

Perfidy in the flicker of an eyelash. She stood stone still, as if turned to a pillar of salt. Could this be happening yet again? This intent to subjugate, violate, her body? If Fletcher Neville had won her affection with words and deeds, that might have made the difference. Had he but given her a choice even.

But involuntary submission of her body . . . that constituted rape. A repeat of the horror, even if she was attracted to the Englishman. More than she should be, more than her heart could bear. Mother of God, help her.

CHAPTER EIGHTEEN

Puerto de Luna, Territory of New Mexico
June 1878

Mhaire fought her constraints. Not prickly briar or wrist chains but merely fine linen sheets, musty from closet storage. Dripping with perspiration, she shoved upright on her bedroom's richly appointed featherdown mattress.

This most recent dream was so real, she could not awaken from it. It was as if she were living dual lives occurring at the same time, though separated by . . . what? . . . nearly two centuries, if she recollected her Irish history correctly?

Two lives connected by two self-serving males with smiles to make the angels sing, and eyes the blue green of both the holy well, Tobar Na Croí Naofa, and the Blue Hole . . . and a home in both centuries that were no longer hers.

Despair glooming her mood, she disentangled her limbs from the damp, clingy bedsheets and padded to the water closet and tub with its promise of heated, life-restorative water. She should be grateful for this, at least. So much better than the chilling dip in the acequia that looped from the Pecos, around Elsa's adobe home, and back to the river.

And there that word was again to reinforce her lack – home. Even the small, austere adobe home was not hers. She had no home to call her own.

Dawn's light still slept for another hour. Dressed but yawning, she headed downstairs to prepare the morning's meal – and passed a sleepy looking Finian, striding in through the front door. In one hand, he swung an object by its cord. Taken aback, she tucked her chin and arched one brow with disbelief. "Is that a *hat* box?"

As he sailed past her, the ends of his mustache lifted in a sheepish grin. "That it is, lass."

Her eyes widened. Then, despite her uneasy lassitude, a semblance of a smile crimped the ends of her mouth. "Ahhh, another conquest fer ye, eh? The Widow Singletary?"

Mounting the staircase to his bedroom, Finian flicked a cheery wink over his shoulder. "Not a conquest, lass, but an interlude of delight I was most fortunate to render."

A romp in the bed would doubtlessly be good for him and the lusty widow. And most likely for herself, as well. But, Jesus, Mary, and Joseph, she wanted to be special, not merely some . . . some conquest . . . which was what her dream's alter ego, Merrow O'Mordha, was facing, had Mhaire not awakened in time.

Miles strode in fifteen minutes later and paused at the kitchen doorway, watching her. She wished she was less conscious of his masculinity. "What?" she asked, halting her whisking of the raw eggs and wishing her stomach was not doing summersaults.

He stepped inside the doorway. "Don't mind me. I can't help noticing." His clefted chin, smudged with morning bristle, pointed toward her head. "Your hair."

Her hand groped for what must be messy strands somewhere astray – only to realize that this morning, in the after fog of her distressed sleep, she had failed to pin up her hair, that it fell loosely to the small of her waist. Immediately, she dropped the whisk and shoved both hands into her tangled locks. Quickly, she fashioned an untidy knot at her nape.

His mouth twitched, and his words ground like a farrier's rasp. "I should learn to keep my mouth shut. Better to leave it loose. It's right comely like that."

He was so close, she could smell his masculinity – the earthy, early morning redolence woven in with the heat of arousal, for that was clearly was she saw in his expression . . . the flare of his nostrils, the dilation of the blue wells that were his pupils. Deep and dark and haunting.

Addled, she swerved her attention back to the cast-iron stove and the frying eggs, and he swung away. Both he and she rattled by desire – and both at a standoff.

Desire. Never had she experienced such a stirring feeling like it . . . and everything tumultuous accompanying it. Shyness. Confusion. Vulnerability. Uncertainty. Every thought and feeling now constantly turned toward him like a weathervane in a storm. She wanted her life to return to its easy placidity before Miles Neville's arrival at Puerta de Luna.

But did she? Did she truly? Would she forego this enrichening, this deepening, of her feelings, be they pleasure or pain? Her spine stiffened. She merely would have to prove herself a worthy foe in this, as she had in previous hardships.

Twenty minutes later, as she set the table with tomatillo salsa, bacon, and sunny-side-up eggs, the way he liked them, he strode in, freshly shaven, his lashes spiked with wash water. Swishing the linen napkin across his lap, he helped himself to the sterling coffee pot.

"My bedlinens need changing." Casually, he tonged his usual two lumps of sugar into his delicate china cup.

Leaning around to set before him the gravy boat, she slid him an incredulous look. "Why, I changed them yesterday."

"Pity that." He tipped cream from its small pitcher into his strong coffee. "Nonetheless, they need to be changed again."

Her hand itched to reach for the closest of the table's pair of silver candelabrum and bash his arrogant brain to bits. He was peering up at her from half-masted lids, awaiting her reaction. She schooled her expression to unconcern. "'Tis yuir succubus soiling your sheets, eh?"

Now it was his turn to stare. "What?"

Finian entered the dining room and pulled out one of the table's ornately carved chairs. "Ye know, me laddie – the folktales about the devil in female form possessing yuir dreams."

"I know what a succubus is, Finian." Annoyance flattened Miles' temptingly full mouth to a blade-thin line, and he nailed her with a suspicious glare. "I want to know what *you* meant."

She allowed innocence to flit across her face. "I warned ye did I no' about the cures and curses of Puerto de Luna." She turned from him and Finian, flinging over her shoulder. "I'll see to changing your dirty bedlinens."

Her response was all but ignored. Miles had fallen into a discussion with Finian about getting the bank construction underway that morning.

If only she could figure out Miles. She wanted to know him better. To understand the rare species of manhood. He might never give up his preoccupation with the gold, but he *had* given his word about the Pecos Pool. Still, she uneasily sensed there was something about that promise, something harboring deception, though she could not put her finger on just what. It was not a promise made of steel but of silk, which deteriorated over time.

But there was something so femininely foolish within her that wanted to trust him, to believe in him.

Dishes washed and kitchen cleaned, she gathered sheets and pillow slips from the linen closet and made her way up the staircase, each step a heavily preoccupied one. A decade before, her footsteps had flitted the stairs, and her thoughts had been lighthearted ones – of beating Riley at chess or secretly swimming sans clothing at Blue Hole . . . of persuading her mother to subscribe to the scandalous suffragist <u>Woman's</u> <u>Journal</u> or her father to purchase from Guido a thoroughbred with which she had fallen in love.

Alas, with youth's folly, she had taken so much for granted.

In the master bedroom suite, once her parents', Miles's masculine essence overrode the memories of them. Permeated everything. From his accouterments – his hairbrush, tooth powder, razor, and leather shaving strap – to his armoire with its clothing redolent of him. The rumpled sheets smelled faintly of his subtle lime and cedar cologne, and his strong personal scent – that of the untamable and unnamable, peculiar to him only.

Dropping the pile of sheets and pillow slips, she flung herself face forward on the bed, arms outspread, and wept with unspent grief that was knotted in the hollow parts of her chest, in the back of her eyes, in the depths of her throat.

She wept for the loss of her parents. For the loss of herself. For her loss of belief in the possibility of love. Because Miles was most certainly a desecration of her heart's yearning. Why could she not settle for the noble, capable Guido, a man she had always cared for and respected?

Wiping her damp eyes with the backs of her hands, she pushed off the bed and began changing its linens. Foolish it was to yearn for something that did not exist. She shoved one of the goose down pillows into its sham.

Even more foolish knowingly to mope for that something. She slammed a pillow at the head of the bed.

Most of all foolish it was to let her moping ruin her day – she heaved the matching pillow to the other side – much less ruin her life.

She marched back to the staircase and the kitchen duties that called below. She was grinding the dried chiles and cilantro for the pintos beans she had soaked overnight in the cast iron pot when the rap on the outside kitchen door distracted her.

Through the screen door, she peered out at Tom Broadbent. The wheelwright stood on the stoop, dusty derby in hand. "Tom, me apologies. I dinna hear the front door knocker."

"Uh, no. I came around back. I . . . uh . . .wanted, you know, to talk to you . . . uh . . . ."

"I understand." Sighing, she wiped her hands on her apron. "Ye dinna want anyone to see you talking to me. Is that it? Well, then, what brings yeself here?"

"Our baby – Clara – her eyes are infected."

"Hae ye tried potato slices on her eyes, like I told ye?"

His jutting jaw laboring anxiously, he nodded. "But they are still crusting over."

"Then, come back around this evening. I'll have a honey potion prepared fer yuir bairn."

Relief flooded his rectangular face. His head bobbed. "Thank you, Mhaire. How about I stop off at the Turquoise door straightaway and repair that stable gate in payment?"

"That would be grand, Tom."

That he had to sneak around to seek her services these days . . . she wanted to hiss, to spit, to hurl something.

She tried not to fixate on her ebbing rapport with the community and concentrated instead on her myriad duties that afternoon – a button to be sewn she noticed missing on one of Finian's shirts, the dusting away of sand that invariably slithered inside somehow, running washed clothes through the wringer without pinching a finger, and pressing the household linen without burning a finger.

Later that day, she set about preparing the honey potion she had promised Tom, along with Finian and Miles's supper – cornbread the color of ripe piñon nuts, beans, and poblano stew. Spitefully, she thought about flavoring the stew with a glob of crushed chile, enough to set fire to the lint in the navel.

Not even a breeze stirred through the screen door to cool her. Her lower back muscles were knotted from her workload that day. As a happy child, she had not known how her life would take such a difficult turn.

Just before sundown, both Tom and Miles, along with Finian, arrived outside at the same time. At the sight once more of the wagon bed's shovels and picks – as if they were responsible for her woes, for her soul's discontent – her back muscles rebelled, writhing up her spine to the base of her skull.

Wordless, she thrust the mason jar of potion at Tom, shot a glare at the exhausted and dirty Miles and Finian, and stalked back inside and upstairs, not even bothering to serve the dinner. Somewhat later a knock came at her bedroom door. Whoever it was, she ignored it.

Her sleep that night was disturbed again, this time by those bloody damn shovels and picks . . . no, pikes, this time.

CHAPTER NINETEEN

Blackwater Vale, Eire
July 1691

Hers was not the kind of beauty that could make a man's jaw drop and his cock rise. No, Fletcher thought, watching Merrow O'Mordha, as she moved among the lower tables, serving the dozen or so of his boisterous soldiers that evening, her beauty was elusive.

The way she held herself . . . with confidence. The way she walked . . . with graceful certainty. The way she could glance from the corner of her eyes rather than swivel the neck. And, by all the saints, what an exquisite neck. And then there was that gloriously red hair.

At his side, Nielsen quaffed the last of his ale. Without glancing at Fletcher, he muttered, "You err, son, if you think yonder maiden will be an easy conquest."

She was no maiden – at least, from the information elicited from Fletcher's inquiries of the local tradesmen and peasants. A couple of his predecessor's soldiers had taken her by force. Yet her spirit had that virginal quality, that untouched resilience, that he could only humbly admire.

"That is precisely why I want the maiden, Nielsen – because she will not be an easy conquest."

Even more than admire her, he wanted her. He might have a will of steel, as the King claimed, but she was his magnet.

He wanted her and no amount of plowing the furrows of the county's females, who avidly crawled into his bed, seemed to satisfy him. Something was lacking. Not in them, per se, but in himself. A consuming want that could not be quenched . . . at least, as easily as it seemed to be for others.

But then he had been a base-born bastard, his father long gone, and, thus, raised always wanting. Food . . . clothing . . . approval . . . parental nourishment.

When Fletcher was seven, his mother had been beaten to death by a drunken sailor she had been servicing. Fletcher had been forced to fend for himself like a wild animal, until a year later he had found work and food, laboring on a castle mote.

Nielsen cast him a smug grin. "Ahh, but I suspect it is more likely the *vena amoris*, the vein of love, that pumps into your heart these days, rather than the juices that pump hard your fleshy weapon."

He jabbed a knife into a hunk sawed from the smoke blackened venison and staked it on his wooden trencher. "You have drunk too much, my old friend. Or else, you would know I have no heart."

"Oh, is that why the meal's leftovers are given as alms to the village's poor?"

He huffed an aggravated grumble. "You're going to be the death of me yet."

When, in fact, Nielsen Buxtehude had reprieved him from certain death.

By the time Fletcher was thirteen, hard labor had developed him into a bruising two-fisted youth, who could pass for sixteen or seventeen easily. Seeing no future as little more than a manor serf, he readily joined the Duke of Monmouth's brigade to fight the combined forces of the Dutch Republic and Denmark in Holland.

The English grenadiers had been flinging explosives and flaming shells stuffed with oil to protect their brigade's advance. But when the brigade futilely tried to cross the ice of the Water Line the Dutch had constructed for defense, Fletcher was bayonetted in the gut. Coming to sometime later, he found his fingertips and one cheek frozen to the ice by his congealed blood.

From his horizontal view on the ice, a pair of bladed skates stood between him and the fallen bodies of his red-tunicked comrades-in-arms. Painfully and slowly, he peeled his cheek off the ice, leaving a scrap of flesh and beard scruff. He lifted his head only slightly. His gaze traveled from the ice skates up navy blue woolen tights to encounter a battle-scarred, weather-beaten face of a Danish sailor.

The massive soldier, who looked to be somewhere in his forties, fingered his flintlock and muttered in English. "So, you are not dead yet, eh?" He lowered the flintlock muzzle to poke it in the center of Fletcher's forehead.

This was not how he had seen ending his young life. Falling in the fierce action of combat, yes. But not ignobly executed like chicken for the boiling pot. Since he figured he was about to die then and there, he grinned back manically. "Dead? Hell, no. I was fishing and slipped and knocked my noggin on the ice."

The soldier grumbled some kind of Danish oath. "*Pokker!* A boy with balls as brazen as yours deserves to live a little longer." He tucked the musket beneath his leather belt and scooped up Fletcher.

He yelped at the sharp pain shearing his freezing flesh, but the steamy heat coming off the Dane afforded some comfort and consolation.

From that day forward, Nielsen had taken him under his wing. A surrogate father, Nielsen trained him. And tutored him, yes. For Nielsen's own father had been a renowned composer and organist and Nielsen had been given an education par excellence, even while his sailor's spirit thirsted for the sea. The River Blackwater assuaged that longing somewhat.

Nielsen signaled Merrow for a refill, and Fletcher steeled himself, his features reflecting mere indifference.

Pewter pitcher in hand, she sauntered to the dais, her floor-length, food-stained apron swishing around shapely ankles encased in white woolen hose. Moving with grace and elegance, her chin was held haughtily high, her back as straight as a queen's scepter. She looked to-the-manor-born, which she was. And which he wasn't. Her contempt for him fueled the very obsession he would deny.

"Wench, I'll have my tankard refilled, as well."

The look she gave him would blister the hide off a horse. The small pleasure he felt at putting her in her place was mitigated by the shadows beneath her eyes. Perspiration dribbled down her heat-flushed cheeks,

He had arranged to install her with the bawdy chambermaid Phebe in one of the vaulted undercroft's quarters. Though cramped, they would be far more comfortable, he thought, than the mouse hole in which Merrow presently lived with her remaining brother and the beekeeper's daughter.

And yet he continued his tactics of taunting her relentlessly.

As she leaned between Nielsen and himself to pour the ale, he was fortunate neither his raging blood nor the hammering of his heart blood could betray him to her. Instantly, he jerked back his forearm, its sleeve purposefully slit to reveal the fine linen shirt underneath. He was wary of touching her even indirectly. He could not afford to lose control. To let his men, to let her, see his weakness, this terrible debilitating wanting of her.

She shot him a startled glance. "Do I assault your senses, sire?"

Was she that perceptive? Had she intuited his weakness, his seemingly unquenchable desire for her?

Her voice had smoky edges. "If I reek of sweat, my lord, it could be the kitchen fires. Or the chickens I plucked and singed earlier. Or, mayhap, the long hours today."

So, she did not suspect the tender chink in his armor, where the smoke of yearning seeped through. Instead, she mistakenly thought he had insulted her. Relief eddied through him. Lifting his tankard, he delivered a coolly dismissive smile. "Then I would heartily suggest bathing. It works wonders to remove the stench of one's . . . drudgery."

She looked mortified, then her eyes flared. She went to swing away, but her pitcher clipped his knuckles. Ale splashed over his lap, and he jumped to his feet. "God's blood!"

Her gasp was feigned. Of that he was quite sure, as well as, her profuse apology. "Oh, my lord, tis quite sorry I am."

Whisking down the soiled linen hand towel draped over her shoulder, she squatted on her heels between his legs and began dabbing at his drenched doublet of watered silk decorated with parchment lace . . . then paused.

He caught the halt in her ministrations. There was no mistaking the rapidly engorging mound at his crotch, incited by her touch, by her mouth so close. Her head tilted back, her gaze raised to meet his in a female's triumphant glance.

He knew he would repent his determination to have the last word. "Alas and alack, if only your betrothed was here today. Regrettably, I have sent him back to England to fetch a *proper* wife for me – one of *aristocratic* bearing – the Duchess of Montague."

She could not possibly mistake his emphasis on his wording nor the condescending glance he settled on her, kneeling as she was in the subservient position. Off to his side, Nielsen rolled his eyes.

King William had arranged Fletcher's marriage with the Lady Elizabeth's father, eager to plant a foothold in Ireland, but her miniature forwarded by the Duke portrayed a whey-faced daughter with squinty eyes that foretold of a cantankerous nature.

Merrow rose, hand towel still in hand. He had the distinct feeling she wanted to lash it across his face. Instead, she let a sly smile play across her lips. "Ahhh, then, you'll have no need of the *droit du seigneur*, as I doubt your duchess would approve."

"My point exactly. Why dally with a mere scullery maid when a Duchess seeks to pleasure me?"

She blanched. Inhaling sharply, she sank her teeth into her lip until he thought she would draw blood, then swung away.

Watching her storm toward the dais stairs, he knew he had been right . . . yes, repent his words, he did. He would gladly wipe them from existence . . . as his tongue would gladly wipe the blood from her lips.

But he had scrambled to survive to this point in life, and he would not ease up now. Most of all, not now, not when royalties and riches were his to ensure for the rest of his life.

"Oh," he called after her, "there are the chamber pots yet to be emptied and cleaned."

CHAPTER TWENTY

Puerto de Luna, Territory of New Mexico
July 1878

At the mumbling moans, Miles paused at Mhaire's bedroom door. Almost nightly, he overheard the whimperings. And sometimes sighs. But this was close to dawn. Was each night entirely one of disturbed sleep for her?

He had thought that with her return to the Luna House, things might be easier for the spunky lass, but mauve shadows were smudged at the inner corners of her eyes, and haunting hollows were hiding beneath her high cheekbones. At times, by candlelight, her slender frame appeared eerily wraithlike, as insubstantial as a dream.

Several times, he had been tempted to check on her. Even though she kept the door locked, he had its master key. But, God help him, he did not trust himself to get anywhere near her, not when she was in such a vulnerable state. Not when he wanted her. Her bed, his bed, it did not matter. He just wanted her. Just about every damn minute of the day.

And the thought she might prefer the ridiculously righteous Guido was incomprehensible. Clearly Miles was the better man. He reckoned he might be a lot of dastardly things, but he did not hide behind the skirts of the morally superior.

He continued on downstairs. In the morning's rosy half-light, Finian was already reloading the buckboard with tools – adz, hammers, saws, a nail keg – these meant solely for today's bank construction.

Puerto de Luna's menfolk would be turning out early from

their squalid little houses to help convert the cooper's abandoned workshop to a bank, before they attended to their own daily chores.

The workshop was next to the cooper's abandoned home, now the meeting place-cum-church for the Catholic community. Miles grinned dryly. How convenient. An opportunity throughout the next few Sundays to keep an eye on both the Catholic gawkers and his heartbreakingly beautiful housemaid– when he wasn't searching for Coronado's cache.

A foolish treasure hunt, Miles's father would have derided.

The cooper's workshop with its caved-in roof and peeling stucco walls was a shamble. For startup construction, about a dozen men had gathered. Lumber supply was not a problem, as wooden casks, hogsheads, buckets, tubs, troughs and other staved containers littered both the workshop and outback, where a stove had been used for heating the staves to pliancy.

Fortunately, the wheelwright, Tom Broadbent, and Benicio Moreno, the farrier, would be great assets in fashioning a vault, teller cage, and office.

Unfortunately, Benicio's daughter was dogging Miles's every step. He had thought himself safe from her pursuit when he swung himself up to straddle one of the remaining beams.

"For you, señor," Alma said, offering up to him a tin cup of water, drawn from a barrel set up in the adobe's nearest corner.

He looked down at the pigtailed lass with the dark, limpid eyes. The morning was already hot, and he had shed his shirt. "Shouldn't you be at the schoolhouse or something?" She couldn't be any more than thirteen or fourteen.

"Tengo diecisiete años, señor." She simpered, cupping her mouth with her hand.

Seventeen? Bugger! "Gracias." He dropped the emptied cup into her upstretched palms and, ignoring her disappointed expression, went back to hammering a truss.

From the corner of his eyes, he saw Benicio frown at his daughter. Wiping his hands on his pigskin apron, the man called her away. With a last fluttering of lashes at Miles, Alma sashayed off, and he sighed his relief.

By the time of the sacred hour of siesta, what was left of the volunteer help had one by one drifted off, as well, so that only Miles and Finian were left to work on their own.

Miles figured, at the most, five weeks would see the bank's opening day. As much as he wanted to find the gold cache, signifying he had finally outdone his old man, he couldn't help feeling but a little pride at the small achievement of opening his own bank.

Strangely, he felt a protectiveness toward these provincial investors, trusting him with their capital. That susceptibility of his worried him. He could not allow that weakness to stand in the way of his goal.

A hot and humid gusty wind pitted Finian and him with sand but did not cool the sweat drenching them. Clouds were boiling above the red mesas to the west. Nail fixed between his lips, he mumbled, "What I wouldn't give to shuck my pants right now."

Finian broke off with his sawing, and his long mustache turned up at the ends. "What? And have yet another woman, the Widow Singletary, hustle over to ogle yuirself?"

"Hmmm. Know her that well, do you?" he teased. He was fully aware that his old friend had gone missing one night. "Know her, as in carnal knowledge?"

But his attention was distracted by the approaching horseman. He trotted his horse between the maze of scaffolding to halt directly beneath Miles. Guido Jaramillo. *"Buenos dias, señor."*

Miles stared down. "Since it's a little late in the day to be volunteering your work here on my bank, I take it your visit has to do with my Luna livestock? I hear Chisum's cattle are sick from eating too much green grass."

The leather-brown face grew solemn. "That is not why I am here. You know I do not approve of the woman I love – *la curandera* – living in your house."

"*Her* house, originally." Thoughts of her avalanched in his mind. Her hair needed to come down. Her skirt to come up. Her dancing smile meant for others needed to be turned on himself. At once, he ceased his woolgathering. This wanting of her, needing her beneath him, congealed into a thick knot of self-disgust.

It began to sprinkle and raindrops beaded his bare back. "But you have known that all this time. Mhaire's pedigree and her calling. So, what brings you to visit this afternoon?"

He swung down from the beam, and, with Finian's help, spread a waxed cloth to protect the tools and lumber from the weather.

Guido dismounted, and Miles motioned for him to have a seat on a nearby nail cask. Exhausted and grateful for the respite, Miles and Finian sank opposite him onto a stack of rafters. He and Finian sorely needed Guido's greased canvas rainslicker.

Guido shook his dark head. There was an aspect about his features, something infinitely agitated. "*Si*, I do not approve of Mhaire living under the same roof with you, but that is her choice – to return to her house as a servant. I merely wanted you to understand my feelings before I explain why it is I call upon you."

Grudgingly, Miles had to admit a certain respect for the proud hidalgo. Reports were the man's hacienda and outbuildings were well maintained, his estancia's fences stood sturdily, and his black Andalusian horses and creole cattle vigilantly attended. In 1540, Coronado had brought those cattle's predecessors to New Mexico as a walking commissary. But it was not Coronado's cattle but his gold that occupied Miles.

Wearily, he suspended the hammer between his spread knee. "Understood. And I agree, that is Mhaire's choice."

Guido's expression turned as morose and sullen as the afternoon weather. "Your coming to Puerto de Luna has brought nothing but heartache for everyone here."

Miles cut a glance at Finian, who raised a raven brow flecked with white. "Get to the point, mon."

Guido spat in the dirt, pitted now with rain-like pellets. Yet none of the three moved to take cover. "One of my sheepherders brought word he had found a body. Benicio Moreno's. Swinging from a mesquite."

"What?" Miles's could feel his countenance crumbling like rain-soaked adobe brick. "Benicio was here only this morning, helping."

"There is more. His . . . his cojones had been hacked off and stuffed in his mouth. I go now to tell his widow and daughter, Alma, of his death."

Finian swiped at the rain dripping from his mustache. "He told me when he left he was riding out to Burt Lowry's place to tend a foundering horse of his."

Guido stood, and rainwater poured off his concho-decorated

sombrero. "Benicio never made it."

He grunted deeply. His hammer slipped from his grasp, to thunk on the wet ground. "Tell me, did Benicio have enemies?"

"No . . . *si*." Those eyes mutated to the brown of bitter chocolate. "When he fell in with your banco scheme. *Pues*, I think he made an enemy – the Sullivan gang."

"And you . . . which side are you taking, Jaramillo?"

Guido's gazed burned with the fervent conviction of a martyr at the stake. "Duty and loyalty to Mhaire O'Moore – and this holy land – they are all that matter to me."

§ § §

The milliner, the Widow Singletary, used forged nails to secure nets onto her blockheads, and next – according to what Gladys had shared with Finian – she wove strands of donated hair, mostly Mexican, then curled them, using heated rods much like a branding iron.

At his request for a lighter shade of hair, she had resorted to stitching goat's hair. Light brown, it was not nearly fair enough for his purpose. Still . . . .

Hat box in hand, he knocked on the adobe's turquoise door. Waiting for a response, he restlessly shifted the box's cord from one hand to another. He rapped again.

The door jerked open. Elsa eyed him, then, suspiciously, the box. The sunlight, filtering through her thin muslin dress, outlined the graceful lines of her figure. "Vat do you vant?"

"Unlike the Greeks bearing a treacherous gift, me lady, I present to ye a token of me remorse."

"Cease your blather and talk plain." Each word was spat like a tiny, poisonous dart. At her feet, Pork snorted its emphasis.

"If you will permit me." He slipped past her and Pork to set the box on the armoire. "I have brought something that I trust will redeem my ungallant behavior toward yuir personage in the Luna kitchen, brighten yuir blighted life, and with guid fortune, also, relieve the Luna estates of its seven plagues."

Both she and Pork followed him. "Flapping zat foxy tongue of . . . of yours von't . . . get you . . . any – " Guarded curiosity dwindled

142

her words. "Vat is all zis? Zis seven plagues? And vat is in zat box?" She jabbed a quivering finger toward it.

"'Tis a surprise. Turn around, if ye will, me lady."

Hands planted on her hips. "I am not your lady."

His mustache wagged. "As must have Dulcinea told Don Quixote." He bestowed a grave glance on her, taking in the white scar that ran from temple across one eyelid. "And like Don Quixote felt toward his Dulcinea, I find myself fascinated with ye."

Rage quivered her jaw and palsied her lips. "I vil not be made fun of. Enough is enough!"

With jeweled-green eyes big and soft and beautiful – and boiling with hot resentment – she was a bird with a broken wing. "Nae, I speak but the truth. Ye fash too much about other people's pity and horror. When, the truth is, wherever ye go, folks stand in awe of ye. A stalwart-hearted woman, strong of limb and strong of spirit. Ye are both feared and respected. Me lady, I seek only to earn yuir guid will."

Her mouth curled with bitter scorn. "And remove curses you believe I have placed on you and your friend?"

He bowed low, then straightened. "Please, I request you indulge this fool and turn around. There is no one here to witness what will only take a minute."

He saw her clenched jaws ease, saw her swallow, saw her lips screw, as if taking a vile tasting potion. Slowly, reluctantly, she yielded to her curiosity and presented her back to him.

A splendid spine it was, even concealed by the harsh black of her dowdy day dress. Straight and strong, her back supported shoulders that could bear whatever weight life demanded of her.

"Merely one impersonal adjustment," he murmured, quickly coiling her braid and anchoring it low on her nape with a hairpin from his pocket.

Like a racehorse chomping to bolt at the drop of the flag, she tensed at his touch.

Lightly, he clasped a restraining hand on her shoulder. Lifting the hat box lid with the other, he withdrew the wig and settled it over her head. "With this crowning glory, not even Helen of Troy could compete with yuir beauty."

She stiffened and tried to wrench free. "Vat? Vat are – "

"Patience, me pretty." He slipped around in front of her to

view his Pygmalion efforts. She was the storied statue, her eyes wide, unseeing, her full lips compressed. "With but a wee touch here and there . . ."

Deftly, he rearranged the tendrils of goat hair around her forehead and temples, so that they blended better with the golden wheat shade of her shorter curls that evaded on the right side the wig's constraints. "And voila!" He kissed his bunched fingertips.

Her work-varnished hands slipped up to explore in blind, tentative touches. He knew she both desired and feared to see herself. On his past visits to the Turquoise Door to check on his convalescing laddie, Finian had noticed no mirrors. So, now, he reached behind her to retrieve the tarnished shard of mirror from the box bottom and held it up before her.

She stared. She gaped. Then, she gasped. Next, hot, bitter tears crested her palely lashed lids. "Uff da! I vil be the laughingstock of Puerto de Luna. Putting on airs. I vant no truck vit zis!"

Her fingers went to remove it, and his free hand latched onto her wrist. "Me lady, at least give me gift some consideration." Releasing her, he dropped the mirror back into the box. "Take me gift from the box, here in the privacy of yuir domicile, and don it when ye wish to feel as beautiful as ye really are."

She slapped him. "I vil not be mocked!"

Edging toward the door, he fingered his stinging jaw. "And as fierce as Thalestris, the legendary Amazon warrioress, ye are, also." He grinned cheerfully and shut the door behind him.

CHAPTER TWENTY-ONE

Assigned the easier duty of repairing the household bedlinen, Merrow set cross-legged on the ramparts that overlooked the bailey, where Fletcher's various units of soldiers drilled respectively with pike, swords and flintlock muskets.

A gloriously late afternoon it was to be out from under the watchful eye of Beatrice, the grumpy head cook. Short and thick in build, the middle-aged widow wore a perpetual disgruntled expression.

The fading rays of sunlight cast a golden, magical glow over the Castle's bastions. Recent rains had turned the vale a vibrant lime green. Herring gulls and crows sailed on currents around the turret's pennants. Birdsong reminded one that life was ever renewing.

A wistful smile tipped the corners of Merrow's mouth. Once, as a child she had stolen away here, her needle flashing like a miniature sword, requisite for a lady's lessons in needlepoint, and had watched the exciting drills of her father's archers. Now, for these few precious minutes, she could turn over the hourglass, reverse its sands of time.

But, of course, times changed. Circumstances changed. And she certainly had, though she could certainly not ascribe it for the better.

Not when her errant thoughts protested the creed of both church and patriotism. Not when she wanted to lie with the enemy, to couple without benefit of church blessing or her fellow patriots.

"I have been looking for you, mistress."

The gruff voice behind her taking her by surprise, she jabbed her fingertip with the needle. Sucking it, she twisted and looked up. Arms akimbo, Nielsen stood over her. "Have ye now?"

He nodded at the scissors by her side. "The Lord Justice is in need of a hair trimming. With no resident barber, your service seems to be required."

Her heart skipped a beat. How could she be so unnerved, both terribly wary and fiercely excited, about being in his presence? "He does not fear I'll rip open his throat with the shears?"

He pondered her for a moment. "Tis not your shears my Lord Justice should fear but you, yourself, mistress."

The setting sun silhouetted the Danish mercenary, and she had to squint up at his shadowed face. "And why be that?"

He squatted to eye her directly, a forearm braced across one hosed knee. "Because the superstitious Danish part of me suspects your destinies are in some way intertwined." At that he stood again, waiting.

Collecting her linen, thread, and shears into her sewing basket, she pushed erect. "Destinies? As opposed to fates, which somehow seems to the superstitious Irish part of me to be bleak. Lead on, if ye please."

As they descended and ascended the various staircases toward the keep's quarters of the Lord Justice, tremors quaked her, making her feel queasy, making her feel as if her heart would claw from her body. Fletcher Neville could hurt it no more than it had already endured at the rapacious hands of the Williamite soldiers. But whatever this was she felt about him, this powerful pull, she feared it could crumble her wall of will, so that she might fail her family, her people, herself even.

Aye, the soldiers had battered and bruised her body and left her with pain that passed and a wariness toward men that did not. But she fretted that this man, this Englishman, could do more than merely batter and bruise her heart. He could destroy it.

She maintained the respectful distance of servant behind the giant, who served, no less, as steward of the castle that once was hers. Yet he hesitated for her to draw abreast of him. "Tell me, mistress, how fares your brother and the maid Betha?"

She looked askance at him and started to fret even more. "You have interest in Betha?"

His craggy, earthy profile wore a non-committal expression. "It would seem your little beekeeper is a keeper of people, as well. But, no, tis quite obvious Hugh Harrington fancies the fair lass, while my tastes run toward a seasoned woman, stout of strength and will."

So, that explained his numerous visits to the kitchen, presumably to monitor Beatrice's kitchen duties. Merrow smiled wryly to herself.

But, as they approached Fletcher's comfortable chambers, her smile gave way to a nervous inner clenching. As with the naiads and mermaids inhabiting the Blackwater and the holy wells it fed, she was leery of men.

Lore went that if a mermaid ever fell in love with a man and coupled with him, she would begin to age like a mortal woman, losing not only her youthfulness but eternal life.

By all the saints, take her youth, take eternal life, but give her back her home, O'Mordha Castle.

CHAPTER TWENTY-TWO

Puerto de Luna, Territory of New Mexico
July 1878

With smooth strokes, Miles finished sharpening the blade on the leather strop, attached by a ring to the wall's wainscoted marble tile. The bathroom's appointments comprised a full-sized marble tub and lavatory and a floor of pristine white hex tiles.

After lathering his facial hair, he faced the large, beveled mirror with its black, tarnished edges – like himself – and took up the cutthroat razor.

That was what he should do, cut his throat. Because if he did not do it himself, mercifully, Mhaire would do it violently should she ever discover what he had in mind for the Blue Hole.

Hell, she'd cut his throat violently if she ever divined the thoughts he entertained about her. Day and night. Wickedly fantasizing about the ways he could make love to her, to mark every inch of her skin with his kisses, his mouth, his tongue. To burn his bristle between her thighs. To mark her as his territory. His.

Still, his fantasies were worth a plugged nickel if he did not take the steps to manifest them. And that was why it'd be better he cut his throat, because he feared that much more time corralled in this close proximity with her he would do just that. Seduce her against her will.

And he was dead set that she would first come to him. Before he found Coronado's cache, before he surpassed his late, unmourned father in aggrandizement, and before he departed for safer territory.

He had started over so many times in his life. He could do this. Could best his father, who had never been available and who had *carelessly inflicted suffering and shame on Miles with his words and judgments. In Miles's early years, he had pondered why his father beat him so much. What had he done to make him so angry.*

And Mhaire? Miles hiked his mouth to one side to better shave the stubble at the blunt edge of his jaw. Well, Mhaire was a rare creature, deserving of being neither bridled by the haughty hidalgo Jaramillo – or himself. Yet he found himself persistently returning to her bedroom door to listen, like a love-sick youth, to her nightly moanings and sighings.

Was she pleasuring herself? He felt his sudden arousal press with a throb against the cast iron of the pedestal sink.

If only her sighings were for him. But no, he sensed her moanings and feverish whisperings came from disturbed dreams, dreams about another. But whom? Jealousy assailed him. Surely not the self-righteous Jaramillo.

Miles considered himself by far the better man. At least, he had restored her to her former home, albeit under subterfuge. All right, admittedly, with his own self-interest at play. But Mhaire knew where he stood. No displays of medieval gallantry to muddy the water.

Earlier, in the wee hours of this Sabbath morning, he had heard Mhaire telling her rosary in broken sobs. Later, he had heard her dressing, preparing to attend Puerto de Luna's makeshift church.

And where the hell was Finian? Today, they were supposed to survey the Blue Hole for the demolition layout.

When surfacing from the depths toward the rim of the Blue Hole that magical night with Mhaire, Miles had noticed, close to the top, three words apparently scraped into a rock rimming the pool – *Puerta al Oro.*

Not Doorway to the Moon, as one would expect, but Doorway to the Gold. Or, as pirates of centuries before would proclaim, *X marks the spot!*

Had Coronado ordered rocks dislodged at the Blue Hole's rim and jars of gold hidden behind them, with the anticipation of one day returning to reclaim them – not for His Majesty King Philip of Spain but for himself?

Regardless, the life affirming intimacy that Miles had felt with

Mhaire on the return walk from the Blue Hole that night was like no other. He did not let himself get close to people, Finian being the exception.

The need for Miles to have his way, manipulating Mhaire to within his easy reach, pursuing his plan to find the gold cache contrary to her own aspirations, had destroyed that unique closeness with her. He regretted that more than he would have ever thought. But all his excoriation of his black soul did not change his plans – a fool's errand his old man would denounce. Well, fuck his old man.

Donning his wool socks and undershirt, he shrugged into his chambray work shirt and rolled its sleeves to just below the elbow to better manage the more physical tasks that would be required of him. Then, by the dawn's half-light, he headed downstairs and out to the barn – only to draw up short at the barn doors. A Winchester muzzle pointed six inches from his chest.

His gaze glanced along the barrel to the rifle stock at the other end. Cradled against it was a grinning brown face with a gold front tooth.

And beyond him, near the tack door, Miles espied another man in a sugarloaf sombrero, his dirty yellow hair concealing *his* face. He hunkered with a wire in one hand. Near him was an oblong wooden box that Miles recognized instantly as the blasting machine he had ordered, along with the crate of dynamite sticks.

"Just in time for the party." The gold-toothed man grinned. "Cloyd here is rigging up fireworks for it." And then he pulled the rifle's trigger.

The deadly sound of its clicking coincided with Miles's ramming the back of his forearm hard against the barrel's end. The ear-shattering shot jarred Mile's shoulder. The lever-action Winchester thunked on the floor's mucked straw.

Both he and the gunman lunged for it. Nearer it, Miles was a hair's breadth quicker. He grabbed the Winchester's barrel and swung its stock against the man's throat.

A gagging gasp rent the smoky, sulfuric air. Stunned by the pain, the man's eyes widened in panic. He sank to his knees. He could neither draw in nor exhale a breath.

Miles took the opportunity to kick him in the head. Blood spurted from his flattened nostrils. He swayed, then toppled backwards and rolled, fetching up against a hay barrel.

At that same moment, the other man jumped Miles from behind, and an elbow locked vicelike around his neck. His fingers grasped the forearm and jerked, but all he could do was struggle against the powerful restraining grip. Changing tactics, he rammed his elbow into the man's abdomen, then threw himself backward, so that they tumbled inside the barn doors.

His slamming body weight momentarily dazed the man. A second later, minus his crushed sugarloaf, the yellow-headed ape wriggled free of Miles and was levering himself up with an unsteady hand on each of the terminals of the blasting machine. Bloodthirst raged in his eyes.

At once, Miles seized the opening. He shoved down on the plunger. The lethal electrical charge dropped the man like a clay pigeon at target practice.

Expecting another attack from the gold-toothed man, Miles spun. He was breathing hard. And his shoulder hurt like hell where the bullet had grazed it.

Steps away from him, the man looked like an enraged bull. Snotty blood streamed from both nostrils. He grabbed the first thing at hand, an iron rake propped against a haybale.

Miles balanced on the balls of his feet, ready to dodge, but not quickly enough. One tong gashed his left brow. Blood poured, blinding him. He swiped at the blood and searched for his opponent.

Then he heard the rifle's lever cock, and he stiffened. The fight was lost. Better to go out like this than coughing his lungs out, as had his old man of consumption.

The crack of the rifle shot, so close, was deafening inside the barn. Cordite stung Miles's nostrils. And yet still he stood, though wobbly. He blinked to clear his vision. A fuzzy image coalesced of his assailant, blown back against the stall door. Sliding down it, he left a vertical smear of blood. A death rattle issued from his chest.

Miles looked over his shoulder. Mhaire appeared, the Remington still cradled against her cheek. She was shaking and looked as if she was about to retch. "I hae ne'er killed anyone."

"Better him than me."

"I thought about it, but given that box of dynamite on the veranda, me home was a priority."

He crossed to her. Tears brimmed her eyes. She jammed the barrel against his chest. "Don't. I do no' fear to make one less desperado in this world."

"I warn you, my heart is my least vulnerable part." Gently, he removed the gun from her trembling hands.

Her palm pressed against the sticky blood soaking one shoulder of his chambray shirt, reeking of gunpowder. "You've been shot!"

"It's but a scratch."

"Some say the devil smells of sulfur." And then she fainted, collapsing before he could catch her on the straw in a most unladylike sprawl of those lovely legs.

He knelt beside her and flicked the flecks of straw from the stray tendrils, curling in disorder about her neck. She had saved him. Sighing, he scooped her frail body up against his chest and emitted a growling grunt at the pain of exertion.

He perused her pale face, its freckles washed out, her lashes as raven black as Civil War mourning fans. He stifled another groan. This an inner one directed at this tender feeling, a weakness he could ill afford. Her defenselessness was as dangerous to him as her spirited opposition, damn't.

CHAPTER TWENTY-THREE

Blackwater Vale, Eire
July 1691

Fletcher laid his quill aside the brass and marble inkstand and pinched the bridge of his nose. Piled letters, charters, maps, petitions, warrants, the latest edition of the *London Gazette*, and more – totally obscuring his desk blotter – demanded his attention. As did the fourteen men he was keeping waiting in the Privy council's chamber.

To his ire, his attention was focused on the maiden he purposefully forced to tarry in the outer room of his apartment. If only she were pliant. He anticipated dealing with her as eagerly as he might a toothache.

Unpleasant recollections of his awkward adolescence fore-stalled him from rising to greet her. His status as a bastard base-born was inferior to hers. As early as three years prior, to even look upon her with admiration would be subject to flogging.

A dark connection thrummed the air between them. God help him, if he could but quell the sensual storm with which this proud and passionate young woman unknowingly lashed him.

Alas, he found O'Mordha Castle, despite its pale peach stones and vaulted windows, little better than the cutthroat halls of London's royal court and coffee houses with their clandestine lives of cunning smiles and daggers hidden in sleeves.

No longer able to sustain the tension pulsating through him, he pushed aside a silver salver of invitations and shoved erect from the escritoire. Like a moody bear waking from hibernation, he strode to the outer room's door, throwing it open.

She shot to her feet. Her sewing basket tumped over on the wooden floor, spilling out its contents of bedlinen, scissors spools of thread, and whatnots. "You keep me waiting like a kenneled dog!"

Blasted by her beauty, a glow coming off her skin that drew stares from other men, the anger at himself was immediately doused. He targeted it on her, instead. "You forget your station, Merrow."

Her eyes blazed, and he knew by now that when they got like that, haunting as amber, anything should be anticipated. She was so real, so raw. "'Tis because I am uncertain exactly what is my station. As your minion, I am field hand, undercook, laundress, chambermaid, server – and is it now, barber?"

His shoulders, those shoulders, lifted with a disaffected shrug. "It is whatever I so wish." He wished to couple with her, her vibrant body spread for him on the floor's crumpled bedsheet, her arms reaching lovingly for him. He wished to be the one to stamp upon her features the satiated expression from their lovemaking.

But, awful fool that he was, he wished more fervently for her to come to him of her own free will. Especially, since the soldiers of his predecessor had taken that free will from her when they raped her.

"Bring your sewing basket and follow me." He turned his back, striding through the room he had sequestered for his more scholarly obligations and into to his personal chamber. It was spartan enough, with only the bed, a trunk, an armoire, and a pair of baroque armchairs, which he had brought back from his tour of duty in France.

He went to pull out one of the wainscot chairs, but she forestalled him with an uplifted palm. "Evidently, I have more experience cutting me brother's hair than barbers do yuirs." She gathered up the bedlinen and, with a snap of the sheet, flared it. She let it settle onto the floor, then positioned the chair in its middle. "Sit. No, first, remove your shirt."

His one brow arched, the other, scarred, lowered.

"Ye dinna want hair in yuir shirt itching you, do ye now?"

"I want you to trim my hair with as few extraneous comments as possible." What he wanted was his head to stop spinning when she was near. To think clearly, as his duty called for.

He shed his tailored waistcoat, unknotted his cravat and drew his ruffled, long-sleeve white shirt over his head. Clad only in his tanned skin britches, he sank into the armchair. Not for him the lovelocks of the courtiers. No, his long and heavy hair was combed back and bound with a leather strip to prevent it being blown about by the wind.

Warily, he watched her, shears in hand, circle behind him, so close his nostrils flared at the sensual scent of her femininity.

She leaned close to his ear and whispered, "I could take yuir life, ye know. Bury me scissors in yuir black heart."

If she but knew she had already buried herself in his heart. "Little good it would do you. The guards outside my apartment would be delighted to make use of your lovely body several times over before hacking it to pieces."

Her fingers stilled at the leather strip binding his hair, and he realized his response had not been a wise one. It only pushed her farther away. But was not that what he wanted? To keep himself from hearing her mermaid's siren call? And yet here he sat, subject to her whimsy. Subject to her since first he observed her, gamboling naked at the holy well like some mythical water naiad.

She loosed the thin strip, and her fingers rustled through his hair, spreading it across his shoulders. He tensed. When her hands settled on the rock-like ridges that were his shoulders, their muscles flexed in reaction.

"Relax. I willna be burying me scissors in your heart . . . today, at least."

His ear detected the amusement in her voice. "*Votre beauté a déjà blessé mon coeur.*"

She took up her scissors, her murmur a breath sighing over his ears. "A wounded heart may be guid. It signifies ye have the courage to open yuirself."

"You understand the lingua of France?"

"Understand things beyond needlework?" she asked dryly. "Aye, French was among my required studies, including Latin, Greek, and philosophy. But then I doubt ye know about philosophy when it comes to affairs of the heart."

"'Love comes with invincible madness' – Diogenes, if I recall correctly."

As if startled by his erudition, her fingers paused. "'One word frees us of all the weight and pain in life. That word is Love.' Aristotle."

He mumbled, more to himself, sounding disgustingly like a little boy lost. "If you do not place as much value to that which you love, then it hurts less when you inevitably lose it."

Momentarily, her fingernails grooved the tendons of his shoulders, tight from the repetitive swing on his rapier. Then abruptly her fingers deserted them. "More light is needed."

Granted, the late afternoon sunlight was retreating across the floor, but he sensed she used the excuse to collect herself. She crossed to the chest, where sat a lamp with its glob of lard. She struck a flint to the lamp's wick and paused at the sight of the delectable food he had ordered set out for her, almond cake wafers.

"Avail yourself of the refreshments, Merrow." Despite working in the kitchen, she went hungry more often than not, he knew.

She turned to face him. "No thank ye. Me gullet is all too full of the English . . . pablum."

With lethal grace, yet as silent as the sunset, she crossed to him. The lamplight's glow was a royal corona around her head and its smoke swirled around her like incense, dazzling him. Circling behind him, she threaded her hands through his hair to find the base of his skull, and her agile fingers massaged it. He felt the potency of a whirlwind spinning around him.

"Then you believe the loss of love inevitable, yuir lordship?"

Her voice was a sorceress's spell. He sought to recall his earlier comment, so as not to appear a dunce. "Yes, the death of affection . . . the death of the loved one . . . the loss of love is, indeed, inevitable."

At her nearness, his stomach muscles tightened. Yet his head inclined back into the safekeeping of her hands, seeking the pleasure of her touch. A sensual need so volatile stirred in his groan and threatened his cool composure. Fucking hell, he was obsessed with her.

She ceased her massaging and took up the scissors again. Her fingers, knitted through his overlong hair, then began shoring it.

His eyes grew heavy lidded. Perhaps it was the intimacy of the moment, but he found himself sharing with her, most inarticulately and achingly, something he had not even told Nielsen.

"My mother was a prostitute. She and the man who sired me . . .he was a common laborer . . . they did not live together, you understand. A year and a half after her murder – ”

Her question was delivered in a sharp inhalation. “She was murdered?”

“Beaten to death by a client. My father heard I was running wild on the streets, in the woods, wherever. “

“How old were you?”

“By that time, I was eight. Well, he arranged for me to work with him. You cannot imagine my joy at having him come into my life, someone who cared. We were digging a moat with our pickaxes and shoves . . . and I saw the castle's retaining wall we were working on give way. The crumbling earth buried him alive.” He could feel the acid burning in his throat and swallowed over its thickness to finish harshly. “So, aye, I believe the loss of love is inevitable.”

He thought she might have sighed, her breath a warning of a coming storm in his ears. He could only admire the love and loyalty she demonstrated for her family and friends. He did not want to hurt her despite the despicable darkness gnawing at him. The darkness of duties and obligations. Yet, with piercing resolution, he was determined to withstand her beauty and the charm of her quick mind.

Her hands, dusting the trimmed hair from his bare shoulders, hesitated. What was she thinking? He forced himself to assume the infuriating patience which his men often decried.

“If ye are the one giving the love, yuir lordship, well then, there never is a loss.” Then, her fingers began to gently knead his shoulder muscles, knotted with the accumulation of nigh a lifetime of disappointment and heartache . . . and, aye, fear. Monstrous fear.

Helpless beneath this sensuous onslaught, his head sagged forward now. It was all he could do to keep his lungs from bellowing with the serrated edges of his desire. He was defenseless against this enemy of England.

Especially, when a moment later he felt what he thought were her lips brushing his nape. So swiftly, he wasn't sure. Perhaps it was merely her fingertips. But her fingers lay lightly upon his shoulders, as if prepared to take flight. His hands slid up to capture hers and draw her around him and into his lap, her skirt draping her hobnailed boots and his polished ones.

He pressed a kiss on the backs of her fingers. “No webbing between them, I see.” The words were tossed off lightly, but his heart was thudding. "Perhaps then you are no sea siren."

Her heated palm pressed against his bare chest, where the hair wreathed one nipple, and the muscle there flexed in response. Her eyes, shielded by her dense, dark lashes, gradually lifted to counter his fierce, possessive gaze. "I would not trifle with the Irish fairy world, yuir lordship. The inhabitants of *Tir fo Thoinn*, the Land Beneath the Waves, can cast a magical spell on ye, then disappear before yuir verra eyes."

He should give her the opportunity to flee. But he wouldn't. Couldn't. Rapture had overtaken him.

CHAPTER TWENTY-FOUR

Puerto de Luna, Territory of New Mexico
July 1878

Aheadache beat like a medicine man's drum inside Mhaire's skull. She stirred, shifted her shoulders, flexed a wrist that had gone to sleep beneath her cheek, then peered between her lashes. Twilight slanted through her bedroom's delicately laced Nottingham curtains.

Vaguely, she recalled earlier in the barn feeling faint, feeling blackness closing in, feeling arms that caught her as she slid into darkness.

And she recalled regaining consciousness in her bedroom as those arms lowered her onto her mattress. Recalled gazing fuzzily up at Miles's fretting expression . . . his fingers trailing lingeringly across her collarbone, then withdrawing swiftly . . . his far-off voice murmuring, "Rest, you need it . . . today you certainly earned it."

Like a blown-out candle, she had instantly fallen into the deep sleep that these days seemed only to aggravate rather than to restore her vitality. To drain her life energy.

Wearily, she levered herself onto her forearms and stared unblinkingly into the room's unearthly semi-light for so long that she momentarily moved beyond it and time. To another man's other arms that held her, another's hands that pleasured her. Even now, her entirety was still reacting to the smoky heat stirred by that male, Fletcher. If was as if summer lightning was still striking through her muscles. But no more so than the electrical current arcing between herself and Miles.

She felt a correlation existed between these two lifetimes, the reality and the dream world, she was experiencing. A correlation between her and Miles and Merrow and Fletcher. A correlation between this part of the Pecos River and that Irish part of the River Blackwater.

Something had to be changed. Either in the past or in the present. Because her body and emotions could not sustain this fever pitch. She was a but a burning candle nub, its feeble light flickering out. But how to change what was already set in motion by forces she could not divine?

From somewhere near, she heard indistinguishable voices. Was she still dreaming? She rolled to her bed's edge and pushed upright. She waited for her head to clear and along with it her vision. Waited for her pulse to slow its galloping. But the muted voices, she still heard them. Standing, she shoved a swath of sweat-tangled hair back from her face and summoned the wherewithal to search out the origin of the voices.

Down the long hall, she found Miles and Finian in the billiard room. She paused at the doorway. From her limited viewpoint, she could see only Finian, cue in hand and bent over the billiard table. "No' as many townspeople have been showing up lately to help with the buildout, laddie."

"Not only are they deserting quicker than fleas off a dead horse but they are reneging on their deposit pledges." Miles stepped into her sight for a better angle of the shot. "Benicio's hanging has pretty much sealed the bloody deal and killed any hopes for the bank."

Now she knew what single thing had to be changed, in order for everything it affected to be changed. Stepping forward, she clung with one hand to the doorframe for support. "Dinna ye see? Tis the curse I put on ye."

Both heads whipped toward her. Miles scowled. His charged vitality flirted with an inexplicable combination of melancholy and mystery. As if he, too, was no stranger to this insanity of the steel bonds that bound their souls. "You should be resting."

"Me curse – that what ye wanted would ne'er be yuirs – tis why nothing has gone right for ye."

The glance Miles cut Finian brimmed with incredulity. "We're nearing the 20th century not the Medieval Times, Mhaire."

His smug scoffing infuriated her. "No, ye have it arseways." She found herself gravitating across the parquet floor toward him. "'Tis both. Then – and now. One and the same. Curses dinna know time."

His bemused expression lightened the blue depths of his eyes and curled the tips of his beautiful mouth. He braced one end of his cue on the floor and a fist on his hip. "Do tell. And I am quite sure you have the cure to counter the curse?"

She drew up close, feeling small and inconsequential in the face of his larger, more muscular frame and dominating presence. Her breath was corked in her throat. She could only nod.

He hiked a brow, and she noted that dried blood on it traced a line of a fresh cut. Then, she remembered. The fight in the barn . . . and the man she had killed. Miles's smile was mockingly encouraging. "And that is?"

She swallowed. This double life was wearing on her. She had to end it, here, now. "Restore my ancestral castle and its estates to the O'Mordha descendants still living in the River Blackwater area of Eire."

His low peal of sonorous laughter nigh buffeted her. "I would be a fool to buy into that."

"Ye self-absorbed eejit! Can ye risk no' to? I tell ye truly, all that you want, all happiness that you seek, will be forever denied you if you dinna do this."

Dead silence weighted the stale air. She imagined she could hear the stampeding fury of his barbed heart.

Then, from behind him, Finian said. "Think of it, laddie. What do ye have to lose?"

Miles flashed a disparaging glance over his shoulder. "You're talking seven-hundred acres and a castle worth easily £60,000."

Finian shrugged his oxen-yoke-sized shoulders. "Ye're talking besting yuir da. Can ye do that – really do that, laddie – if ye hold on to what was once his?"

"No, what was once my mother's." A tortured look fleeted across his face. He spun and hurled his cue against the wood paneled wall, where the stick splintered and clacked onto the floor.

Startled, she and Finian shot furtive glances at one another before looking at Miles, his back still to them. His shoulders, nearly as wide as Finian's, sagged. He palmed one shoulder, shrugging it slightly, as though throwing the cue had hurt its muscles.

Then, she remembered – the fight in the barn! She wanted to reach out to him, to touch him, to comfort him. But she knew he did not want her comfort any more than he wanted to accept there was anything beyond his control.

He scrubbed a hand over his face, then turned to confront her. She could see where he had opened the scab on his brow. This time she did brave his wrath.

She reached up, touched the brow now oozing blood, and he winced. She mustered a jocular expression, hoping to distract his attention from her affectionate gesture. "You clumsy oaf. Hurt yuirself in the fight, did ye now? Sacred water from the Blue Hole would – "

"Spare me your silliness, Mhaire."

His voice held the rawness of a fresh wound, but she could not help but take offense at this slight. Her chin shot up. "Silliness is it – when your bullet wounds healed the instant you fell into the Blue Hole?"

His brows collided. "Fell . . . or was pushed?" He raked a hand through his hair. The corners of his mouth curled down morosely. "I'll have my solicitor draw up the papers. I am assuming a search of local descendants will take time. When will so this . . . so-called cure of yours . . . take effect?"

The agony in his face tore at her. She owed him much. Owed him her life restored as it was to the Luna House. He had been nothing but kind to her. Moreover, she was drawn to him, wanted him, wanted him in a way that made her heart – aye, even her body – ache intolerably.

She answered honestly. "I dinna know. Remember, time is naught in the other world."

§ § §

Mhaire figured if Jesus Christ walked in the desert for forty days, she could certainly walk the four miles to Puerto de Luna that day. Besides, the walk provided her much needed time to think. Like Jesus, she was facing temptation – the devil in disguise, Miles Neville.

Balmy she might be, but she had to question seriously if,

indeed, her soul was at stake. These days, it seemed like she moved about in a fog. She could attribute it to the lack of sleep. The nightly dreams had a stranglehold on her mind, if not her body and spirit.

She wore her floppy straw hat against the high desert's scorching sunlight, yet that very sunlight was restorative, as well. With slow, lazy wing beats, a Great Blue Heron skimmed the river a little way off to her right. To her left, a dust devil danced next to the cinnamon-red cliffs of an imposing canyon. It harbored within its stone walls maples whose sleepy sap still flowed.

Real life was here . . . not in a netherworld.

Siesta had cleared Puerto de Luna's plaza of all but a few determined mortals. A donkey lazed in the shadow of an alley cutting between the saddlery and blacksmith shop. Just beyond was Grzelachowski Mercantile. Its cool, musty interior was a welcome respite from the searing heat.

"Miss Mhaire."

Her eyes adjusted to the dimness, and she saw old Alex, hailing her from behind the counter.

"Your package, it arrived, at last."

She smiled her gratitude. "Aye, Tom delivered yuir message yesterday."

Along with her jar, refilled with honey in gratitude, that her remedy for his bairn's crusted eye had worked – surprising even her, when none of her other curatives did these days. But then the honey potion was a common enough one. Perhaps, the bairn's natural resilience had resolved the minor health problem.

Still, the bairn's improvement offered her hope that possibly she was on the right track in requesting Miles's restoration of the Blackwater castle to the O'Mordha descendants still in Ireland . . . if he had even bothered to start the process.

She wended her way through boxes, barrels, crates, and even a coffin. The front counter was littered – a coffee grinder, cheese wheel, humidor and apothecary jar filled with lemon drops and peppermint hard candy. Nudging aside his cash register ledger, Alex plopped next to it a cardboard box. A pencil was tucked behind his ear, tufted with hair. "Want me to open it for you?"

Another gratuitous smile for the curious old codger. She was even more curious. Would the cardboard box contain not only the answers to her disturbing dreams but solutions, as well? "Um, no, thank ye, Alex. Better not to open it. I am afoot back to the Turquoise Door, and ye know how sand creeps into everything."

"Must be something fragile?" His curiosity was getting the best of him.

"Oh, that it is."

Outside, she ducked her head against the blinding sun . . . and must have collided with the portico's cedar post. Or so she thought, until her palms felt thick cloth and her eyes adjusted to the bright sunlight. With mild shock, she stared up at Guido's tortured face. She did not know which of them looked the worse, him or her. He was suffering, and she knew she was the cause. Her smile came out weak. "Guido, good to see you."

His leather gloves on her shoulders steadied her. He nodded over his shoulder at the dusty plaza, empty but for his buckboard and a mangy mutt, curled up under the scanty shade of the plaza's only tree, a native soapberry. "I can take you home, Mhaire. Give me a few minutes to pick up the salt licks I ordered."

She cradled the flat box against her chest. "No, I shall be fine, Guido."

Beneath his sombrero, his brows hoisted in his brown face.

"Truly, I need the walk." She did not want to give him any hopes there could be anything further between them than friendship now. Now that her heart was on fire. And he had not been the tinder's spark that set the conflagration.

He dropped his hands. "What you need is commons sense, Mhaire." He yanked off his sombrero and slapped it against the cedar post, causing her to jump back a step. "*¡Maldito sea!* What you need is a priest's absolution. Not only are you selling your body to Neville in return for your home, but you – "

She slapped him. "What Miles and I do is none of your business."

He fingered the rapidly fading imprint of her anger. However, his own was not fading but escalating. "*Quizás no, pero – *" He reverted to English. "Maybe not, but his desecration of our land's holy water is. For that you are selling your soul."

She spun away. He gripped her elbow and jerked her back around. He wore the patient and noble expression of a confessor. "But

I shall yet save it. Save the holy water and your soul from damnation, Mhaire."

She shoved his hand off her elbow, her free hand drawing her skirts away from him, as if he were a leper. Her words were spit like a hissing cat. "Yuir saintly convictions be damned. Understand me well, Guido. I'd rather burn with Miles in the radiant flames of hell than experience eternal boredom with ye in heaven."

She turned from him, striding into the sleepy plaza . . . and ignoring the pleading scored in her called-out name.

CHAPTER TWENTY-FIVE

Blackwater Vale, Eire
July 1691

With dismay, her body aching as much as her heart, Merrow watched as Alfred, holding aloft the lady Elizabeth's palm on the back of his hand, led her, her lady-in-waiting, and her cortège to the Chair of Estate.

There Fletcher sat. The new hollows beneath his cheeks but emphasized the challenging curl to his lips, as he waited like the spider for the fly. The codswallop.

At least, it was the Lady Elizabeth whose fate was doomed and not Merrow's own. Unless . . . unless she was with child. Fletcher's child. It was too soon to know.

Only three days since that afternoon they had coupled . . . three days since she had experienced a unique kind of gratification she did not know existed.

Merely cradled by him in the wainscot chair . . . with his caressing touch . . . had come something unexpected. Something she did not want. Not from him. It began in eddies. Then undulated into ripples. It slammed her with engulfing waves. Her heart's defenses staggered against its tidal breakers.

Mother Mary. She had gritted her teeth, clenched at his forearm beneath her kirtle. But his lightning and thunder had burnt through her rigidified muscles, setting fire to the region below her navel.

With but his hand stroking between her thighs, Fletcher had

brought her unsuspecting, unprepared body, to a state of grace that surely surpassed the ecstasy experienced by saints at death. His lips moving over hers had smothered her outcry. Then, later, there on the sheet, his bristly jaw had burnt paths of fire on the delicate, furls of flesh between her thighs.

At last, he relinquished her from his oral torture, only to mount her with his feral lean body. Hooded gaze, his eyes sparks of flint, he rusked in his rich English voice, "If you think to feign indifference, Merrow, you are mistaken. I can feel your flame arcing toward me whenever we are in the same room even."

Moving his hips against her, he surely must have encountered her betraying wetness. And then he thrust inside, jolting her. She might no longer possess a maidenhead but except for that violation three years before, her untouched body since that time still retained a virginal quality. Such was her wanting of him, she barely noticed this new pain. Then, finding his rhythm, he began a slow, steady conquest of her.

She found herself gasping against her will, and her body joining his in lust's duet. For, surely, it could not be termed love's duet. Merely an incredibly strong attraction . . . or an alchemical reaction arising from their first meeting there at the holy well?

His lips had flattened into a hard, dangerous line. "You are mine."

Her body might submit, but not her will. "For now."

Against her ear, his breath was an approaching storm. "For now, for always, if I should want." Then his decadent mouth, sweet and minty, brushed her lips, back and forth, as he coaxed her ever closer into sublime abandon.

With what little dignity she had left, she wrenched free her mouth from the dominating pressure of his. "And what if I should want differently?"

He merely shrugged, but his dark brows slanted low. "I won't give you up."

"Yet will you give up the duchess to whom you are betrothed?"

"You should not vex yourself. There has been no other woman in my mind since first I saw you naked, there at the holy well."

But even as he had brusquely rolled her onto her belly to pleasure her in yet another fashion, she was dimly aware he had evaded her question – as evidenced by the Lady Elizabeth, moving now down the aisle jammed on both sides with spectators.

Even at that moment, trumpets atop the castle parapets announced news of the betrothal. Below the pennants snapping on the turret, six-horse coaches lined up with dignitaries waiting to present their opulent gifts. Within the castle, silk finery along with velvet capes of blue, crimson and gold dazzled the eye. Sweet cakes and ale and brandy whetted their palates, while outside peasants went without meals.

The young woman appeared about the same age as Merrow, mayhap a year or two younger. She wore a richly brocaded silver dress with sleeves ending in lace just below the elbow and an overskirt drawn back to reveal the ruffled lace petticoat. The low, broad neckline displayed all but her nipples.

She looked mightily pleased with herself. Of course, she would be, what with the brawny and virile male twenty paces in front of her, receiving her as his betrothed. While no beauty, neither was she a troll, which was what Merrow wished upon this Lord Justice who now possessed her home and everything pertinent to it.

She was bitterly hurt by what Fletcher had done, bedding her then taking another as his betrothed. If only a tourniquet could bind the heart's bleeding. The next clootie she hung on the rowan tree would accompany the fervent wish his body would combust to mere ashes that the *Sídhe*, the Celtic fairy folk of the wind, would blow to the four corners of the earth.

How utterly hopeless her situation was. Trembling with rage and disappointment and flagging spirits, she could take no more. Threading through the room's crowd of gawkers, she made her way to the kitchen duties that awaited.

She headed down the stairwell, lit by the rush torches. The manor-castle was of the older style, built without a separate kitchen, and it could be an inferno. That day, she could even feel its heat on the sooty stone wall at the bottom of the staircase. Obnoxious odors of rubbish, offal, rancid fats, and smoke assailed her nostrils.

At a flash point, she yanked the blackened pot off the huge timber beam that served as the hearth lintel. One of the undercooks was adding egg yolks for a Torte de Bry mixture. Beatrice was chopping turnips on a table hardy enough to survive a lifetime of thumping. Her ruddy face formed a frown. "Where have ye been? We need all the hands on deck now."

"I basted the potatoes with herbs – they are in the oven now."

"There still be the trout to scale and fry."

Phebe, spooning almond meal into her marzipan bowl, flitted a catlike grin at Merrow.

None of the staff remained from the days when the O'Mordha's ruled and she had played with dolls, ordered specially for her from the most prestigious dollmakers and with tailors paid to make her dolls' wardrobes.

Of course, by now her identity had spread to the castle's reduced staff, and most took the opportunity to lord it over her, to make her life even more difficult. Especially, Phebe. Merrow suspected Phebe not only resented Merrow's prior status but, also, fretted that the Lord Justice was finding favor in her.

Favor in the amorous sense, mayhap, but not the cherishing that came from a caring heart. That was as likely to happen as the Golden Trout appearing in the *Tobar Na Croí Naofa* and turning her into a mermaid.

She sighed, restored the pot, and went to collect the string of fish and a spoon to scrub off their scales. For a moment, she halted over the strung-out trout, staring with dismay at her reddened and callused hands. With the back of one, she swiped the sweat from her eyes, burning with salt. Her foolish susceptibility!

Her lower back ached abominably. How much longer could she endure this? Others in servitude toiled their entire life. Was she so flagging in body and spirit?

No, it was her spirit that rebelled against this subjugation. She could wretch with its acidity. Difficulties be damned. She swallowed and turned to Beatrice. "My stomach is ailing. Heading for home, I am. Let Phebe scale the trout."

Phoebe's eyes went as wide as the dead fish. "Ye think ye're too good for domestic duties. I am not stupid."

"If you say so."

The heavyset Beatrice looked from Phebe to Merrow, then nodded as if perceiving more than passed before the eye. "The Sabbath does not begin until midnight." Then, though her flinty expression did not soften, her huffing tone did. "Be gone with ye."

Merrow thumped the spoon on the board and swung away.

Surprisingly, she left the creeper-clad castle unchallenged by an ogling guard. Just before sundown she passed through its south gate, jammed with carts hurrying to get inside before sundown.

By the time she reached Betha's hut, the moon was rising. Twilight shafting through the hut door, left open to dispel the heat, combining with the soft candlelight from inside, illuminated Betha and Patrick. They sat cross-legged, in front of the hearth, playing hazard.

Her spirits rose at this small semblance of a family left to her – as did her hunger at the sniff of potato pudding. It went without the luxurious benefit of the recipe's wine ingredient. Nor the exotic spices of the Far East like sugar and cinnamon. Nevertheless, this pudding smelled far more tantalizing to her than the rich marzipan Betha was making.

"I nicked!" Patrick crowed at Betha, then, spotting Merrow, swooped up the pair of cast dice and jumped to his feet. "Merrow!"

At once, out of deferential habit, Betha stood. Her small bowed lips widened in a smile. "So, Lady Merrow, the Devil let loose of ye early, did he?"

She pressed on the girl's bony shoulder. "Sit." Exhausted, she plopped, as well, before the hearth. She wrapped an arm about Paddi's thin waist, drawing him down beside her. "No, I left on me own."

Betha gasped. "Withoot a 'by your leave, sire,' from the Lord Justice?"

Fiercely, she hugged her brother's head to her chest. What had she wrought in her selfish action to walk away from her duties? Would Fletcher Neville make good his hint to conscript Patrick? The Englishman, fluent in both French and Danish, was dangerously smart and cynical to a fault. He was notorious for his courage, desperation, and savagery – as she had witnessed that day when he had impaled the ironmonger Alroy with such disregard.

"Merrow!" Patrick protested at her smothering hug.

Playfully, she knuckled his cowlick, then groaned softly at what she felt. "Nits! Ye hae nits again, Paddi!"

"Ouch," he bellowed as her fingernails began scraping his scalp mercilessly in hunt for the pests.

"Ye must be frayed." Betha went to rise. "Let me fetch ye a bowl of pudding."

"Nae, save it for later." Merrow grinned and, leaning first to one side, then the other, withdrew from the pockets tied beneath her apron the sustenance she had purloined. "Trout meant for the Lord Justice." She passed them over to Betha. "Best ye fry them quickly, mayhap with any mustard you might hae, afore they spoil."

"Spoiling is the least of your worries, Lady Merrow," came a male voice. All three turned to behold Alfred Dunhill's husky frame, blotting the moonlight from the doorway. He strode on in, glancing about the gutted cottage with dismay.

She sprang to her feet. "How did ye find me, Alfred?"

His chest, the size of a keg, heaved a sigh. "Not without a lot of questioning. From the stable groom to the spinner to the miller. Look, I am weary. Might I sit a spell?"

Stripping off her apron, a symbol of her servitude, she indicated one of the stools and chose, this time, to sit on the one bench, her back regally straight. She rubbed her sweating palms on her skirt's dirty brown linen. What fate awaited her for her rebellious impudence? "If not the trout spoiling, then for what should I worry, Alfred?"

He flipped back the skirt of his jacket, which like his cravat was made of the finest silk, and braced his forearms on his full breeches, open at the knees. "Your father. He is plotting to overthrow the Williamites."

Patrick piped up. "But papa – Merrow, is he not in the Kilmainham Gaol?"

Awaiting execution, but she said naught. Instead, it was Alfred who answered. "Aye, but he has contacts who will set their plot in motion that will set him free."

Her lashes nearly met in her lids, narrowed. "What kind of plot?"

He fished the snuff box from his waistcoat pocket and, opening it, added a pinch of tobacco to the back of his hand. "At the Harvest Festival, where Neville will preside." He inhaled the snuff, then continued. "After the villagers, their devotions performed, fall into their drunken dancing and carousing the rest of the day, you will draw the Lord Justice away from his guards and his shadow Nielsen."

"Me? What makes ye think I hae such sway with Fletcher?"

At her familiar use of the Lord Justice's name, Alfred's protruding eyes widened even more. He ducked his chin, doubling it, and peered at her with a look that she couldn't quite fathom. A reluctant look? An apologetic one? "He wants you in his bed, Merrow."

So, word had not spread yet of their liaison. She should have been offended that Alfred would so willingly bestow her in another man's bed. But she felt only a prickly repugnance for this man in the periwig sitting opposite her, her betrothed. A man she had once esteemed. "He has the Lady Elizabeth to bed."

Besides any other female of his choice. All were avid for his attention and his vaulted prowess between the sheets – of which she could bear witness, to her eternal shame and heart's suffering.

"Not until their marriage at November's Martinmas. Afore that, at the Harvest Festive, you have merely to entice him away from his obligations, from his betrothed and his guards. Get him alone. The murder itself, we'll take care of."

"Murder?" A shiver rattled up her spine.

As though sensing her aversion, he said, "Think of your father, Merrow."

She was. And of her soul's eternal damnation.

CHAPTER TWENTY-SIX

Puerto de Luna, Territory of New Mexico
July 1878

Around midnight, the persistent thumping against the Luna House's brick wall aroused Miles from an exhausted sleep. An analytical investigation revealed the source of the thumping to be outside the casement window. The wind was gnashing the oak's gnarly, twisted limbs.

As gnarly and twisted as his soul.

He flipped over onto his back, hands clasped beneath his nerve ticking nape, and stared into the darkness of the master bedroom's ceiling. With its ornate molding, it was reminiscent of another area, another era, than the stark, spare territorial architecture. It seemed to him that Mhaire was, also, of another era.

Mhaire.

He was furious with her. She had cornered him into agreeing to forfeit his estates back in Ireland. No, worse. She had forced him to confront his past, his daemon, his father.

In setting out on this quest more than a decade before – at that time a determination to outdo his old man – he had known somewhere in the back of his mind he always had his inheritance to fall back upon. A source of wealth he had obstinately refused to ever touch.

Now, thanks to Mhaire, he had only his own wits and skills. So little to fall back on when one wanted to – no, needed to, had to – prove his mettle, his self-worth. In a sense, it was a matter of his soul's survival.

Even the mere thought of his father could rouse an anxious breath out of him, plunge him into irrationality, erect a wall of anger. Had he been that difficult of a child? Had he deserved to be struck so often?

And, damn it, he had Mhaire to thank for resurrecting his past anxieties.

For thirty heedless, reckless years, he had lived without so much as dreaming that such a female existed as she. All this time, all these years, he had regarded females as rare and wonderful creatures, but serving a purpose and only for a while. Mother, servant, sister, or lover.

But she was far more. Something preternatural about her nudged him to question all that he had learned as a child from adults and in church.

Each day, interacting with her, he had to question if there was more than the eye could see, the ear could hear, the finger could touch.

Did other realms exist? He was haunted by the ethereal image of her leaning over him as he sank from sight in the Blue Hole, her expression fey.

Other conflicting images of her made it difficult for him to think about her even in an orderly fashion. That day she had risen before him from the rush-lined banks of the Pecos like an avenging angel . . . since then, every day, she had beleaguered his existence with recollections darting in and out . . . her spoon-feeding him as he lay deathly ill . . . shaving him . . . saving him with a single blast from the Remington.

Or had she, in truth, been saving her precious home?

He was lying, denying to himself that he did not want to physically possess her. And if he possessed her, would she have served her purpose? Both the assuagement of his lust and the cure for this curse? Or worse, was she his curse? His folly?

The bedroom door opened, and she stood framed there, wearing that damned virginal white nightgown with its dainty lace at her neck and wrists. She held a candle sconce, and its soft, wavering flame cast an otherworldly glow on her striking features.

"Yes?" His eyes raked over her calmly, as if her coming to his bedchamber at that time of night was ordinary.

Her head canted, swaying her unbound hair around her waist

like a scarlet curtain teased by the wind. "Yuir eyebrows clash together like hairy black caterpillars."

Buying time, he shrugged. "They grew in this thick early on. I look neither like my mother nor my father." At that, he suppressed a wince. Just whom did he resemble? O'Mordha Castle's master-of-the-stables, dismissed abruptly before Miles's birth? No one ever knew for certain who had fathered him. Least, of all, and most importantly, the Earl.

Mhaire stepped to the unlit fireplace and sat the candle on the marble mantel. Rubbing her palms nervously, she slowly crossed to the foot of the four-poster. She bit her lower lip, hard enough to stain it the color of a red rose. She looked around the room, as if she would find the right thing to say tucked somewhere among its richly appointed furniture. She returned her gaze to his alert one. "I am grateful."

He sat up, legs crossed beneath him, Indian fashion, and, hands planted on his thighs, leaned forward slightly. He gritted out his words. "I don't want your gratitude."

Her eyes met his courageously. "But ye want me."

It was a bold statement, not a timid question. Heart thudding, breath held, he held out his hand and waited.

§　　§　　§

Mhaire would most likely be coming to visit after church, and Elsa knew how much the young woman like *buenuelos*, especially when laden with a surfeit of sugar and cinnamon.

Uneasy, Elsa paused in rolling out the dough to a thin layer. She heard nothing, detected nothing, unusual. And, obviously, neither did Pork, snoring in hiccoughed snorts on the sisal rug by the hearth.

After a moment, she resumed her work. She took pleasure in the hypnotic rhythm of her hands. Despite the periodic arthritic swelling of her knuckles, her graceful, unveined hands were probably her only redeeming feature. They had cooked potions and cleaned vomits, caressed feverish infants and soothed dying adults.

Touch. It was important. She missed it. Missed Mhaire's impulsive hugs. The animals . . . Bray and Neigh, and Pork and Gruff and Cock . . . just patting them helped stave off her starving flesh.

She felt someone was drawing near the adobe. For as long as she could remember, certainly since her scalping, she had an acute sense of knowing things. Nothing she could call upon at will. No, to her regret, or maybe not, she was subject to the vagaries of the veil.

Still . . . .

Exasperated with the nagging feeling, she huffed, then set aside the rolling pin, wiped her flour-dusted hands on her apron, and crossed to open the door. She peered out into the predawn, that time of day when nothing stirred.

A light mist rose off the distant acequia to wreath about its feathery pink salt cedars. Even the birds had yet to begin their morning psalms and the rooster to recite his cocky crow. Gruff curled up like Rip Van Winkle against the yard's desert willow.

Uneasily she went to close the door. From the corner of her eye . . . had she sighted a phantom?

A chimerical image emerged from the scrim of alders and cottonwoods, the alamos of the acequia. Her throat worked. It was him. One hand clutching the door, the other braced on its frame, she waited with a trip-beating heart.

He crossed to stand within a broomstick's length before her. His gaunt frame seemed, nevertheless, to minimize her strapping one. His jaw was set resolutely, his eyes focused intently on her. "I've come to take ye to the church today."

"You valk four miles to tell me that?"

Gruff, awakened, trotted up to investigate. "I walked four miles to tell ye that and see ye again, wearing me gift."

Grunting, groinking, Pork padded to a protective halt beside her. She hugged her elbows. "Vell, I never go to church. And I vil never vere your ridiculous gift."

"Ye're a long time deid, me lady."

She stiffened. "Vat do you mean by that?"

He scrubbed the back of his neck and peered at her from beneath his thick, grizzled-black brows. "Listen, do ye mind letting me in to rest? I'm plumb knackered after the walk."

Could she maintain her protective wall in his plaguing presence? "Vell . . . for a few minutes only."

She stepped aside, and, as he passed into the cool interior, she could smell his maleness. Healthy sweat, pinewood, leather, and sunlight. It assaulted her senses and went straight to her head. It smote her so hard that, closing the door, she had to cling to its latch at the small of her back for support.

He hooked his tweed flat cap on the ear of the nearest chair, painted in a rainbow of colors. Then, he settled onto its thatched seat and stretched out his lengthy legs. Satisfied the visitor meant no harm, Pork plodded back to plop on the rug.

She said nothing, waiting, all the while her heart pulsing fiercely.

"Me bones may be weary, but, by Jove, *I'm* not deid yet, so I could do with a bit of water, if ye don't mind."

Her lips pinched, she crossed to the hutch to find a chipped glass, filling it with water dipped from the olla that was suspended from one of the roof's vigas to keep its contents cool. Feeling his intense gaze, she sloshed the water in handing him the glass. Her fingers brushed his. Instantly enfeebled by a feeling new to her, a sensual wanting, she sank into the chair opposite him.

His pewter-gray mustache, drooping at either side of his staunch lips, twitched like whiskers of a stalking cat. "Wide eyes that smolder with bitterness could smolder with desire. Beautiful full lips that scorn could smile . . . and buckle me at the knees, Elsa."

It was the first time he had called her by her given name. Her mouth twitched fitfully. "I vill not let you make a fool of me again."

He leaned forward and grabbed both sides of her chair seat, scooting the chair forward so that his dusty brogans cradled chair legs and her knees were wedged between his.

"Mr. Selkirk! You go too far! I demand – "

His large, roughened hands framed her face. With infuriating patience, he slanted his head, and her alarmed gaze watched as he lowered his face over hers. Her lids fluttered closed. She felt the tickling of his mustache on her trembling lips. Felt his lips grazing back and forth over hers, as if importuning. For what? She experienced an urge strange to her. A sweet panic of need. And next another fiercer, stranger urge. That of yielding.

She just did not know how.

The tip of his tongue took advantage of her parted lips to caress inside them. Startled, she gasped at these new stimulating sensations rushing through her. A long forgotten feminine instinct took over. Mindless, she clutched his shoulders for support, while her kiss responded in kind.

Before she could grasp what was happening, he had scooped her from the chair and cradled her against his broad, bony chest, where she could detect the heavy thudding of his heart. He carried her into the bedroom and laid her on one of the two straw mattresses, she wasn't sure which, with as much gentleness and care as one would place a cherished heirloom ring on the fourth finger.

Looking up at him as he levered himself beside her, she summoned a gruff tone as protection against her fragile emotions. "I varn you, I am still a maiden . . . and, uhh . . . entry may be difficult."

Surprise crossed his ruddy face, then he grinned. "Entry is not my concern, lass. Tis pleasuring your flinty spirit that is my goal."

She wept, tears running down her ruined face. Wept from the fear of surrendering . . . and from the ecstasy in surrendering.

§　§　§

Mhaire partially slitted her lids, her lashes tangling with . . . with the soft tufts of Miles's chest! Sudden memories of her wanton behavior during the night, long after the candlewick had sputtered out, sizzled through her.

Beneath her cheek, his solid chest muscle flexed at the ticking sensation from her lashes. She froze, not wanting to wake him. After a few seconds, she cautiously moved her leg, draped in helpless abandon over his thigh.

Those thighs had anchored her hips in his final foray of introducing her into the pleasure of her body's passionate responses . . . until she slipped free to clutch her own thighs about his waist, lock her arms around his sweat-sheened shoulder muscles . . . until, staring up into his triumphant eyes, she screamed out his name as the peak of his pleasuring vibrated through her . . . until the whole world faded away in the magical afterglow . . . until she felt the heavy breathing of their hearts, at one in tempo . . . at least, for that wondrous space in time.

Facilely, she could explain her descent into the realm of sexual passion as one of mere duty, of obligation. Miles had kept to his part of the bargain, already issuing inquests regarding Ireland's surviving

O'Mordhas.

She had felt the need to rectify the imbalance of their relationship. But she was not that featherbrained. She had never been among the fainthearted. Since her father's suicide, she tried mightily to be upfront with herself and others, as he had not been with her, going through her mother's inheritance and the prostitutes in Lincoln with such spendthrift disregard.

So, the truth of the matter was she wanted Miles Neville with every fiber of her body. She was attracted to *his* body, aye, but to his brilliant mind, as well. To his humor. His determination . . . which might, also, be a part of his dark side.

"I love you most when you are nude," he lazed. His hand reached out now to palm one of her breasts. "They are smaller than they look . . . and everything I had fantasized about. The color of your nipples, their taste . . . peaches. Ripe peaches."

Quickly rising, she dragged up over her nudity the still damp sheet, in complete disarray and redolent with his virile sweat, her virgin blood, and their lovemaking.

He raised a brow in that familiarly questioning and occasionally mocking way. "As I lamented before, I should learn to keep my mouth shut." Yet he was watching her intently, as if waiting for something further from her.

"'Tis the Sabbath. I need to . . . to ready meself fer church. A bath I need."

To wash away this latest sin.

If she expected him to protest the desertion of the place of their torrid, torching lovemaking or inquire if she would return – ever – to his bed, she was disappointed.

He rose, stretching his sleekly muscled body, silhouetted in the dawn's early light. "While you draw bath water, I'll hitch the team to the buckboard for you."

She sensed he was looking for an excuse to escape her presence. Was what had transpired between them, something that shook her foundations, her world, of so little consequence to him? Was he bored with her now that he had bedded her?

She wanted to believe her surrender had been merely payment for a just debt – the restoration of O'Mordha Castle to its rightful heirs, when located. But she knew better. There was the appallingly guilty memory of the near unbearable pleasure beneath him, astride him, on all fours in front of him.

Even as she leaned over the zinc tub's wooden casing and flooded the tub with water, she ruminated on what she had done, willfully, and where this new aspect of their relationship would go.

She felt in one sense replete, and in another, weakened – because she needed him now. Like a tick, his lovemaking had itself attached to her untried, vulnerable body – an itch that no amount of scratching would satisfy without his particular and arousing touch. The saints help her.

She divested herself of the maidenly nightgown, almost as easily as she had divested herself of her maidenhead. What a fool she was. She should crawl on her hands and knees, like the faithful did on the mountain road to El Sanctuario de Chimayo outside Santa Fe at Holy Week, and beg forgiveness for her sin of fornication, not to mention all her smaller ones.

Instead, she would go to the little slapdash church here in Puerto de Luna this morning and do penance. She was weary from the struggle between her and Miles and utterly weary with her struggle within herself.

She pinned up her hair and went to step into the oval tub – and paused, sensing another presence. Glancing over her shoulder, she inhaled sharply and grabbed to bunch her skimpy nightgown as an inadequate shield.

Miles, his shoulder braced against the door frame and arms folded, was studying her with an admiring note. He wore only his denims, settling low on his hipbones, and the skin of his chest and upper arms was white where the sun had not bronzed it.

"You're back." How utterly inane of her.

His scrutiny was focused on her face, especially her eyes. "Given the magic of night, you're beautiful enough, but you are really a sight to behold unclothed in the bold light of day."

Quickly, she slipped into the tub, beneath the covering of its steaming water. The water's heat was scorching. She crossed her palms over her breasts. "Please. I am not accustomed to bathing in front of . . . a male."

He loosened his denim buttons. His smile was mocking, but she was not certain if the mockery was directed at her or himself. "Me neither. That is, in front of a female. Well, not often, anyway."

"Bray and Neigh, they are waiting."

The tiredness etched around his nimble mouth would deceive others into believing he was like any other man. "They can wait. I can't seem to."

Her lips could formulate no reasonable objection as he swiped a precious bar of lavender soap and crouched into the tub, knees doubled opposite her. His eyes turned the shade of blue one could drown in. They scorched the cleavage of her breasts, visible just above the lapping water. "The necklace you wear."

Automatically, her fingers fluttered to the leather cord. Paltry the age-eroded gold cross with its turquoise nugget might be, but it meant everything to her.

"I would have expected a pagan amulet, given your proclivity for casting curses."

Curses and potions of which he was obviously becoming warily and respectfully aware. Curses and potions of which she had not the slightest notion of their power. "Belonged to me mother, the necklace did. Well, the cross did. An ancient artifact, I am told. I took it from her rosary beads before we buried her with them. Tis all I have left of her . . . of me childhood . . . me home . . . me family."

As if to dispel her melancholy, he clasped her right calf and, lifting it, began gently lathering its length. "I find it interesting – and delightful – how very fine hair is found on the female as opposed to the course and profuse hair on we males."

He drew her eyes into his, making it impossible to resist. So completely under his male's spell was she, she could only submit to this new form of pleasuring.

His fingers moved lower to massage, first, the arch of her foot, then each of her toes, one by one. She contained a sigh of utter bliss but, relaxed, and, lids closing, sank a little lower into the gently lapping water.

"Wondrous," he mused. "Your tiny toes. They have not been cramped into ugly contortions by women's bloody, constraining shoes."

Rebuttal at this intimacy was difficult when one's pleasure places were being stroked. "Huaraches are easy on the feet," she found herself murmuring inanely. "But then, I go barefooted often."

He grinned. "I am hoping you will be willing to go bare-assed naked often." His hands released her right leg to begin their ministrations on her other. "Around me, that is. While Finian is away, courting that Valkyrie that is your friend."

That final comment detoured her momentarily. "Finian is courting Elsa? Ye are sure about this?"

He chuckled. "Well, trying. He's back at the Turquoise Door this morning, giving the courting his best."

"She's harder on outsiders than shoes on the feet."

Which brought her back to the moment, his thumb pressing insistently against her foot's sensitive arch. Both painful and, oh, so pleasurable. How did the body, the emotions, tolerate both, at once? Through the steam curtaining her and Miles, she beseeched him in a wild whisper. "Ye hae to know that, while, I canna imagine denying ye . . . anything, I hae to, want to, reclaim the Luna House as me own."

"And I foresaw as much." His hand forsook her arch to travel up her left calf, past her knee, and began gently kneading the back of her thigh's taut muscles. He seemed not to recognize the crisis between them. "I have signed over the Blackwater deed to an Irish strain of O'Mordhas, because I won't have the past interfering with here and now, between you and me. As for the future, I'll sign over to you the Luna House when it is time for me to leave."

His leaving. Of course, she had known to expect it. But her heartsickness faded while his fingers slipped farther up her thigh to fondle between her ultra-sensitive, furred folds.

All thoughts of Church and repentance for this heavy sin of fornication were forgotten for that singular exquisite moment.

CHAPTER TWENTY-SEVEN

Blackwater Vale, Eire
July 1691

Before dawn, Merrow, at last, found Phebe, whose bleak undercroft compartment she shared. The young woman was curled in a dank corner of the garderobe. The stench of the bodily waste was staggering.

Like a fist, opening and closing, the girl writhed with her bloody flux. "Crikey, cramping something awful, I am, Merrow."

While the pretty chambermaid could not be called amicable with her, Merrow could certainly empathize with the lass. "I'll light the fires for ye this morning and tidy up the rooms."

Phebe looked up hopefully. "And empty the chamber pots?"

She sighed. "Aye." Emptying the odorous chamber pots, even scrubbing them with a vinegar-soaked rag, would be less irksome for her than her own specified task that morning – the burdensome lugging of water buckets up flights of stairs. The Lady Elizabeth requested a bath.

The water well, located in the castle's huge courtyard, was cloistered with its storeys of high arches and pink stone. After several trips between the kitchen and the keep's well, Merrow's shoulders ached fiercely. And the morning was still early.

Drawing up yet another bucket of water from the well, Merrow could not help but stare at the ancient Celtic goddess carved into a gray stone opposite the well. Wearing a cheeky grin, the half-squatting woman, her thighs spread-wide, proudly displayed her own well, the gaping symbol of feminine power between them.

Surely a sign, Merrow thought, that she should wield her own power. But, nae, her power had been seized by Fletcher. That and her family's castle.

Stifling yet another oath, she hoisted the buckets onto her carefully balanced shoulder pole and returned to the kitchen.

Beatrice was nowhere in sight. Quickly, Merrow set the buckets on the hearth to heat and pilfered a freshly baked, hot biscuit. She painted it with orange marmalade and crammed it into her mouth.

Barely had she swallowed, than Beatrice waddled back into the kitchen. "Is that marmalade on yer lips?"

Merrow's lips crimped in a forced gulp. "Tis Betha's honey, Beatrice. To keep me dry lips moistened."

Setting out smoked herring and cheese, Beatrice pursed her lips impatiently. "Be sure ye collect the dovecote's eggs forthwith."

Merrow hefted from the hearth onto her shoulder pole the four sufficiently warmed buckets for bathing. "Aye."

Aye, Grumpy-lumpy. Merrow knew she should be more charitable toward the woman. When the River Blackwater flooded five years before, the woman had lost her three sons and husband. But, saints alive, Merrow could use a wee bit of charity herself at the moment.

She toted her buckets of heated water up the stairs to the solar that had once been hers and was now occupied by Lady Elizabeth.

Merrow's bed. Former bed.

With over thirty bedrooms in the castle, she would have thought the steward Nielsen could have installed the young noblewoman in any but Merrow's own.

At her discreet knock on the half-opened door, a feminine voice bid her enter. Elizabeth was still abed in the great four-poster. She left off stroking her lapdog, a pug that lay warming her feet beneath her drawn up knees. "Oh, it's you."

Merrow was quick to consider the young woman's slightest frown. After all, the welfare of her father and Paddi's could depend on Elizabeth's temperament. "Ye had requested the bathwater, Lady Elizabeth."

The young woman gestured with beckoning fingers to enter.

Merrow circumvented the four-poster to unburden herself of

the shoulder pole, biting into her tender flesh, and emptied the first bucket into the copper tub. She felt Elizabeth's eyes inventorying her.

"You look well bred."

She did not know how to answer that. Quickly, she emptied the next three buckets, and went over to bank the hearth's morning fire.

"Once, I shared sleeping quarters with another well-bred girl in a convent where we had been sent for supposed safe keeping."

Distinctly uneasy, and she knew not why, she dropped a curtsy and retreated toward the doorway. She could afford no further antagonism within the castle. "I'll fetch further buckets of heated water."

But still the narrow-faced woman detained her with a sly smile. "I played the male part with the girl. She had no experience in this sort of dalliance but took to it like a camel to water."

"Guid day, me lady." Hastily, she closed the door.

Alas, her body had been deflowered by an English soldier, bartered off by a fiancé of English stock, and now coveted by an Englishwoman with Sapphic proclivity. Merrow thought it would seem she should have had enough of the beastly English.

Yet, she could not deny this absurdly strong and torching connection, something exceeding mere attraction, that she felt with the Englishman, the arrogant and autocratic Lord Justice Fletcher Neville . . . the Englishman who so masterfully made love to her body.

CHAPTER TWENTY-EIGHT

Puerto de Luna, Territory of New Mexico
August 1878

Briskly, Miles strode across the hardwood floor of the Luna House office and tossed the tape measure on the desk. Even though the morning was still early, excitement galvanized him. He knew he needed to rein in on his enthusiasm. To generate some form of practicality.

He fished from the pocket of his chambray shirt the notes of calculations he had taken at the Blue Hole. Sitting back in the tufted swivel chair, he propped his water-washed and mud-speckled boots atop the desk, his spurs just avoiding its edge. Hands locked behind his nape, he stared up at the ceiling's decorative tin tiles, which must have cost a fortune. Mentally, he reviewed his plan.

If his theory was correct, the Blue Hole's water level had been lower when Coronado had cached the jars of gold behind the rock walls with the plan of returning for his loot. Centuries later, the damming of the Blue Hole's outpour had risen the water level, concealing those same rocks.

Miles jackknifed forward and reviewed the notes he furiously scribbled, estimating the approximate weight of rocks to be dislodged, the combustion heat anticipated, which should equal the approximate amount of dynamite needed. The one case he had ordered from Grzelachowski's should suffice – the case of which Sullivan's flunkies had hoped to obliterate The Luna House – and himself.

Finished with further rapid computations, Miles settled back in his chair. He should be elated, but he was dissatisfied. Words like estimated . . . approximated . . . and anticipated . . . were woefully indefinite.

So, what if in safeguarding the jars from the explosion, he took out a part of the Blue Hole's natural rock formation? The water would still flow from its aquifer's endless supply. That bloody water so sacred to Mhaire and her community.

His brain would pick that moment to resurrect the memory of Mhaire's beautifully nude body, stepping from the tub . . . and how he had buffed it dry with attentive care to each curve and crevice. If only, the confounded donkey team and church had not been demanding her attention. The stimulating image was hard to envision without his body also becoming hard.

As if to compound his dissatisfaction, Finian, the ends of his long mustache turned down like a horseshoe, blotted the doorway. Miles sighed. "What? What's got you in a sour mood this early in the morning?"

After all, the big old Irishman had seemed quite delighted by spending recent nights with Elsa. He propped his rawboned body in one of the pair of leather campaign chairs facing the writing desk. As always when agitated, his knotty fingers worried his mustache. "Tis the townsfolks, laddie."

"What about them?" He tamped down his impatience like tobacco in a pipe bowl. His life-long friend deserved his full attention.

"Rumors are flying thicker than flies on a dead horse."

"Come on. Out with it."

"Laddie, I've watched ye do yuir fair share of pollenating – and more, but this . . . this seduction of the lass, Mhaire . . . ."

Miles felt his tendons and ligaments rigidify, as stiff as his determination.

"The other lasses, they were naught like this one. I hae seen ye grow in mind and body over all these years, and if ye're the man I think ye are . . . well, then . . . ye'd know ye hae her honor and reputation to protect."

"Meaning?"

Finian eagle-eyed him. "Ye know what I mean."

Simmering indignation was usurping his impatience. He was no longer the whelp to be scolded. In an effort to diffuse his anger, unwarranted as he knew it was – at least, toward Finian – he delayed responding. He scrubbed his jaw. In his haste that morning to check out his Blue Hole logistics, he had not shaved.

"As much as I value all that you have been to me, Finian – mentor and quasi father – my relationship with Mhaire is entirely between myself and her – and not town gossips. Furthermore," and at this he smiled dryly at Finian, "It might do well to practice what you preach."

Not surprisingly, Finian did not take umbrage at Miles's implication regarding the spinster Elsa Anderson. Finian understood him all too well. Shoving his lanky frame off from the chair, Finian bestowed a smile of gentle reproof. "I know ye'll do right by Mhaire O'Moore, laddie."

§ § §

The hour was not yet seven in the morning. Miles expected to find Mhaire preparing breakfast, but she was not in the kitchen. Irritated, he wandered through the house, looking for her.

He thought she might be in the music room, but, no. Nor was she in *their* bedroom, as he thought of it, where he had singed himself on the pyre of their lovemaking. Now, she was a furnace boiling his blood. He abhorred the insistent nudging of rationality . . . that he might need her, want her, so much that he would risk opening his heart . . . well, bloody hell, it would be the same as opening his veins.

He found her in the library. She was still wearing her nightgown, her legs curled up beneath it on the tufted chair. Her magnificently red hair disheveled, her face wan, she looked up from the book opened on her lap. Her hands trembled. Had his ravishing of her brought about this? Given, they had not slept at all the night before.

Alarmed, he crossed to drop on one knee beside the chair, his face on a level with hers. His glance took in the title heading the top of the page: *Recurring Dreams and Their Interpretations.*

His searching gaze delved into her dazed one. "Is this what has you thrashing and moaning at nights – a recurring dream?"

Her lips parted, and a barely audible word breathed over them. "Doppelgangers."

"What?"

"In Spanish, *alma gemela* – soul twins. Us. Yeself, me. As vivid as this verra moment in time, but centuries in the past."

He would try to humor her. "Mhaire, Mhaire. Au contraire."

"Do no' patronize me, Miles Neville."

Well, then, another tactic was required. A more direct one. Practicality. "And these dreams rob you of your sleep? These lucid dreams?"

Her lips, a paler pink than usual, quivered. "I fear the dream's past may rob ye of yuir future." She swallowed hard. "Yuir verra life."

He could feel the darkness descending on her. He knocked the book from her hands and, gathering her up in his arms, strode from the library toward the staircase. Reaching the master bedroom upstairs, he deposited her on the mattress's still tousled sheets and stretched out alongside her.

He cradled her frail body against his, as if to infuse her with his strength, and his hand captured both of hers, pressing her palms against his chest. "Feel me, Mhaire. Feel my heartbeat beneath my skin, beneath my chest muscles and ribs. I am real. Here and now. No doppelganger. And I am stronger than any curse you murmured, anything you conjured in your dreams."

Her thick, dark lashes fanned up, and she stole a hopeful look at him. Her fingers crept through the whorl of hair matting his chest. "Love me, Miles. Love away my dreams, my fears. So that there is only ye."

§ § §

Languorously, Mhaire stirred her limbs, well-loved and now entangled in cumbersome sheets. Miles' lovemaking was passionate, intense . . . and, aye, soul stirring. Soul stirring for her, at least. She was not certain the passion and feelings their lovemaking invoked plumbed to the depths of his own soul.

At least, his lovemaking kept away her disturbing dreams.

"That's it, Mhaire," he had cajoled time and again in panting, urgent breaths, "come for me. Come *with* me."

Dear God in heaven, if what was transpiring simultaneously within the framework of her nightly dreams approached the intensity of these consummations with Miles, she did not know how her body . . . nae, even her poor heart's emotions . . . could sustain both over any lengthy duration.

For Miles never mentioned marriage. And for that matter, she continued to be in denial of that other gut-wrenching matter . . . what if he had gotten her with a bairn?

"You're awake." His voice, soft and low, worked her as he did his fishing line. Taut with tension one moment, languid and flowing the next.

"I drifted off. What time is it?"

"We've whiled away half the day, luv." His muscle-corded arm encircled her waist, drawing her against the warm length of his naked, suntanned flesh.

She shivered, and he drew the rumpled sheet up over their hips. His hand cupped her chin, and he stared down at her in the afternoon's muted light with troublesome seriousness and half sighed. "It seems I am cursed with this insatiable need to be close to you. Within you. Whenever, wherever."

Somehow, his lovemaking had dispelled the heaviness of her haunting dreams. "I warned ye, did I no'?"

He shot her a wry smile. "That you did, my Lady of the Twinkly Eyes."

She reached a fingertip beneath the sheet's edge to tap his groin, near the hipbone, and, incredibly, that flaccid part of him leapt to life yet again. "The bullet wound – its scar is gone."

He grinned. "How much better my body's other scars would have fared had they been subject to your ministrations."

Her forefinger traced the one-inch puffy nick left on his shoulder by the recent bullet wound. "This nasty scratch is healing nicely – as well as, the one over your left brow. She tapped the old scar scoring his right brow. "This other one, is it from a knife fight?"

He chuckled. "Hardly that dangerous. Caught a fishing hook on it while Finian was teaching me to cast. But the hook came bloody near to ripping a path through his mustache, as well as, my eyebrow."

As if satisfied by her easy laughter, he released her and sprang from bed to stretch his gloriously muscled arms and shoulders.

The curve to her lips remained, but her heart rumbled with the heaviness of her solemnity. "I love you, Miles." Of course, she did not expect him to respond in kind. It was not in him. Oh, she knew he cared for her. Cared deeply. His actions said as much. And did not actions always speak louder than words?

Bending and bracing a palm on the mattress at either side of her waist, he brushed his lips ever so lightly across hers and murmured, "By the way, love, now that my cast has hooked the Golden Carp, I plan to keep her."

§ § §

Miles considered himself a logical and reasonable man., a man who never stopped working the angles, as Mhaire so diplomatically had once described him.

The trick was to keep the opposite – emotions – at bay. Because emotional pain hurt far more than physical. Feelings were fickle, inconstant. Subject to change daily. Hourly.

Although, Mhaire had countered this haphazardly expressed comment quite confidently. "Dinna ye know, me Miles, ye go by faith, never feelings?"

And so, here he was, trailing the Pecos River south to Fort Sumner like a love-struck lad to fetch the priest.

Well, to arrange with Father Ignacio to perform the marriage ceremony before the month was out.

Well, *after* Miles retrieved Coronado's cache on the morrow, if things went as planned.

It was important to marry Mhaire, to make an honest woman of her in the eyes of Puerto de Luna – but to do so after he had the jars in his possession. So that she was coming to him for what he had earned in his own right, not to recover her family land grant. That he planned on returning to her, regardless . . . once the gold was his.

Not that she had given any indication she was interested in marrying him. She was fiercely independent. Like no woman he had met. She might have confessed her love for him. But, as he well knew, love was another volatile emotion. Here today, gone tomorrow. And it could beat the hell out of you while in residence.

Nevertheless, she was a keeper. A fish he did not want to let get away. That was why he was giving no fair warning of his marital intentions. If she suspected of his plan for the Blue Hole, she might

191

balk. Flap out of his scooping hand and escape into the river, once more.

He thought of how they had started out, at odds with one another, the calamity of the barn's burning, and immediately recalled a quote of the Japanese poet he had read that single year at Oxford – "My barn having burned down, I could now see the moon." Perhaps, because of Mhaire he could see things he had missed – or dismissed – before.

To his disappointment, Father Ignacio had ridden out on his donkey from Fort Sumner's chapel and forty square miles, until recently an ill-planned prison camp for the Navajo and Mescalero Apache, to dispense his blessings elsewhere.

Miles had spent more than half a day in travel for nothing. Both he and his sorrel needed a respite before heading back to Puerto de Luna. While waiting for the sorrel to quaff at a nearby trough, hoisting a glass of golden lager seemed infinitely in order for his travel-weary bones.

Nearly a decade earlier, Sumner's old military fort had been charged with the internment of the Navajo and Apache but had since been closed. Lucien Maxwell, who had only surpassed James O'Moore as the largest landowner in the United States, had purchased the fort from the government, and a town had grown up around the fort.

Windblown brown tumble weed bounced down its main street. Miles sought the shade offered beneath the portales of the Issues House, where Indian captives had once lined up for food and supplies. In front of the Issue House, despite the blistering August heat, a game of croquet was in progress on the patch of dirt, the former parade grounds.

Leaning a shoulder against one of the portales's splintered posts, he paused to watch the men with their mallets at play. He caught the drifts of conversation from the other spectators who had gathered. Bets were being laid on one player in particular. The skinny, swaggering kid was the much gossiped about Billy Bonney, a friend of Pat Maxwell, Lucien's son.

Evident from the word of mouth, the kid earned a certain respect. He had been a part of the Regulators who had taken on Sullivan's gang. All eyes were fastened on him. He wore a dusty black felt hat, a dirty red handkerchief, and baggy pants tucked into his boots.

He moved with quick steps among the wickets, joking with Pat as he took a swing at his ball.

Miles's attention picked up at remarks from nearby, one from a drunken sodbuster, who looked tough as a leather shoestring. "Heard tell, there's a $500 reward out for the Kid."

The man next to him, a drummer, if the trunk he toted was anything to go by, shrugged shoulders that nearly clipped his big ears. "Yeah? Far as I've heard, he's never held up a bank or a train. Or a stagecoach, for that matter."

The drunk leered. "It don't matter. Five hundred is five hundred." He lurched from beneath the shaded colonnade into the harsh sunlight.

Miles possessed the unfortunate disposition to be inclined toward support of the underdog. Mallet in hand, Billy would be hard pressed to protect his self-interest. Miles stepped forward. "Say, that's a fine looking six-shooter you have."

The drunk blinked, shoved back his braided, curl-brimmed hat, and narrowed wary eyes on Miles. "Well . . . yeah?"

"Can I see it?"

The man hesitated then reluctantly forked over the pistol. Casually, Miles accepted the revolver, hefted its weight in his hand as if checking for balance, then spun its cylinder so that its next shot would be an empty chamber and handed it back.

Revolver in hand, the man wove an unsteady path among the stakes and then almost lost his footing on a resting yellow ball. At that point, he halted abruptly. Leveling his six-shooter at the kid's back, he shouted, "You're a dead son-of-a-bitch, Billy Bonney."

The trigger's click sounded hollowly around the parade grounds. In the next second, Billy spun and fired. Like a bagged turkey, the drunk crumpled atop the yellow ball – ironically and incredibly shooting it off cleanly through the nearest stake.

The onlookers hurried to gather around the dead man and Billy, smiling widely at his good fortune.

Miles swung away. He had seen enough murders during California's gold rush that he was indifferent to yet one more.

Tethering his sorrel to the hitching post in front of Beaver Smith's rough saloon, Miles braced a foot on the brass railing and ordered a lager. It was warm but wonderfully quenched his thirsty throat.

Brooding, he stared vacantly at the bison head above the bar. He wanted to wrap up this marriage thing with Father Ignacio, to solidify his bond with Mhaire before anything else could go wrong. He needed her. She reassembled his fragmented soul. She made not only his body but his spirit feel better. She was the warming sunlight and the lively rain and the vivid desert starlight.

Damn it to hell, his good sense and prudence were all trussed up with her foolish mermaid sorcery. But how to dismiss as foolery the roar of his pulse in his ears when near her?

Someone sidled up beside him, and he turned to see the bucktoothed Billy. "I heard what you did for me."

Miles shrugged. "I believe in a fair chance." Not that either player had an equal chance to succeed, but he believed that both, at least, should play by the same set of rules.

"Whatever, I owe you one, mister. An Englishman, are you? My late good friend Tunstall was an English nobleman. I hear you've stood up to Sullivan and his cow patties."

At that, Miles had to smile. "If you, in fact, owe me one, you could begin by telling me where to find Father Ignacio."

"The plastered priest? Why?"

"Plastered or not, I want him to marry me and Mhaire O'Moore."

"Why, that's one debt I won't make good on then. 'Cause I'd love to tie my own self down with that fine piece of calico."

Miles rolled his eyes, then grinned and yanked down on Billy's dusty black hat, so that it covered his eyes. "Then, good luck, kid – you can count on that happening the day Father Ignacio ever sobers up."

CHAPTER TWENTY-NINE

Blackwater Vale, Eire
August 1691

"**O**n my oath, my Lady Merrow, tis no superstition!" Betha's good hand was busy, patting out the dusting of flour on the cottage's crudely made table. "But it only works on the eve of Lughnasa, like I told ye."

Droll amusement curved the ends of Merrow's mouth. The Celtic time known as Lughnasa celebrated the first day of harvest, but this peasant custom she had never heard of – a slug leaving a beloved's initials in the flour dust.

"Try it and see," Patrick urged. "But ye 'ave to fetch the slug yeself."

"And meanwhile I'd suggest ye scramble to the loft and fetch the *eggs*, Paddi."

With her faithful Rory accompanying her, she had only to go a little way into the wood from the cottage to find a slug that afternoon. Dredging the moist soil beneath a pile of oak leaves, she unearthed one gooey body. Cradling it within one purpling ash leaf, she made her way back to the cottage.

Yet again, she had stolen away from her duties at the castle. Beatrice would be stewing at this moment. Or maybe not. The head cook seemed to be oblivious to her periodic absences from the castle.

The castle might have been Merrow's home, but now Fletcher's energy, raw energy it was, branded itself throughout the castle, as he had branded her as his own with his merciless, yet tender and captivating, lovemaking.

Within but a few minutes, she returned to view from the cottage doorway a hearty barrage of grenades – eggs hurled from the loft by the gleeful Patrick at Hugh, below. Hat in hand, he nimbly dodged two, then a third one that, instead, pelted her chest dead center, where the leather strings loosely laced her kirtle.

"Crikey, Paddi!" She swiped inside her cleavage, damp with cracked eggshells mixed with slithering egg white and yoke. "Hae ye ne'er heard of waste not, want not? And dinna make that impish face at me!"

Rory was busy licking up the splattered eggs. Patrick, Hugh and Betha – emerging from her hiding place behind the table – were all grinning.

Betha tore her blissful gaze from Hugh. "Aww, Lady Merrow, we were just having a wee bit of fun."

Merrow caught the yearning exchange between the two. Some of her strain, the sensual tension between her and Fletcher that was slowly building to a broil, momentarily ebbed back to a simmer. "Welcome, Hugh." She held out the leaf bundling the snail. "Betha and I were testing the divination of this wee creature in regard to a True Love's initials."

Hugh raised a flummoxed brow. "True Love's initials?"

Betha of the beautiful hair slip-slided an utterly wistful smile at him. "Aye. Me lady, if ye'll but place the slug at the edge of flour. Then, we have only to wait a few hours to see what initials of your intended love your snail traces."

Merrow thought this was too good of an opportunity to waste. Hugh may have come calling on Betha on whatever pretext, but Merrow intended to keep him in the cottage as long as possible. Nudging the snail off the leaf onto the table, she said, "Meanwhile, Hugh, would ye partake of some mead with us?" Already, she was headed for the wooden cups.

When she turned from the cupboard, Hugh was looking down at Betha's upturned face like a man too long starved. "Whose initials did yuir own slug leave?"

Betha gnawed at her lower lip, lowered her lids shyly. "I have no' tried it yet."

His chest expanded, as if gathering air for a fight. He glanced from her to Merrow and, lastly, Patrick, descending from the loft with his wicker basket of remaining eggs. "My initials or no', I would gladly make ye three my family. Care for ye . . . protect ye. That is, if ye will have me as your intended, Betha."

A wee bit precipitous, Merrow thought. He could have plied Betha with a few more romantic gestures over time. But then, no one ever knew how much time was allotted them, did they now?

Betha's cheeks were splashed the color of rich red wine. She grinned joyously, indifferently displaying her missing tooth. "Aye, I would like that, Hugh . . . verra much."

Patrick emitted a whoop and a pumping of his fist. "I knew ye'd come through, Hugh!"

Hugh took Betha's deformed hand in his. "Ye are a boon to me heart, fair Betha."

Relief sighed out of Merrow. Betha and Hugh would be happy together, this she knew. She lifted her cup in a toast. "To our new family."

§ § §

Alfred had not only delivered Fletcher's intended, the Lady Elizabeth, but had, also, delivered King William's message for Fletcher to ready his forces, following the wedding with the Lady Elizabeth.

As if Fletcher could ever bring himself to bed the harpy. Refined as convent lace, as she was purported to be, she nattered enough to drive a man mad. And her perfume, heavy enough to cover the sickening stench of death, did little to encourage him.

Many times he wondered what made him tick. Like now. When he should be occupied planning a renewed siege of Limerick. William's ultimate strategy to finally win the war in Ireland was to crush the remnants of the Jacobite resistance, centered in that city.

A bold plan. But Fletcher was war weary. A feeling utterly foreign to his nature. Warfare was his mead.

But, lately, the blood on his boots, the stench of gunpowder in his nostrils, the horror in his sleepless eyes, being shot at in the trenches and trampled by soldiers' mounts – all this was wearing down his spirit. Watching womenfolk cry over their dead sons, husbands, and fathers . . . he was no longer certain that warfare could make things right, that might made right.

And, worse, was the knowledge of the atrocities his own soldiers most likely committed on hapless females, spoils of war, despite his strict countermanding order. Exactly what had happened to Merrow, the despoliation. His teeth ground audibly in his ears.

Fuming, he wouldn't pretend to understand her. She mystified him. Refinement. Strength. Poise. And confidence. Those qualities he grudgingly admitted she possessed. But something more. Something more elusive than merely her quick wit sparring with his verbal jousts.

Hell, he never laid claim to understanding females. His indifferent mother had totally lacked nurturing skills, and his campaigns had never permitted him residence long enough to form any kind of meaningful relationship. Besides, the kind of women he encountered in the embattled towns were more interested in his coffers than his caring.

Instead of preparing for the battle ahead, he left his officers, loyal to their lives to him, cooling their heels – while he tracked down his errant servant woman. Nowhere was Merrow to be found within the castle's thick, angular walls. She could be anywhere in Blackwater Vale. He began with the cottage belonging to the beekeeper's daughter.

The gods help him, it had been but mere days since he had possessed Merrow. Fifty-eight hours since he had made up his mind to keep his distance, lest she possess him completely – body, mind, and soul.

For the ensuing hours, he had chaffed without her . . . without her mouth eagerly accepting his invasion with both tongue and cock, her stroking fingers unwittingly soothing his troubled heart beneath his hair-matted chest.

The day's thick fog had been burnt off by the evening's sunset to reveal a soft cloudless, azure sky. He was resolved to win the day or lose all.

Hand palming his rapier hilt, he paused at the cottage's open door and took in the lighthearted scene within. A twinge in his heart signaled his envy for the close-knit group. He had never experienced this bonding, this trust to open his feelings so freely, as the four seemed to be doing as they stood around the crude table . . . joking, talking, laughing.

The thought crossed his mind to retreat to where he had

tethered his horse before the cottage's occupants spotted him.

But Merrow's bewitching voice deterred him. "Ye canna really believe a slug's trail on Lughnasa reveals a beloved's initials, do ye now, Betha? Hugh?" She stared up at the one-armed man with a skeptical but sweet expression.

Hugh Harrington, the castle's former gatekeeper. Fletcher had investigated the man after he had so boldly stepped up to her defense at the threshing floor and then later danced with her around the maypole. Obviously, he, too, had fallen under the spell she spun as fine as Mulberry Silk.

Still, Fletcher, irritated by his unwarranted reticence, tried to resist the tugging toward the cottage. But next the Irish setter, having detected him, came bounding through the open doorway to greet him. Fecking Furies, there was nothing to do but go within.

Patting the setter's head, he ducked the lintel and strode into the room's smoky dimness. All four faces swiveled toward him. He cut a curt bow but affected a pleasant demeanor when straightening to confront the startled four. "Pray tell, what is this about a slug's trail and one's beloved?"

The radiant smile of the beekeeper's daughter exposed a glimpse of a missing tooth. She swept a deformed forearm with its lovely hand toward the room's rustic table. "Why, we're waiting to see which lover's initials the slug leaves in the flour for me lady. I am Betha MacLiam. Ye are the Lord Justice, are ye not?"

Fletcher's scarred brow rose. "*Which* lover?"

Hugh stepped in between. He nodded duly in differential respect. His jaw was set firmly in his thin face, as if ready to take a blow if need be, but his tone was congenial enough. "Her intended, sire, whoever he may be."

He bared his teeth in a humorless smile. "Fancy that." He moved even deeper into the room, into the snare of Merrow's sensuality and splendor. Affecting ennui, he plucked some kind of honey and nut confection from the sideboard and popped it into his mouth. Her stare cut into his guts and loins.

The maid Betha beckoned with her finger. "Come, sire, let us look."

Merrow, battered wooden cup in hand, moved forward. Her lovely and unpredictable lips painted a smile. "Nothing of import.

Naught that could be of interest to yuir lordship."

Lordship? When, her neck arched, his hands fisted in her hair, she had cried out "Fletcher" in the throes of his taking her beyond herself? He smiled thinly. "By all means, yes. I am highly interested, as I am sure would be your intended, Lord Dunhill."

He crossed to stand between her and Betha and Hugh at the table. Rory padded behind.

Hugh set a lantern on the table. Eyes adjusting to the light, Fletcher stared down at the snow-white table top. A slimy yellow path wound through the flour dust.

Merrow's brother, bordering on manhood, interrupted in a voice that shot to a high squeaky pitch and dropped back. "Whose initials, Merrow? Dunhill's, ye think?"

Fletcher peered closer, trying to decipher the squiggles – as if he believed in such nonsense.

"That – there toward the corner," Betha said, "it could well be a D."

Hugh cut Fletcher a curious glance. "Or an N. See how the tail of the marking dinna quite close?"

Beside him, Merrow, with the back of her hand, brushed across the table, sending a flurry of flour dust among them and upending the lantern.

He restored it to the table. "You're much too intelligent for foolish superstition."

Her irritable gaze darted from Hugh to Betha to the lad and lastly to himself. She shrugged. "I agree. Child's play!"

"Granted, child's play. But not your absence from the castle. Derelict at your duties – that is serious. I am here to fetch you back."

"And if I refuse to accompany ye?"

The small room's atmosphere was suddenly heavy with tension as hot and flickering as summer lightning.

He chose his words carefully. "The rub of it is, considering your status – not only castle minion but castle mistress . . . former mistress, that is – then you could be deemed a traitor."

Traitors were consigned to the breaking wheel and tortured by spinning them around while a hammer smashed their bones. Something he did not want to happen to her lovely limbs, if he could avoid it.

But he possessed information that Dunhill was working both sides. Soon, very soon, the rat would be caught stealing the cheese, and Fletcher would spring the noose on the rattrap – the bait being Fletcher himself. And he fervently hoped Merrow did not let herself get involved.

Her eyes narrowed, her words blistered. "Pray tell, how could I be a traitor, when I have ne'er been yuir subject?"

The want of her was too potent for him to pretend indifference. "But you are mine, nonetheless." He stretched out his gloved palm. "I have come for you. Don't make this unpleasant for yourself – and the others here."

A low growl, almost indistinct but mongrel-like, could be heard coming from Hugh, yet Fletcher never took his gaze off her rebellious one. He should feel contrition at this summary treatment of her today, but how could he when he relished her nearness?

However, clearly anxious to forestall an eruption, she placed her hand in his. Her smile was frosty. "Ye are quite right. Tis late and time I return to me duties."

She made her goodbyes, hugging the huge dog lastly, and he led her outside. As if echoing the storm within the cottage, the western sky was broiling with dark clouds, and the stars, normally his guideposts for navigation, were hidden. The wind had picked up, and thunder rumbled in the distance. Finally, the long-awaited rain was arriving to moisten the parched countryside.

His hands easily encircled her waist, and he lifted her onto his great steed's saddle. Then, climbing into the stirrup, he mounted behind her. She held herself stiffly away from him.

He leaned forward, his lips close to her ear so that he could clearly make himself understood. His face was lashed by her hair, the long thick strands of her sensuality that was tugged loose from its knot by the wind.

"Merrow, I am petitioning King William for clemency for your father – that his life may be spared." A letter under the seal of the sovereign, often meant imprisonment without trial and all hope for reprieve denied. "But his freedom . . . I can tell you now William will never stamp his royal seal on a full pardon for Jacobite gentry and noblemen."

And the best he himself could offer was his protection of this rare young woman, this naiad.

Her sigh might well be mistaken for the wind's gust. Then, her body settled against his, her head nudged into the cradle of his shoulder and neck, and her fist opened to drop and palm his hand, splayed across her flat belly.

They were one another's foe. Thus, he would have to be content that her body craved his, as he needed hers . . . and her mind and spirit.

The splattering rain both offered promise of renewal for the war-scorched earth and his innocent boyhood's yearning, to be loved beyond measure.

CHAPTER THIRTY

Puerto de Luna, Territory of New Mexico
August 1878

The way Miles looked intently at Mhaire during mealtimes, it was as if he took possession of her mouth with a mere slant of his gaze. And the way he looked for her at other times throughout the house . . . touched her, if only her shoulder, when he located her . . . it confirmed their lovemaking had become indispensable for him, as well, as for her.

It was not yet dawn, and she had slept none. She lay in bed, entwined with Miles, having unraveled in his arms . . . and replete, as always.

Only the morning before, he had come upon her in the kitchen, bent over the stove door to take out baked apples bubbling with cinnamon and sugar. His hands had first caressed her bottom, then circled round to palm her breasts, and his teeth had nipped at her nape.

Her sigh of delicious, wanton wanting encouraging him, he had grasped her waist, maneuvering her away to the working table. And there, shoving up her skirts, his hands anchoring her hips, her palms braced atop the knife-notched table, he took her. Her hips had rocked to rebut his rhythmic pounding, and she had groaned out her spiraling pleasure.

He released her now and sprang from the bed to stretch his gloriously muscled arms and shoulders, then leaned over to swat her on her buttocks.

"Ouch!" Her lower lips thrust out in a petulant and feigned glower, but she could feel the corners of her mouth threatening to tilt upward. That happy, that content, this man made her.

"The pain I deliver you can nowhere equal the torture of your exquisite pleasuring, my sprite. I expect you do be waiting right here for me when I return this evening."

"Tis Sunday." She raised on one elbow, trying to hide the disappointment in her voice, as she watched him dress.

In an enthusiastic mood, he quickly shrugged into his cotton underdrawers and denims. "And a glorious Sunday, it is."

She stewed now. Had her previous aversion to him been but a challenge? She did not know his varying moods well enough yet. Might now her love bore him? In effect, he had bought what he once could not have. As a result, was the spell he had declared she cast upon him broken? "Where are you off to?"

The people she loved were always leaving, it seemed. Her mother, her father. Her brother. She'd like to think Riley would have returned, with her dowry, had he not frozen to death in that late winter storm.

"Meeting with Guido." He paused, drawing on an old buckskin shirt. "About some tick-infested cattle."

Her teeth worried the inside of her lip even as her fingers worried her necklace's gold cross. "Miles . . . be careful. Around Guido. He . . . he's been hot tempered lately. About your desecration of our watershed. And my . . . relationship . . . with you."

"He owns neither the water . . . nor you." Leaning over her, he framed her face. She closed her eyes. He braided his lips with hers in a sweet, lingering kiss. The kiss deepened, their breaths sharing. Then, straightening, he grabbed his boots, padded to the door and turned to fix her with a glinting smile. "For that matter, neither do I. Own you. But, please, no disappearing on me, my love. You are no Golden Carp."

At that, she adopted a cryptic smile. "Dinna be so sure, sir!"

But after he left, with hours still left before church, she snuggled back between the sheets, seeking a snatch of sleep of which she was so deprived lately . . . and seeking to stave off the inkling she might be denying the truth, believing Miles, trusting him, as she foolishly did.

CHAPTER THIRTY-ONE

Blackwater Vale, Eire
August 1691

Lughnasa marked the beginning of the harvest season, when, at dawn, Blackwater villagers did their stations barefoot at *Tobar Na Croí Naofa.*

Since Fletcher was not due to preside over the festivities in the town square until noon, Merrow joined Betha, Patrick and Rory – and a crowd of villagers – in the barefoot trek to the Well of the Holy Heart.

She opened herself to the fresh, calm air with its hint of earthly aroma, so unlike the stench of the village. The trees were resplendent in their festival clothing of sundry greens. Here and there, the first orange leaves of autumn, along with chestnut burrs, were crushed by the bare feet of the penitents.

Autumn, the grand finale of labor by both the villagers and nature. Too soon for autumn, it seemed. Time was swiftly passing, too fast for her. And that second nature in her that sensed what others overlooked whispered another sort of grand finale was approaching.

She did not know what she had expected from Fletcher when he had whisked her from Betha's cottage to return her to the castle, but it certainly was not to be given summarily into Beatrice' keeping with not even a fare thee well last night. But then mostly likely there was his intended, the Lady Elizabeth, awaiting his attentions.

Merrow had not seen him that morning. But she had seen the evidence of her monthly bloodletting that morning, and for that she was thankful.

At the river's well site, she knelt alongside the holy spring with the others. The faint odor of wood smoke wove in and out among them. She found it difficult to concentrate on the prayers and invocations. She did not, could not, love Fletcher, she repeated silently with each bead of her rosary that passed through her fingers. Enthralled with him, she was. That and no more.

As though sensing her agitation, Betha joined her, kneeling at her side, and whispered, "Can ye really go through with this?"

She knew what plagued Betha. They had discussed it over the morning's ale the day before – Dunhill's idea to lure the Lord Justice into a trap that day. Her voice was an equal hush. "I have to."

"'Tis far too dangerous."

She latched onto Rory's neck to keep him from romping in the water. "Nae, not so dangerous – I only have to draw him away from his guards." But, after all, what she was involved in would be deemed by English courts as high treason.

How could she not follow through with the plot? Not only her father's freedom depended on this but that of Eire, its countrymen, her neighbors.

Her heart rendered up a ragged prayer. Like a condemned person quartered by four horses, her loyalties were yanked between her love for her family and her feelings for Fletcher. Feelings? How could this mere caring for him, this mystifying bonding with him, be stronger than her love for her family?

Their devotions performed, the hundreds of pilgrims quickly began to shod their bare feet, eager to return to the village to begin dancing and carousing the rest of the Harvest Day, as if they were celebrating the Bacchanalia rather than the memory of a favored pious saint.

Standing on first one bare foot, then the other to don her hobnail boots, she was reminded of Fletcher, of the day he had returned them to her. She might have feared him, but she knew . . . as well, he did . . . that they both had wanted to see one another again. That lust-longing between them was undeniable, unavoidable, unstoppable.

On the journey back to the village, she stooped to gather a purple clump of michaelmas daisies, whose beauty had caught her eye.

Patrick wrinkled his upturned pug nose. "Better ye give those to the Lord Justice, Merrow."

Giving a michaelmas daisy symbolized saying farewell, perhaps in the same way as Michaelmas Day, the last day of harvest was seen to say farewell to the productive year. But, looking at the rather insignificant, common flowers she clutched, she suddenly trembled, struck by the reflection that the michaelmas daisies could be a sign.

If St Michael was celebrated as a protector from darkness and evil, just as the daisy fought against the advancing gloom of winter, then surely somehow, some way, she could stand between Fletcher and his assailants, just as he was standing between King William and her father's execution.

How could her heart deny what her soul knew — that she had loved Fletcher before ever they had met and would love him for a thousand years or more to come?

Foolish as it was, since he was soon to wed another. And with the beginning of their wedded life, her own lonely life would begin as well. But no one else would ever satisfy her. When you loved someone, you risked it all, you sacrificed body and soul.

By the time she entered through the town gates, ale sellers were already hawking from their booths in the square. Shrilling trumpets, horns, and pipes taunted revelers to plunge into an excess of drinking and dancing.

Along with Patrick and Betha and a frisky Rory, she joined the hot press of humanity watching the armed infantry parading past, a display of power staged by the Lord Justice to impress the populace, no doubt.

A stand had been erected, where Fletcher now presided in the Chair of the Estate, transported from its place in the Castle's Grand Hall. Nielsen stood watchfully behind him. The Lady Elizabeth, wearing the colors of Saint George, was seated at Fletcher's side. Her beringed hand lightly capped his, reposed on the chair's scrolled arm.

He appeared to be reviewing the rank and file of his military might. But intimate exchanges with his betrothed occasionally distracted his attention. The sight of the couple carved the insides out of Merrow. She nearly doubled with the pain. What a blithering, heartsick eejit she was.

Still, another urgency diverted her focus. Warily, she scanned the multitude of onlookers for sign of Alfred. But then Fletcher's assassin could be someone designated by Alfred instead. Someone among them armed with a primed pistol, easy enough to conceal in the congestion of people.

She could not stand by and do nothing. Yet to warn Fletcher put her family and friends in jeopardy. What she could do was place herself at his side that day, always between him and the assassin.

She turned to Betha. "Take Paddi and Rory and mix with the crowd."

Restraining Rory with a calming hand, Betha placed her withered one on Merrow's shoulder. "I dinna like whatever it is ye're about."

"I'll fare fine, Betha."

Chagrinned, her friend's little mouth twisted like a crushed rosebud.

Patrick's grubby hand latched onto hers. "Dinna leave, Merrow. There is still the St. George and dragon play to see."

She tousled his thatch of russet hair and forced a grin. "Betha will take ye, Paddi. I shall rejoin ye two later."

She lost herself in the milling crowd, with its stench of sweat and ale, and circled to the newly erected stand, smelling of fresh-sawed pine. Heart thudding like mill paddles on water and her knees weak with both wanting and fear, she climbed the short flight of stairs.

At the top, two red-coated guards immediately barred her way with their pikes. Smiling at the beefier one, she held aloft the michaelmas daisies, their purple heads now drooping in her sweaty clutch, and announced loudly, "For the Duchess."

Past the soldier, she saw Fletcher's betroth cut both the wilted bouquet and her a look of surprise, followed by a speculative appraisal. Next to Elizabeth, Fletcher straightened attentively at the sight of her. He nodded at the guards. "Let her pass."

Shakily, she made her way to the pair of chairs, dropped a curtsey worthy of high court before Elizabeth, and held out the daisies to her. Fletcher's warm gaze locked on Merrow like only a lover's could. She fervently hoped he could read the urgent appeal in hers.

Elizabeth was quick to take note of the exchange of ardent glances. She wrinkled her nose and waved Merrow off with a negligent flick of her beringed fingers. "Whatever can you be thinking, my lord, to allow a scullery maid join us here?"

"A kind gesture should never be turned away." He gestured for Merrow to approach.

She drew even closer to him, dipping low, her skirts flowering around her. Without rising, she lifted the bouquet to him. He took it, their fingers brushing, and she had to wonder if he felt the jolt she did.

In a muted tone meant only for his ears, she leaned closer, so that her upturned face was near his inclined one. "Your life is in danger today, Fletcher."

His heavily lashed lids narrowed, his gunmetal-blue eyes searching her features, as if her beseeching expression might render up information. He nodded. Still holding the daisies, he stood, one hand extended to assist her in rising.

"Fresher flowers would be better for my Lady Elizabeth. Show me where you picked them, my lady."

She blinked rapidly. He had called her his lady.

Gaped-mouth, Elizabeth stiffened. "My lord, I care not for flowers. They send me into violent fits of sneezing."

His dark expression could have been interpreted either as solicitous or sarcastic. "Then perhaps I shall return with holy water from Tobar Na Croí Naofa to cure your . . . violent . . . fits?"

Elizabeth's voice was as muted as Merrow's had been but laced with vitriol. "This is unseemly. To desert the review with this . . . this mewling maidservant . . . on a capricious search for holy water."

He looked over his shoulder at Nielsen. "Pray keep my betrothed company in my absence. I shall return anon."

The Dane frowned, stepped closer, and lowered his voice. "Not a good idea, my lord."

Merrow had to agree, but she knew not what else to do to protect Fletcher. Her voice dropped to a pleading whisper. "Heed me, please, sire. A hired assassin could be anywhere. In the crowd. Even when you think to be alone."

His hand captured hers, both drawing her with him and supporting her as she descended the three steps alongside him. He lowered his head, his face grazing her hair. "Why?" He was leading her away from the crowd, back through the castle's outbuildings and through the outer defensive walls. "Why risk aligning yourself with me?"

She couldn't let her susceptibility to his charm throw her off guard. "Told ye, did I no'? I am no' yuir subject. I am no' aligning meself with ye." Beyond, the majestic view over the woods below gave flashes of the coal black river between their green leaves.

His smile was softly mocking. "But you would give yourself to me."

She tore her gaze from his caressing one. When she realized he was taking her down the 100 steps, cut into the solid rock, she shivered apprehensively. *Why, the uneasiness — when she could recall the jovial times she had played with her brothers on these steps? One moment, they would be fisticuffing one another, and the next discussing the best fishing bait.*

Her family . . . how could she turn her back on the two decades of love and attention and care they had provided her in exchange for these few but precious months of both breathless delight and deep despair that Fletcher had rendered her. The overwhelming urge to turn and flee, to leave him to his just deserts, seized her mid-step.

She half-pivoted, when he lifted her hand to press a kiss on the back of it. "I fear to lose my hold of you," he murmured, staring down at her from beneath thick lashes as black as a dungeon, "lest you disappear like the fireflies with the deepening darkness."

Deepening it was, with the night's scintillating stars soon to come down around them like a vast velvet cloak. She bit her lip, tried to offer up a smile, tremulous though it was. When, where, at what time, had she fallen in love with her tormentor?

Thrice, she glanced over her shoulder to assure herself she and Fletcher were not being followed. "Do ye no' understand, Fletcher — there may be conspirators who want ye alone, away from yuir guards?"

He gave her a patronizing smile that held the power to infuriate her. "I anticipated as much. This morning, I ordered the quay and both sides of the river patrolled for Jacobite parties."

Her mouth dropped open. "Then, you knew — you knew all this time?"

"About Dunghill's plot to overthrow me?" He leaned close, his hands framing her face, and she inhaled his dizzying masculinity. "You are quite exceptional, my love. Courageous, even when divided by loyalties."

"Nae, I am quite weak. I canna resist whatever it is that draws me to ye, Fletcher."

"Nor I you, I fear." He leaned his forehead against hers momentarily, then drew her along with him.

They reached the steep bank of the Blackwater. As a child she learned to swim in her shift there, and her father joked she could outswim the fish. And her father and brothers used to fish there. They had cut alder branches for fishing poles and dug worms for bait.

She knew where to find the salmon and brown trout that slivered around shadowy bends. More importantly, she knew when and where one might spot the shapeshifting golden trout, sluicing through the current, if one was most fortunate.

As yet, she had not been.

Still, she worried for Fletcher. True, no creaking timber of ships creeping into the quay's docks could be heard *that evening* and *no packet boats trawled the river.* Here and there, it was dotted only with paddling ducks and scattered along its banks fresh beaver cuttings. A reassurance that life continued placidly, though interrupted periodically by loss, heartache, betrayal, and . . . death.

Near a silver stack of driftwood, he removed his purple velvet mantle and, spreading it on the tufted grass at the river's edge, settled himself on the cloak, his arm hooked around one drawn-up knee. He patted the cloth. "Come, my luv. Sit."

She hesitated, then dropped down, tucking her legs beneath her and leaned toward him, praying he would take her seriously. "Ye must heed me, Fletcher. I dinna know how much I can share, but Alfred came to me and — "

Leaning forward, he captured her chin between his thumb and forefinger and looked deeply into her eyes. His own were dark with a passion that swallowed the eve's remaining light. "I care naught about Dunghill. Tis you, only you. You, who have changed my world. That you would risk your all for me . . . . you are teaching me what the power of love between a man and woman truly can be."

She had waited it seemed forever to hear him declare that he loved her. She detested her perverse neediness but could never return to the unfulfilled life she had known prior to his invasion of it. Even if it meant awaiting him off stage, while Elizabeth played his wife on stage. But, oh, the price. "Fletcher, do ye no' see? Ne'er can we bridge our differences."

Grinning playfully, his long fingers rustled through her unbound hair draping one breast, and it tingled at this touch. "Be damn the blasted bridge. Have I not captured myself a mermaid with this magical red cap that will enable travel between the two, water and dry land?"

He leaned forward to kiss her, and her eyes soaked up the gradations of sun-touched gold that illuminated his handsome, hungry face. For this she had awaited her entire life, awaited his love. It was a feeling, a love, so enormous, such as she had never known.

Then, through the evening mist, she glimpsed something else . . . something behind him. Alfred, cowardly Alfred, rising from a dense shrub of black dogwood. Starlight found its way through the mist to fall on the flintlock pistol he held in his hand.

She lunged, shoving Fletcher aside. The ball only grazed her shoulder, but she lost her balance. "Merrow!" Fletcher shot to his feet, grabbing futilely for her.

His hand was out of reach. Still, she knew how to swim. Her arm stroked forward, even as the Blackwater's dangerously swirling current tugged at her dragging skirt and heavy boots. She swallowed water. Coughed and swallowed even more water. Her arms did not obey her but thrashed wildly. Her lungs protested at the watery influx.

She was sinking deeper, feeling things growing darker. Struggling seemed an effort not worthwhile. This dying thing was not that hard, that painful.

She thought she heard Fletcher's bellowing shout or maybe it was Rory's distant howling.

CHAPTER THIRTY-TWO

Puerto de Luna, Territory of New Mexico
August 1878

Miles wasn't so sure that the naiad who had invaded every part of his life, leaving him no room to dodge her druid charms, wasn't, indeed, the fabled Golden Carp. Absurd, he knew.

Still, he felt uncomfortable about his objective that morning, when it was a glorious one for accomplishing his goal. Buckets full of sunshine splashed the high desert.

Nevertheless, the annoying creaking of the saddle, the damned drone of grasshoppers, the enthusiastic chirping of the mockingbirds, the endless burbling of the Pecos off to his left . . . they each irritated him irrationally.

He tried whistling, but he had the uneasy sense this time he was whistling past the graveyard. He eased Bronco back into a slow trot, wanting time to . . . to what? To find reasons to justify what he was about to do? Rationalize that what he would do would not violate Mhaire and the Puerto de Luna citizens' ridiculous notion of the Blue Hole's sanctity?

Bloody hell, had he not already deep-sixed the plan for dynamiting the site to retrieve Coronado's cache? A much easier and less dangerous approach to achieving his goal than the current one he had substituted – holding his breath and diving repeatedly under water with a crowbar to loosen the inscribed stone he had sighted during his initial plunge.

Ingenious, how the conquistador had managed to loosen the

rock, store the vessels, and replace it, marking it for future retrieval. But at that time El Rito Creek had not been dammed, raising the Blue Hole's water level.

Hell, finding the Holy Grail had to be an easier aspiration than this. But he was certain he was correct in his theory, wild ass though it might be.

As the sorrel drew near the Pecos's confluence with El Rito Creek, first the thunder of hoof beats, then a shout from behind, caused him to haul in on his reins. One work gloved hand braced on the sorrel's rump, he shifted in the saddle to glance back.

A horseman skidded his mount down the cliff on the river's far side and splashed across, heading in his direction. He recognized the cowboy, drawing up to halt just short of him. "On the lam again, Billy?"

The kid yanked off his hat and fanned his narrow, flushed face. "Figured I owed you a helping hand after you saved my bacon." His hand patted his pistol. He nodded at Miles's holstered scabbard. "A rifle would serve you a sight better than that there crowbar."

"Well, that depends on what I'm aiming to do."

"Stand off 'gainst Sullivan. And his hired guns. And that is if you're bound for the Blue Hole."

"Why?" Instinctively, he palmed his nearly useless Smith & Wesson. "What's going on?"

"Heard tell at the No Scum Allowed Saloon over in White Oaks that Sullivan is planning on dynamiting the Blue Hole today."

He frowned. "Why? For what purpose?"

Billy planted a bony wrist on his pommel and uttered a tuckered-out sigh. "Reckon, he has an ax to grind. Shift the blame to you. That way the good citizens of Puerto de Luna will tar and feather you 'fore they run you out of the Territory. That way Sullivan has it all to hisself again."

"Bloody bastard!" Wrongly placed the dynamite could blow to hell the stashed gold. "That's not going to happen!"

§   §   §

After Miles left, Mhaire bathed and dressed for Sunday mass. She intended to stop off afterwards at the Turquoise Door and visit with Elsa. That was if Finian wasn't also . . . visiting.

How curious, that relationship, Finian and Elsa's. The past week, he had returned each day a little after dawn to the Luna House, his mustache lifted by his cheery smile. His only comment came yesterday. "What a treasure your friend Elsa is, lass."

Upon entering the adobe-cum-chapel, she at once sighted Finian's shock of hair, the shade of charcoal. She was somewhat surprised he had not already departed to join Miles – and even more surprised by the unknown female seated next to him on the bench, around whom he casually wrapped his arm. And Mhaire knew every female in the area, or so she thought.

Lately, all parishioners' eyes had followed Mhaire censoriously, living as she did with Miles, without the blessing of the church.

Today was different.

Rather than attending to the mass's droning First Reading, led by Guido, all the parishioners' gazes seemed to be darting with interest to the mysterious fair-haired older beauty. She wore a feathered, beribboned, and crushed satin chapeau. A bright candy-apple red, its wide-brimmed was slanted provocatively across her forehead.

Mhaire, her head covered with her pitiful straw hat, felt positively drab. Overcome with piercing curiosity, she sought out that pew to seat herself next to Finian. She lowered her voice. "I thought you would be with Miles." And Guido, for that matter.

"Nae, lass. Miles is off to the Blue Hole – uh, fishing, ye know."

Fishing? When he had said he was checking on tick-infected cattle? Still her curiosity got the better of her. She was trying to peek around the Irishman at the woman on his other side, her chin held defiantly high.

Leaning forward slightly, the woman now turned her head toward Mhaire, who gasped in recognition. "Elsa!" she breathed. Never, in Mhaire's most far flung imagination, had she expected to see Elsa at church. And this . . . this Elsa, with her splendid bonnet framing abundant hair. "Ye . . . ye've changed."

Elsa shrugged and draped her work-burnished hand over Finian's, placed strategically on his thigh, close to hers. "Ja, love can do that, *havfrue*."

He flashed Mhaire a smile. "Thanks in goodly part to the talented Miss Singletary behind us."

"Sssshh!" hushed the people around them.

Trying to absorb the enormous change wrought in Elsa, Mhaire glanced over her shoulder at Gladys. The milliner preened with unsuccessfully suppressed pride.

Miles and Finian's arrival at Puerto De Luna had certainly wrought changes. How wonderful they were, she wasn't sure.

While her brain told by rote the novena, "Hail, Mary, full of grace, I humbly beseech you through your immense love of this repentant sinner," another part of her, that wild druidess part of her, whispered she had been lied to and used.

Her fingers forsook her rosary's cheap wooden beads to clutch her necklace's gold crucifix, and she murmured the litany, "I beseech the ancient harmonies of the untamable sea to be true to my divine self . . . ."

She felt hemmed in there in that small adobe, consecrated to serve holy purposes, felt the need of her restless spirit to retreat to that wild part of nature, the waters inhabited by druids of yore.

Seated at the end of the bench, it was easy enough to slip out before the parishioners congested the only route out at the end of mass, the room's single doorway.

However, old Alex Grzelachowski, already at the door, forestalled her escape. He grinned broadly through his luxuriant beard. "Mhaire, good to see you, gal."

She smiled and moved to step around him. "A guid day to ye, Alex."

"By the way, would you let the Earl know he overpaid for that box of dynamite he ordered."

Guido, sombrero in hand, joined them, but she ignored him. "Did ye say it was Miles who ordered the box of dynamite, Alex?"

"Why, yes."

Then . . . then, the box had *not* been planted at the Luna House by Sullivan's gang. She turned to Guido. "Are ye no' to meet with Miles today – about the cattle tick infestation?"

A puzzled frown notched a line between his eyes, eyes that still wore the shadow of a man wronged and hurting badly. Slowly, he shook his head. "No . . . I think not. Pues, not today anyway."

Finian's remark traipsed through her tumbling thoughts . . . he had said Miles had gone fishing at Blue Hole. It struck an uneasy cord with her. Then, her mind stuttered at the preposterous idea that followed . . . Miles's odd, offhanded mention that he wouldn't be surprised if Coronado's gold was somewhere in Blue Hole. Her gut instinct shouted it was not a preposterous idea, that she wasn't wrong in her suspicion.

Bile churned in her stomach. Her whole world was shattered. Foolishly, she had invested all that she believed in, all that she was, all her hopes and dreams and plans, in a clearly distorted image she had fabricated of a monstrous soul.

The bile reached her throat to bubble as scalding fury. She could only nod Alex and Guido a curt goodbye and shouldered past them, muttering madly, "Mary, Mother of God, the eejit's going to blow up Blue Hole!"

Blinded by rage, blinded to everything going on around her, she loped in the direction of her wagon, parked alongside buggies and tethered horses. She was appalled by this act of sacrilege. But so deeply hurt even more by the realization that Miles's love for her was a mockery. He had been using her to get to the gold he believed to be hidden at the Blue Hole.

As she went to climb aboard the buckboard, Guido caught up with her. "We'll make better time if you ride with me, Mhaire." He tightened his sombrero's drawstring beneath his jutting chin, tense with righteous purpose.

Heart thudding, she watched with bruised eyes as he went to his chestnut. Something in her hesitated – shifting loyalties as it seemed to her, from Guido to Miles.

Eeejit! Get over this yearning for what does not exist. Miles Neville has pulled the wool over yuir eyes.

She accepted the gloved hand Guido held down to assist her astride behind his saddle. Not a ladylike position, with her skirts bunched around her calves, but then she was not longer a lady, was she? She had lost that status when, unwed, she surrendered her maidenhead to Miles. And her heart. But not her soul, by God.

The river had shaken off it its morning mist. Galloping along the River Road, clutching Guido's barreled ribs, she fought to shake off intolerable, painful images of Miles the night before.

His sweat-sheened body braced on his forearms over her trembling and spent one, later his nose breathing into the soft, springy curls protecting that private part of her, and even later his lips whispering words of passion that incited her once more.

But not words of love.

But then, love never made anything nice and tidy. Nae, broke the heart, it did. Called one to be more than it was possible to be. Immolated the heart on the bonfire that came with loving the wrong one. And that was the poignant truth, she loved the wrong one. Miles, not Guido, the worthier one.

And that love had brought her to this under the eternal New Mexican sun . . . weary to the bone and hollow with despair.

Somewhere along the breakneck ride, the wind ripped away her straw hat, ripped away her despair – and whipped to a flame the coals of anger buried behind the sockets of her eyes. Incalculable hurt and frustration choked up inside her. Had she a pistol, she would kill Miles Neville.

At last, Guido's chestnut crested the bluff above Blue Hole. Below, she sighted Miles with Billy – faced off across its rim against four other men. One, she recognized. Emmet Sullivan.

The chestnut half scrambled, half slid, on its hindquarters down the rough outcropping of bedrock and *skidded to a halt at* the bottom. She skittered off the chestnut's rump to sprint toward the Blue Hole. At its rim's limestone scree, Guido caught up with her.

Suddenly, Billy was fanning his six-shooter, so fast it was a blur. A man wearing an eyepatch tottered, then fell. Another cowboy she did not recognize slid limply into the Blue Hole's far side.

At the same time, defying the eye's tracking, Miles and Sullivan were exchanging gunfire. The shots reverberated like cannon boom among the cliffs. Horrified, she couldn't catch her breath. Nausea roiled up through he at the carnage unfolding.

Gun smoke and flurried dust wreathed the duelists. Dear God, let her heart's betrayer still be standing. Then, a slight, sulfuric breeze partially cleared the air. At the limestone's rim, Billy stood over the man with the eyepatch. The Kid's boot nudged the man, and the body tumbled over the side.

Urgently her gaze swerved, searching through the haze for Miles – and spotted him, next to a dynamite detonator. He was hauling Sullivan to his feet. The Irishman looked bloody eyed and bloody fanged. His fingers whipped to the knife at his belt.

Miles intercepted the hand with a vice-like grip, while his other hand fisted a punch to the stomach that dropped Sullivan to his knees. He doubled over, retching. Not finished, Miles delivered a kick to his head, keeling him over backwards.

Then Miles swung around. Staggered toward the detonator, its plunger rising menacingly from its top. Her heart was thunderous in her ears. He was going to do it – blow the Blue Hole into eternity.

Instead, he reached, yanking loose the wire. That close now, but a few yards away, she could see his chest rising and falling with his labored breathing.

"You're a dead man, Neville!"

Guido's gritted shout whirled Miles toward him and her. Next to her, Guido wore the contentious expression of a holy man wanting sainthood in behalf of a noble cause – protecting the well – when it was obvious Miles was trying to save the well. Or was it to save the gold he believed buried there?

Guido's hand went for his Colt Dragoon.

On the edge of derangement, she could feel her scream entombed behind her teeth. To her horror, her dreamtime was being reenacted in this lifetime. Here – now! In another time, another place, she had sided with Fletcher in the name of love – for naught. Now, the tragic nightmare in this lifetime.

Next, everything was a kaleidoscopic swirl.

Sullivan lurched to his feet and hurled his knife. It spun, haft over blade. Miles jerked. He reeled. His hand groped over his shoulder. He yanked at the heft of the knife imbedded near his shoulder blade.

Then, a shot – it must have come from Billy – dropped Sullivan dead.

But it was Guido who drew her attention from the horrific slaughtering before her eyes. He had leveled his .44, its barrel pointed at Miles. Oh, dear God! She hurled herself against him. "No, Guido, no!"

Two more shots resounded. Billy's bullet punched Guido back a step. And Guido's slammed into her breastbone. She faltered, then wobbled against him to clutch his charro jacket's lapels for support. With disbelief, she glanced down at the medal of blood pinned to her throbbing chest, then back up at him.

Dropping his pistol, he clapped his hands to his face. "What have I done?!" His exclamation was but a repentant breath from his crimson-foamed lips. His eyes staring vacantly like a statue's, he swayed.

It was her turn to try to support him. Then, she saw the pulsing wound near the base of his throat. A soprano scream tore from her. "Oh, God, Guido!"

"Mhaire! Mhaire!" Mile's alarmed yell drew her gaze from the blood on her fingertips. Hers or Guido's, she was not sure.

She looked up. Miles was sprinting toward her. The steps she turned in his direction stuttered. Another step she managed. So close was she to him, the air crackled around them, as always.

Then she lost her balance and crumbled. He grabbed for her – only to rip away her necklace.

Next, she was falling, falling into the water. Sinking. She peered up. Above, she saw his tortured face. She thought she heard the deep bass of his slow, tortured shout. "Noooo, noooo!"

Or was this merely another of those turbulent dreams of hers? Was it Fletcher's shout for Merrow that Mhaire dreamed she was hearing? Could there not exist a link between these two lives – was it not possible for the soul to bind them together?

She stretched her hand up, toward Miles's water-distorted one. He was kneeling, reaching for her again. Their wavering fingertips so close . . . . But then a whirlpool of water was engulfing her.

"Mhaire – "

She thought she heard his agonized voice cracking on his next words, whatever they were. She knew, she knew. *Wait I will, my darling, as I always have. All this time. All these centuries.*

Her last blurry glimpse was that of her beloved, crumbling on the limestone rim of the holy well.

CHAPTER THIRTY-THREE

For a week, Elsa and I kept watch over Miles, hovering between this side of the veil and the other. It was me Elsa's fierce determination and curative skills that kept me laddie from the netherworld. He eventually recovered from yet another body wound. But apparently not his mind.

Come each nightfall, he lit his lantern and set out from Luna House. He could easily have ridden his sorrel or driven the buckboard, but it was as if me laddie felt driven to walk the distance as a pilgrim in penitence.

He might have been Diogenes with his lantern, searching for a truthful man. But, nae, Miles Neville with his lantern was searching for the Golden Carp. Return, he did, before each dawn. But looking the worse for the wear after each outing -- his eyes red-rimmed and haunted, his cheeks sunken and unshaven.

Of course, I knew where he went each night, to be sure. 'Cause I followed him each night. Stayed a respectful distance, I did. Watched him, as with lantern lifted aloft, he prowled around the Blue Hole for maybe half an hour or so before and after midnight. Watched him collapse each night to his knees and sink his face into his hands with despair. And then would come his inhuman howl of human heartbreak.

I dinna think me laddie knew I kept my nightly vigil, so knackered was he. And, maybe, I was, too. Me arthritic bones tucker out more easily these day. Beat up with the rheumatism I am, crookeder than a knotty limb. Fear sometimes I'll never walk again.

Anyway, propped as I was against this rocky ledge, I'd swear me peepers, they closed only momentarily. With a snort, I jerked awake. 'Tis the awful stillness that bothered me. Frogs, crickets, the nightingales . . . all deathly silent.

Anxiously, I glanced around me, then scanned around the Blue Hole's perimeters. On its far side, the lantern still cast its golden glow. A relieved sigh eddied through me auld body. Me peepers almost closed again — and then snapped wide.

The lantern sat there, on the limestone shelf. But Miles was nowhere to be seen. I shoved to me feet. Ignoring me groaning bones, I hustled over to the lantern. Fear was hammering painfully in me skeletal chest and cold sweat marbled me back.

Alongside the lantern, I saw lying a neatly coiled leather cord with its ancient gold cross. Mhaire's precious necklace. Mary, mother of God!

Like struck by a lightning bolt, my heart stopped. I was incinerated. At that moment, I realized the lass and her pendant's source of old gold were there all the time, had anyone but taken notice. Coronado's gold passed down through the offspring he had sired.

Dreading to, but doing it anyway, I peered over the edge. Nae, I didna see the Golden Carp, but I do believe I might have seen me son, Miles, sinking from sight in the turquoise depths of the Blue Hole.

Aye, me son.

As the Blackwater estate's head gamekeeper, I had come from a middle-class family with a good profession as head gamekeeper assured me the rest of me life and plenty of lasses eager to take me name.

But, nae, I had to go and fall in the love with the Duchess of Blackwater, the beautiful but frivolous Lady Kathleen Neville Drummond. And to protect our lovechild's right to the vast inheritance controlled by the widower Drummond, I had to deny Miles me name. Many times over in the past six months, since me laddie came into his inheritance, I had thought to reveal me paternity, me pride as his father, but I forced meself to a patient wait, until he came into his own, here in the land of enchantment.

Madness. Sheer madness. All of this.

§   §   §

Paris, France
August 1940

Sorcha O'Moore heard the man's timber-rich, American voice before she opened her eyes. " . . . took in a lot of water."

Then another voice, that of an old Frenchwoman, maybe. "Good that you dove in the Seine when you did. The Nazi patrol boat's prop would have made liverwurst of her."

"I was fishing the Canal St. Martin for redeye or white carp, not a mermaid."

Mermaid – her contact password! Sorcha's hand feebly flailed for her purse strap – and the five counterfeit passports. Gone!

Her water weighted lids slid open. She supposed she wasn't surprised at the image that coalesced before her – below dark brows, one plowed by a puckered scar, a young man with eyes the shade of the deep blue water of her hometown's Tobar Na Croí Naofa were studying her with concern . . . and wonderment . . . and perplexed recognition.

Naiads and mermaids inspire us. From them we learn that to choose love is to choose forever. And when two hearts are meant to be together, no matter long it takes, how far they go, fate will reunite them.

T h e E n d ~ or not?

ABOUT THE AUTHOR

    I'm dancing on sunshine because you have dropped by my little part of Parris's Paradise. We have some things in common ~ that we believe good overcomes evil; that love triumphs over everything, even death; that we love a tension-packed story; and that we feel the best books enhance our lives.

    I write for the reckless of heart. Not surprising, I identify with my novels' characters, both the protagonists AND antagonists. I suffer with their angsts and bewilderments and rejoice in their joys and triumphs. And I believe that if we heroically hold fast to our own vision for ourselves in the face of our journey's confrontations, then Life WILL manifest our dreams and goals and visions, as it does for my characters in my novels.

    Parris Afton Bonds is the mother of five sons and the author of more than thirty-five published novels. She is the co-founder of and first vice president of Romance Writers of America. Declared by ABC's Nightline as one of three best-selling authors of romantic fiction, the award-winning Parris Afton Bonds has been interviewed by such luminaries as Charlie Rose and featured in major newspapers and magazines as well as published in more than a dozen languages. She donates her time to teaching creative writing to both grade school children and female inmates. The Parris Award was established in her name by the Southwest Writers Workshop to honor a published writer who has given outstandingly of time and talent to other writers. Prestigious recipients of the Parris Award include Tony Hillerman and the Pulitzer nominee Norman Zollinger.

Subscribe to my mailing list to receive a FREE novel, as well as, notices of new releases and Free E-Book giveaways. Your information will never be shared, sold or given away.

http://parrisaftonbonds.com/subscribe/